DEATH
FOR OLD
TIMES' SAKE

A. J. Orde

FAWCETT CREST • NEW YORK

A Fawcett Crest Book
Published by Ballantine Books
Copyright © 1992 by A. J. Orde

A. J. Orde has lived in or near Denver for decades, and knows many parts of it intimately. Despite this, the author chooses to use fictional locations to avoid giving offense through unflattering references to specific addresses, neighborhoods, or places of work.

Library of Congress Catalog Card Number: 91-26841

ISBN 0-449-22193-8

This edition published by arrangement with Doubleday, a division of Bantam Doubleday Dell Publishing Group, Inc.

Manufactured in the United States of America

First Ballantine Books Edition: January 1994

It was almost midnight before I got back to the shop. I felt tired but not at all sleepy, so I dumped the papers out on the kitchen table, put some coffee beans through the grinder and made a pot, poured a mugful and then sat down to see what I had to take care of. Inside a big blue envelope was a stack of canceled checks. Big checks. All made out to someone named H. Fixe. All signed by Jacob. I'd never heard of any H. Fixe, which puzzled me a little. Still I wasn't upset until I turned the envelope over and saw written on the outside the word *Extortion!* The word was in firm black felt tip, in Jacob's curly hand. *Extortion!* Underlined. Exclamation point.

I tried to figure it out, feeling inexplicably hurt by the little mystery. Hadn't he wanted to bother me? Didn't he want me involved? You don't write ten-thousand-dollar checks two or three times a year for almost ten years without reason!

Also by A. J. Orde
Published by Fawcett Books:

A LITTLE NEIGHBORHOOD MURDER
DEATH AND THE DOGWALKER

one

M Y FOSTER FATHER, Jacob Buchnam, died quietly on a
February night with snow falling outside and the
world muffled and still. He was eighty-one. A series of little
strokes over a period of years presaged a bad one in late
November. Once that happened, we knew him well enough
to know he wouldn't live long. He simply wouldn't want to.
When I got the early morning call from Jacob's nurse and
companion, Francis Fairweather, I was shaken but not surprised.

Grief had been waiting in the wings, so to speak. It came
surging in, and I sat there immersed in it, using the pain to
expiate all the opportunities lost, all the kindnesses unac-
complished. I suppose everyone does that. People die and
we use our hurt to assuage the guilt of all the things we could
have done for them but didn't. Jacob had been my family,
my anchor, my mainstay since I was thirteen. No amount of
effort would ever have repaid his kindness, and I couldn't
imagine being without him.

So I sat there and hurt, not hearing as Francis spoke earnestly about what had to be done. Finally, I realized he was
repeating himself, and I made myself focus on what he was
saying.

"Jason, remember what Jacob said. He wanted things handled quickly." Francis's voice kept breaking as he reminded
me of Jacob's wishes. "The doctor's on his way, and I've
already called the mortuary. If you want to see him, you'd
better come now."

The Jacob of past years was the one I wanted to remember,

not the shell who had lain in his bed for the last three months. It took a couple of tries to get the words out, but I told Francis it was all right: let the mortuary Jacob had chosen take him. Jacob was Jewish, and though he hadn't been at all observant he'd approved of the Jewish tradition of being buried before sundown of the same day one died. He'd chosen cremation, which is not at all consistent with tradition of course. Consistent or not, traditional or not, I'd promised him I'd do anything he wanted.

Jacob's only blood kin was his niece, Charlotte Grosbek, née Buchnam, a rancher who lived about fifty miles south of Denver. I called her to let her know what had been planned. Like Francis and me, she was up and down half a dozen times as we talked, alternately crying and praising Jacob.

"He was such a really nice man. After Daddy died, Uncle Jacob was always so thoughtful, making sure I never wanted for anything." Then tears would force her to stop talking.

When I told her that Jacob had left her a considerable bequest, she cried even harder. As Jacob's executor, I was to see to the bequests, the ones he'd left to Charlotte and Francis, and the smaller ones to a few local and national charities. The balance of his estate, mostly books and furnishings of no great value, came to me. Jacob had arranged, however, that his sizeable monthly income from his former business (now mine) would end when he died. His death made me sole owner of Jacob Lynx Interiors, the three-story building at 1465 Hyde Street and a valuable inventory. Instead of teetering along in intimate partnership with the loan department at the bank, I was almost well-to-do.

If anything, that made me feel worse. I'd have given it all up and more to have Jacob back. However, no amount of resolve or guilt or grief would do that, so I did what people do when they lose someone: blundered my way through the day, stopping now and then in the bathroom to wash my face in cold water and swallow the lump that kept coming up behind my breast bone, sorry for myself yet glad in a sense that it was over because he had wanted it to be over.

Mark McMillan, my assistant, and Eugenia Lowe, the

showroom manager, kept finding excuses to consult me about things, patting me (figuratively speaking) at each encounter. Grace Willis, who still says she is not in love with me, except when she forgets, took time from what she calls the cop-shop to phone every few hours to ask if I was all right. By evening, they'd stroked and poked me into some kind of shape, enough that I could call Francis and tell him I was coming over to pick up the box of personal papers Jacob had kept in his bedside table. Everything else I might need as executor was already in the old iron safe in the basement of my shop-cum-residence at 1465 Hyde.

Francis made no effort to hide his feelings, and we ended up conducting a two-man wake, getting through half a bottle of scotch in the process. Jacob had been abstemious. He'd had no patience with addictions—whether to alcohol, drugs, tobacco, gambling or sex. I could still call to mind his lectures to the fourteen-year-old Jason about *all* that!—and it was probably the memory of his outspoken attitudes that made Francis and me cap the bottle when we did. Of all Jacob's friends and relations, Francis was going to have his life the most changed. He'd been with Jacob since the first stroke, years ago. Now he'd have to make a lot of changes: whom he cared for, where he lived. He was open about saying he thought it unlikely he'd find another patient he'd care about as much as he had Jacob.

It was almost midnight before I got back to the shop. The showrooms on the lower floor were dark, but I'd left a light on in my apartment upstairs. Bela and Schnitz met me at the back door. Bela is my old friend, a hundred twenty pounds of white Kuvasz dog. Schnitz is a new friend, a twelve-pound Maine Coon kitten, son of Grace's huge tomcat, Critter. Schnitz is an orange tabby with tufty feet, and he'll weigh in at eighteen or twenty pounds when he's fully grown. Not as big as his daddy—there are no other cats as big as Critter— but then who needs twenty-nine pounds of cat.

The three of us went upstairs together. I felt tired but not at all sleepy, so I dumped the papers out on the kitchen table, put some coffee beans through the grinder and made a pot, poured a mugful and then sat down to see what I had to take care of. First thing on the top of a pile was Schnitz, who had followed his usual habit of lying down on top of whatever I am working on. He knows it's an unfailing way to get noticed, especially when he revs up his basso purr, blinks at me slowly, and puts out a fat paw to touch my hand. I gave him a scalp massage with one hand while I fished from under him a thick blue envelope, unsealed. Inside were a stack of cancelled checks. Big checks. All made out to someone named H. Fixe. All signed by Jacob. I'd never heard of any H. Fixe, which puzzled me a little. Still, I wasn't upset until I turned the envelope over and saw written on the outside the word *Extortion!* The word was in firm black felt tip, in Jacob's curly hand. *Extortion!* Underlined. Exclamation point.

It wasn't right. The mood was wrong. I'd been sentimentalizing, floating in memories, and that one black word brought me down with a clang and a shocking flush of red-hot anger, as though someone had set off a bomb in my head. I'd turned the papers upside down when I'd dumped them from the box, so this envelope had been tucked away at the bottom. Despite its location at the bottom of the box, the last check in the series was dated the past November, dated, as a matter of fact, the same day as Jacob's last stroke. Since then, I'd been taking care of his bills and payments because Jacob hadn't been able to. Writing this check to H. Fixe was among the last things Jacob had done!

I knew Francis wouldn't be asleep yet, so I called him and asked if he knew anything about the checks or H. Fixe.

"Jacob paid his own bills and addressed his own envelopes as long as he could, Jason. All I did was stamp the envelopes and put them in the mail for him. You've been doing it all since November."

"Did you mail checks for him the day he had his stroke?"

He heard the anger in my voice. "I may have. Jason, what's wrong?"

"Just something I found here, Francis. Makes me think maybe this guy was bothering Jacob, and I got furious at the thought of it. I never signed a check to H. Fixe. Jacob never mentioned anybody by that name to me. Did he ever say anything to you?''

''Never a word. I always assumed Fixe was an insurance agent or a broker or something.''

I asked another question or two, but Francis really didn't know anything about it. I apologized for bothering him so late and hung up.

Fixe wasn't an insurance agent or a broker, because if Jacob had been paying off a large policy or making some investment, he'd have told me. In fact, if he'd been doing anything usual or ordinary with that amount of money, he'd have told me. Why hadn't he wanted me to know about this? I tried to figure it out, feeling inexplicably hurt by the little mystery. Hadn't he wanted to bother me? Didn't he want me involved? You don't write ten-thousand-dollar checks two or three times a year for almost ten years without a reason! Not if you're Jacob, you don't. And I knew Jacob well enough to know that when he'd written the word ''Extortion,'' he'd meant it. He'd been rigorous about the use of language. Words meant what words meant, and that was that. Extortion was extortion.

There was no address in the envelope. There was no ''Fixe'' in the phone book, either. Francis did remember where the checks had been sent. It was too late in the day to do anything about it immediately. I put the papers back in their box, and went to bed, thinking I might trace Fixe through the banks that had cashed the checks. If I had to. Tomorrow.

As I lay there in bed, staring at the ceiling and thinking how unlike Jacob it was for him to hide something from me, it occurred to me that it was very like him to hand me a distraction. He had often done that when I was a kid, when I was sad or angry or just hating everyone, including myself. He'd find something to interest me, some puzzle for me to figure out, then he'd hang around, asking questions, demanding answers, until I turned from whatever emotion was running wild and began to pay attention to life again. He'd been everything to me any family could have been. When I had wondered who I was and why I had been mysteriously abandoned as a child, it was Jacob who had insisted the "why" didn't matter. Who I was, Jacob said, depended only on what I wanted to make of myself. He told me I was lucky to start with a clean slate, not burdened by other people's desires and failures, not thinking I had to either identify with or rebel against someone else just because they were related.

After a while, I accepted that, though curiosity still reared its head from time to time. Sometimes I still half remember faces or voices. More recent and more troubling than the foggy memories are the half-dozen anonymous letters I've received, all of them mailed over the past eighteen months, letters offering to provide information about Jason Lynx, for a price. I'd been tempted, but Grace and I had talked about it at length, in the end agreeing it was a con. Even if it wasn't—what the hell!—I had Jacob. I didn't need any more family than that.

I'd never mentioned the letters to Jacob, mostly because I hadn't wanted to upset him, but also because I knew what he'd say. Jacob had had a firm rule about traffic in trash, one he'd drummed into me over the years. He wouldn't expend emotion or value on something he called (in a whisper and only for my ears) *dreck*. It didn't matter what other dealers did, buying and selling stuff that was essentially worthless, Jacob wouldn't do it, and he carried the same rule over to his private life. As kids will, I'd sometimes wanted things because other kids had them. It would have been easier for Jacob just to give in to me, as most parents who can afford it no doubt do. He never would. We always had to sit down together and analyze the value of whatever I thought I wanted. As a kid, sometimes I'd been furious with him, but I couldn't remember his ever being wrong.

So, if the checks to H. Fixe had really been extortion payments, I knew the pain and revulsion it must have cost Jacob to write them. I also knew he wouldn't have done it to protect himself. He would have done it only to protect someone else.

My last angry thought, before I fell asleep, was that I

intended to find whoever had been responsible and extract a fair measure of retribution on Jacob's behalf.

Thursday morning I didn't have time for retribution because John and Lucinda Hooper were coming in to see a Federal square-back sofa Mark and I had acquired in bits and pieces at the auction of the Morrison estate. When patriarch Morrison had passed on at age ninety, his children and grandchildren off in Arizona or Florida or California had been more interested in cash than they were in fine old furniture. At the time I had more inventory than I needed, but I went to the auction anyway. If one deals in antiques one goes to auctions. It's obligatory. If your competitors don't see you there, before you know it they've decided you're bankrupt or alcoholic or dying of some incurable disease. Antique dealers are like any professional group, reveling in jargon and fueled by rumor.

So, though the bidding wasn't due to begin until one in the afternoon, by nine that morning I was walking up and down the dusty aisles between piles of great stuff (sternly advising myself that I did not *need* any of it), when I heard this poor crippled thing moaning at me from behind a bunch of dilapidated appliances. It was the strangest feeling. I may have glimpsed it subliminally from the corner of the eye, just enough to make me think I heard this weary little sound, like a tired child crying in a distant room. When I saw what it was, I stood over it for a long time, feeling pity. Such a lovely, elegant thing it was, like a crippled greyhound, lying there among the castoffs with one arm and three of its four tapered front legs missing and the carved frieze coming loose from the top rail. It was a hundred and eighty years old if it was a day, and it was dying.

I raised my eyebrow at Mark when he came browsing by, and we conferred in hasty whispers. Sometimes people save broken parts of old furniture, thinking they'll have them mended later. Sometimes they put the broken bits away and forget about them. Sometimes they put them away in other old furniture. We spent the next hour fossicking around among dusty stuff, like domestic archaeologists trying to do a dig without appearing to be doing anything except aimless wandering.

The missing arm rail, panel, and carved handhold turned up stuffed into the bottom drawer of a 1920's oak dresser under some faded curtains. We redoubled our efforts, surreptitiously burrowing through everything included in the sale. Lo and behold, Mark found the three missing legs at the bottom of a box of brass cupboard hardware. We looked around to see if anyone was paying any attention to us. No one was. Evidently we'd been sufficiently casual about the whole thing that no one knew the pieces were there. The delicate turning and reeding on the legs would have been unmistakable if anyone had been looking. It probably helped that none of my more knowledgeable competitors was present at the time.

When the auction got underway, we bid listlessly for this and that, making sure we didn't get any of it. Then, when the box of hardware and the dresser came up, Mark became less listless (though undetectably so) and got them both for under fifty. When the wreckage of the sofa was sold as part of an aggregation of junk, he bought that, too, while I yawned in a display of complete indifference and made inane comments about the weather to a colleague or two.

One of them, Harold Feddleman, commented, "Pity so many parts are missing on that Federal sofa. Almost be worth restoring it. Nice piece." Harold knew Mark worked for me, and he was examining me suspiciously.

"Very nice," I replied in a bored voice while my heart thubbed away in fear of imminent discovery. "Too bad it's a total wreck."

The only parts of our purchase we brought back to the shop were the disconnected parts of the sofa and the box of assorted brass hardware—which is always useful if one needs to match old drawer pulls or hinges or knobs. There were only shreds of upholstery left on the sofa back, literally shreds, but what was there served to identify the type of fabric used originally as well as giving us a hint as to the original color. There are fabric houses specializing in period fabrics. Once all the mahogany and birch parts were cleaned up and reunited (*all* original parts, mind you, except for one four-inch piece of birch dowel going down the inside of a leg!), and the back and arms reupholstered in silk brocade with an elegant new seat cushion, the sofa turned out to be absolutely gorgeous. Near museum quality. Every time I looked at it with its exposed mahogany top rail and its elaborately carved Sheraton frieze, I felt sanctified by having rescued it.

Since the Morrisons had come originally from New England, my guess was the sofa had been made by Samuel McIntire in Salem, Mass. That made it worth at least twenty thou, more likely twice that. Mark had already worked up a nice comparison chart out of auction catalogues and notations of sales prices on similar items, as well as some information on Samuel McIntire and Salem furniture production in the late 1700's and early 1800's.

At any rate, John and Lucinda Hooper were coming over to take a look. I figured we'd dicker back and forth for some time. Dickering was the greater part of the fun for the Hoopers. They would amuse themselves thinking up new ways to approach the buy, such as trading me back such and such a piece they'd bought last year, or getting me to throw in such and such a piece to sweeten the deal. Eugenia and I had already conferred on what we might use as sweeteners. We could always sacrifice a few small things to make the bigger sale.

The Hoopers played it just as we'd thought they would. Hmm and haw, and this and that, and no decision that morning, though Lucinda cast a worried look over her shoulder when they left, as though she feared another buyer might ooze out of the woodwork the moment she was gone. We had no other prospects for the sofa. Seeing the expression on Lucinda's face, I was pretty sure we didn't need any.

By eleven I was back upstairs in my office staring at the wall, suddenly at a loss.

"You okay?" asked Mark, giving me a sympathetic look.

"Yeah," I said. "Sure." For the moment, dealing with the Hoopers, I'd actually forgotten about Jacob.

"You're going to miss him."

I nodded and swallowed. "We all knew it was inevitable."

"I know. Still."

Right. Still. Since Mark had reminded me, I fetched the box of papers from the kitchen and turned it out on top of my desk, drawing Mark's attention to the envelope with *Extortion!* written on it.

"Pretty firm hand," he said. "I thought Jacob was very shaky."

"That was written before he got sick," I said. "Before I even came back to Denver. The first check was written almost twelve years ago."

Mark had the checks spread out in front of him. "Who's this H. Fixe?" he asked me.

I shrugged.

"You're not looking for a puzzle, are you?" he asked with a faintly worried expression. "You're not trying to make something out of this?"

I leaned over and tapped the word on the envelope. "I don't have to make anything out of it. It's already made. If Jacob wrote that, he meant it. Somebody was holding him up."

"Usually, I'd say go to it," he commented, "but you may be sorry if you go digging into Jacob's life. If he didn't tell you, he had a reason; maybe there was something in his life he wanted to keep private."

"If it was something about Jacob himself, he'd have written the word *Blackmail*. Jacob was as much a stickler for accuracy as he was for honesty. Extortion is a different thing."

Mark sat staring at the envelope. I could follow his thoughts on his face. Though he can do a poker face when he has to, his mobile, handsome countenance usually shows every nuance, every thought, every feeling. He looks like a blond Christopher Reeves, though his lips are fuller and his nose is not quite so sharply classic. He'd have made a great actor.

"Extortion is getting money by threatening someone, isn't it?" He gave me a puzzled look.

I was as puzzled as he. "Jacob wouldn't have given in to a threat against himself, Mark. If he paid to protect someone, it had to be someone else. So who?"

"Who else is there?" Mark asked. "You, or his niece, right."

"Right," I agreed. "Me or Charlotte. In either case, I certainly should know about it. He'd have wanted me to help Charlotte, if necessary, and he'd sure as hell have expected me to look out for myself." Why hadn't he told me about this, whatever it was? He should have told me! It hurt that he hadn't.

Since neither of us could come up with a solution to the problem, Mark went back to his catalogues and I went back to the box, sorting the contents into piles. Jacob's birth certificate. Jacob's military service records, World War II. A picture of me at age thirteen, looking like a hippie. Tough guy. A picture of Jacob in the Colfax Avenue shop with me, age fifteen, wearing shirt and tie and dark apron, my hair long enough to hide the burn scars on the back of my head (the partly healed burns had been there when I'd been abandoned at the Home). After Jacob had caught me trying to steal from his antique shop, he'd hired me and put me to work polishing, repairing, sweeping out, and packing up. Later on, he'd sent me to college, where I'd majored in art and history with the idea of becoming a museum curator. My graduation picture was there, cap and gown and silly grin. A few navy pictures were there, too. I'd been twenty-three or twenty-four by that time. A shot of me with the rest of the guys from scuba school had a "Happy Birthday" message to Jacob written across our wetsuited forms. Nothing like seeing me busy learning to blow stuff up underwater, Jacob had written, to make him feel his years.

Next were two snaps of me in front of the Smithsonian— when I got out of the navy, I'd worked at the Smithsonian for several years—then me and Agatha, then the two of us with baby Jerry. Agatha was dead. Jerry was dead. I had learned to accept that, but still I turned the pictures facedown.

The next thing in the box was a packet of older photos in wrinkled tissue that had obviously been wrapped and unwrapped many, many times. Most of these I couldn't remember ever having seen before, though the first one set off an immediate tingle of recognition. I had seen this portrait—or a copy of it—years ago, hanging on the wall near Jacob's bed. It showed a lovely young woman in her twenties and was signed "Dearest Jacob, all my love always. Olivia." Her light hair was arranged close to her head in those too tight waves women wore back in the twenties and thirties. Her dress had feathers at the shoulders, like little wings, and she wore an ornate crucifix on a chain. The face resembled someone else I knew, but I couldn't think who.

In another photo, a group shot of three women and two men, the same woman stood against a car, her silk dress molded to her slender body in a single fluid line, a man's arm around her shoulders. After staring at it for some time, I realized the man was Jacob, a very virile-looking Jacob, with a full head of dark curly hair. Jacob had been eighty-one when he died; he'd been born in 1911. This picture must have been taken sometime in the thirties. Looking at that lovely, laughing face beside him, I wondered why Jacob had never married. Had something happened to his Olivia? Had she married someone else? Had he gone on loving her, all his life?

Mark came by and peered over my shoulder. "Gorgeous," he said, tracing the line of her body with one forefinger. "Like a Botticelli goddess. She looks like someone I've seen before. Wrong hairdo, though."

I said she looked familiar to me, too, but neither of us could decide who she reminded us of.

"I wonder what happened to the two of them," I said.

Mark cocked his head, thoughtfully. "Didn't you tell me Jacob was Jewish?"

"Yes. Not a religious Jew, but he always identified himself as Jewish."

"She's probably Catholic." Mark pointed out the crucifix, which I had ignored. "Twenties and thirties were very bigoted times, weren't they? Height of the KKK and all that? Her folks probably went through the roof if they thought she was in love with a Jew. Wasn't there a popular stage comedy, way back, about some Catholic girl marrying a Jewish boy and all the problems they had with in-laws? I seem to recall mother making some allusion to it when the son of a friend of hers made a similar *mésalliance*. I'm quoting. At any rate, marrying out of one's class and/or religion wasn't the done thing. Not among good families."

"You think she was from a good family?"

He fanned the pictures on the table. "Look at their clothes," he replied. "I'd guess that's a designer dress in the portrait. Even though feathers were in then, the way these are handled isn't cheap. Look at the car they're leaning against. That's a college crowd in a time when most people didn't go to college. If these people weren't rich, they were well-to-do, at least."

If anyone would know, Mark would know. His family was among the wealthier of my acquaintance, not that they made much of my acquaintance. Mark's father had not yet forgiven his son for being gay, working as a designer, or failing to produce an heir for the family fortune, not necessarily in that order. Since I was the person Mark worked for, I received a full share of the elder McMillan's disapprobation. On the few occasions I'd met him he'd been polite but frosty.

"It's possible it was a prejudice problem," I admitted, feeling sorry for Jacob if that had been true.

I was down to the final two items, the things Jacob had had at the top. One was a list of the charities he had left money to, next to each was a brief paragraph on how he wanted the money used. He'd asked me to visit the local charities on his behalf: the local Planned Parenthood. The Lighthouse center for battered women. Several others.

And finally a snapshot which had come out looking like a

nineteenth-century landscape, full of green and misty distances. I remembered when Jacob had taken it, from the porch of Charlotte's house on a rainy, early summer day. It showed a grove of huge ponderosa pines atop a nearby hill, the land falling away behind in multiple shaded horizons. I remembered the occasion, a family picnic after graduation, just before I'd gone into the navy. Jacob had been about sixty then. I'd been twenty something, home for the summer.

And that was all. There really wasn't a lot for me to do. Jacob had been methodical. He hadn't left a lot of loose ends hanging. I put everything back in the box except the list of bequests, the photos, and the envelope of "Extortion" checks. Those went in the bottom right-hand drawer of my desk where I keep pending matters. There was no good reason for me to assume that the photos of Olivia and her friends belonged in "pending." Maybe I simply wanted to look at her face again because Jacob obviously had, many times.

When Charlotte called later in the morning, I asked her if she recognized either the name Fixe or the name Olivia. Fixe didn't ring a bell, but when I described Olivia's picture, she recalled hearing that Uncle Jacob had had a sweetheart whom he'd never gotten over.

"Daddy told me about it," she said, referring to Harry Buchnam, Jacob's twin brother. "One time I asked him why Uncle Jacob had never married, and he told me about this girl Jacob was in love with, but her family didn't approve of the Buchnams. So they sent her off to Europe where she married someone who got wounded in the war, and later died. It was all very tragic."

"Do you remember her last name?" I asked.

"Olivia sounds sort of familiar," she mused. "But I don't think Dad ever mentioned a last name."

The day passed, Mark and Eugenia closed up shop and went home, I went upstairs to put together an Italian dinner for Grace Willis and me. We had a standing midweek dinner date for any Tuesday, Wednesday, or Thursday she wasn't working, plus whatever time we could spend together on the days she had off. Lately she'd had weekends, which had been nice for us both. Grace is a cop. She says cop. She dislikes "policewoman." She is tiny, blond, eats like three stevedores, has enormous drive and ambition, is honest to a fault and hardworking enough to make me feel guilty. She is about eight years younger than I am, which makes her thirty-two. We are at an indeterminate stage of our relationship. I think she's quit worrying that I may be comparing her to Agatha. I have quit trying to find Agatha all over again. Grace reminds me from time to time that she is not in love with me, though I'm not sure whether she's trying to convince me or herself. We have not talked about marriage, at least not marriage to each other, though I have waltzed toward the subject time and again without much response from Grace.

Grace occasionally says that I am not quite lively enough for her, so she goes out with other men from time to time. However, she tells me she does not go to bed with anyone else. She finds me lively enough in that respect. She has kidded me on occasion about being safe sex. I'm not sure this is flattering, but I'd be a fool to question the status quo. I think at the heart of the issue is that I am not at all gregarious, while she gets a high from being part of a crowd. She likes going Christmas shopping and attending football games, things I consider only slightly less agonizing that being trampled by stampeding cows.

Despite that, we enjoy one another. Sometimes Grace finds me moodier than she likes, and I occasionally feel her unquenchability wearing, but we can say so, and neither of us ever expresses any animosity over these feelings. When I think about it, I find that very lack of irritation a little troubling. It makes me wonder, sometimes, if we are truly tolerant and accepting of one another, or whether we simply don't care quite enough. I like to think it's the former. I'm honest enough not to be sure. In either case, we are very close and fond friends. About that much, I'm positive.

When Grace arrived, I told her what I'd been discovering about Jacob. She got sentimental over the idea of Jacob having an old sweetheart, but when I told her about the "Extortion" envelope, she forgot sentiment and blazed up just as I had. We traded theories on what and who and why. Mine tended to be esoteric, as befits a puzzle lover, while hers were more pragmatic, as befits a cop. Grace often says that most crimes tend to be a matter of ABC rather than the mystery of X. Someone gets drunks, then gets angry, then bashes someone with the nearest heavy object. Or shoots, or stabs, or runs down with a car. Simple. Despite having made this point repeatedly, she couldn't come up with a simple explanation for the checks to H. Fixe.

"I don't think I've ever had an extortion case," she said over the table which had held our Chianti, our antipasto, our minestrone, our veal parmigiana, our linguini, our salad, our cheese cake. I say "our," though three quarters of it had been consumed by Grace. In the year and a half I've known her, I've learned to lay in edibles sufficient for four large men and expect her to eat for three and a fraction of them.

"I did have a guy who threatened to kill his wife if she didn't give him custody of their kid, which was extortion, even though he finally got charged with something else. Felonious assault, I think," she said, polishing off the last crumb of her third helping of cheese cake. "You think Jacob really meant extortion?"

Grace had met Jacob, but she had never had the opportunity to know him. I explained what a stickler Jacob had been for the right word at the right time. If he wrote a word, he meant it. Extortion meant extortion.

"I'll see what I can find out about H. Fixe," she said. "See if anybody with that name has a record."

Then, having temporarily placated her craving for food and crime, she turned her attention to me and we found other things to think about for the remainder of the evening. She fell asleep before I did, on her back, soundlessly as a baby. I lay on my side, my arm across her satiny breasts, my hand curled around her far shoulder, looking at the line of her profile against the light from the hall, thinking about having a family again, starting a family again.

In the Home, all the kids, including me, had constantly

talked about families. Though some of us pretended otherwise, each of us wanted to be adopted. We wanted someone of our own. Most of us were unadoptable. We hadn't been relinquished properly, or we were of mixed race, or we were too old, or we had serious physical or character defects, some of them no doubt inherent, but some we'd acquired during our years of institutional life. In my case, the burns on the back of my head and on one ear (looking, one helpful physician said, not precisely accidental) had left scars on more than my body.

From about age fourteen, I'd worn my hair long to cover the burns. In the year just past, I'd had hair implants and surgery to smooth out the warped ear. In the Home, however, we'd all had short institutional haircuts and I'd been miserably self-conscious about the scars. They had helped convince me I was unwanted and unwantable, which had led me to boasting and strutting and accepting a dare to steal, which had put me in Jacob Buchnam's Colfax Avenue antique shop, where Jacob had caught me at my first attempt.

He could have turned in the brat who had tried to rip off his silver candlestick. Instead, Jacob saw all my cock-a-doodle as mere cover-up and called my bluff. He made me his foster son. He reared me. He sent me to school, he accepted my wife as his own daughter-in-law and my child as his grandchild. When my wife disappeared and my son lay in a lifelong coma, he stood by me. When one was found murdered and the other died, he grieved with me. He had been my family, first and last.

And now I had none. I looked at Grace's quiet face against the glow from the window and thought about asking her to marry me. I decided not to, because I was afraid she'd say no.

Friday morning I made the rounds of the local charities on Jacob's list. He had asked me to call on them personally to explain how he wanted his bequest used. If they couldn't accommodate his wishes, they didn't get it. He'd been very firm about that.

I ended my morning's visits at the local Planned Parenthood clinic, where Jacob had wanted his money used for security against the antiabortion picketers. I recalled visiting Jacob a year or so ago and finding him brooding angrily over a newspaper account of an abortion clinic blockade by some outfit called Operation Rescue. When I confessed puzzlement as to why he felt so strongly about it, he'd been almost angry with me.

"You, of all people, should understand, Jason! How many kids were there in that place where you grew up? Over a hundred? Most of them 'unadoptable,' which means nobody wanted them, right? How many are there now in homes and hospitals all over the country? Half a million, maybe? A million? Minority babies? Half-grown children? Children with AIDS? Retarded children? Children born with addictions? Children who've been abused, as you were? And where is Operation Rescue for them? How many of those children are being rescued from fates far worse than never having been born? Hah?"

"Probably not many, Jacob," I'd said, trying to calm him down. On the rare occasions when he got angry, he trembled all over.

He wouldn't calm. "Oh, it's no doubt rewarding to spend a Saturday morning hunkered down outside a clinic, singing hymns and feeling holy, getting your picture in the paper, taking up the time of already overworked police, abusing women who may be more genuinely religious than you are. It would be too difficult and demanding to actually do something for a child in need! So-called Christians! Pah!"

I certainly had been one of those unadoptable children, which meant I could sympathize with his frustration, even though I couldn't identify personally with the abortion issue. It had simply never come up in my life. Nonetheless, I understood Jacob's point of view well enough to quote him at some length to Cynthia Adamson, the manager of the clinic, actually getting a smile out of her a couple of times. She looked both too thin and too tired, a pale woman of about fifty-five, lines of determination graven around her mouth and eyes.

"We can use the money," she said. "The antiabortion groups like to claim we make a lot of money doing abortions, but we don't. All the nonprofit clinics I know of try to provide abortions at close to cost, because most of our patients are poor."

If the people in the waiting room were any indication, they were not only poor but very troubled. As we had come through, I had noticed a woman sobbing in the arms of a friend. When we had settled into Cynthia's private office with the door closed, she told me the woman already had two children, victims of a genetic disease.

"She can't handle any more. Just taking care of the two she has takes all the strength she has." She nodded toward the waiting room. "The first time that woman came in here for counseling, one of the male picketers grabbed her and started screaming at her not to kill her baby. She almost collapsed. All the poor woman has been trying to do is cope with this damned disease, and she didn't need the compassionate help of the so-called pro-life people, I can tell you that."

She made a spitting motion with her lips, rubbing her forehead as though it hurt. "Sorry. I get so angry at the pain they cause. I wish there were some way to thank Mr. Buchnam for his gift. We need it badly right now."

"Now more than usually?" I asked.

"Yes. A couple of years ago, the police and judges got pretty tired of the demonstrations and started assessing fines that were commensurate with what it cost the city to enforce the law. That stopped the worst of it for a time. It's all very well to shout abuse at poor women and then return to your nice middle-class home for lunch, but spending several weeks in jail among unsympathetic prisoners wasn't what these people had in mind."

"When did it start up again?"

"Just recently. This new bunch is very abusive. Mostly men. The few women in the crowd are usually brought by men. I won't go into what kind of men. Have you seen them in action?"

I admitted I had only seen pictures on the evening news.

"Drive by in the morning," she said. "I'm told we're going to get hit by a full-scale invasion about seven-thirty."

I nodded, more or less affirmatively. I'm not sure whether I was just agreeing that I should or saying that I would. In either case, I promptly forgot about the clinic and did not remember it until very early on Saturday morning when Grace, who'd arrived late the previous evening with a small overnight case, began moving purposefully in and out of the bedroom at about 5 A.M.

"What are you doing?" I asked her in disbelief. She was actually wearing a uniform. Grace had been plainclothes for some time. I couldn't recall ever seeing her in uniform.

"Got to go," she said. "Duty calls."

I knew she had the day off. "What do you mean?" I demanded, furious at her. She had no business going anywhere at all on *our* Saturday.

"It's my weekend at the abortion clinic," she said. "They're going to be blockaded this morning. Some of us women cops moonlight there on the weekends, just to make sure nobody gets hurt."

Oh, great, I thought, still half asleep and completely unsympathetic. "Carrying limp bodies? Arresting protestors?"

"No," she said, kissing me on the forehead. "The guys on regular duty will do that. Those of us moonlighting are inside, to arrest anyone who breaks in or does anything violent. Personally, I'd volunteer, but the department has rules about taking sides in public disputes, like political campaigns or labor union clashes or controversial stuff. Cops are always cops, even out of uniform, even off duty, so I can't volunteer for either side. What I can do is work for pay, enforcing the law."

"Like moonlighting policemen at a concert or football game?" I asked. "Paid extra, but working as cops?"

"Right. I'm not there to take sides. I'm there to provide extra law enforcement. But I donate my pay back to the clinic, which is my right, and that's the best I can do."

"I'll drive you down," I said as I struggled from among the covers, resolving, not for the first time, to be understanding. "It's one of Jacob's selected charities, and I told the clinic manager I wanted to see what goes on. I guess this is as good a time as any."

It wasn't. It was a lousy time. I had only one cup of coffee before we left, because Grace wanted to be there when the clinic opened at six-thirty. I was offered coffee when we arrived, but since it was to be made in a plastic cup from lukewarm water and a spoonful of brown gravel, I decided to forgo a second cup.

Grace and a colleague went off somewhere to decide on their strategy for the day. Cynthia put a green band on my arm to identify me to the staff as friendly, and I sat down in the as yet empty waiting room waiting for something to happen.

First the cops showed up outside. Then a few patients straggled in. Then a cavalcade of cars arrived at the curb, out of which poured the zealots. I watched the whole thing in a kind of frozen disbelief. It was a little like a soccer game, only nastier. The blockaders, mostly male, seemed to be keyed up, rushing the goal. They scrambled for the double glass doors (there were locked steel grills inside), milled around there for a minute, and then hunkered down to begin singing something that sounded neither rousing nor holy.

From inside, all I could see was their backs, shoved up against each other like sheep packed into a stock truck. Out in front of the blockaders roamed the shock troops, evidently assigned to slogan-carrying and harassment.

Inside, the staff and patients went about their business as though nothing were happening. Whenever a patient arrived, clinic volunteers outside the clinic bulldozed a clear path through to a small back door. Someone inside unlocked it to let each patient in while uniformed female cops (Grace and her friends) stood nearby to make sure no laws were broken. They weren't allowed to help, only to warn the protesters to stand back—which they did constantly, because every harasser seemed determined to intimidate the patients with shouted abuse—and to move in and make an arrest if something illegal occurred. After a while the regular duty cops outside made an announcement through a bullhorn. I could hear the bleat but not the content, and assumed the protesters were being warned to disperse. Outside the doors there was some squirming and linking of arms. The bullhorn sounded again. I stood up to look over the heads of the protesters as the uniformed men began taking the blockaders off, one by one. Unlike some newscasts I've seen, the Denver police didn't bother carrying them. They twisted their arms up behind their backs and used pain to get them moving into the police vans. The remaining blockaders screamed about police brutality, but the police handling didn't look nearly as brutal to me as what the harassers had been doing to the patients.

It took about forty-five minutes to clear the doors. I watched as they moved each person until they were down to the last three. A skinny man with wild eyes screamed obscenities at the police. A woman with white curly hair glared at me through the glass as they led her away. The single remaining figure was slumped against the doors in a bulky down coat, shapeless as a walrus, head sagging. As two cops took hold of the coat and shook gently, I thought maybe he or she had gone to sleep, bored by the whole business. Then the heavy figure slid sideways and toppled over. The younger cop yelled something and went off at a run.

Now we had a whole new scene. A doctor, at least one, from inside the clinic. An ambulance. Paramedics. More police. Cynthia went out and talked to the cops. Grace went out and talked to the cops. Grace came in and talked to me.

"She's dead," Grace half whispered, so the few patients left in the waiting room couldn't hear her. "The woman by the door."

So it had been a woman. "Was it a heart attack?"

"We don't know. There was a note in her jacket pocket." She consulted her notebook. "It says, 'She interfered. She's dead.' "

I stared at her, not believing it. "She was killed?"

"Possibly. We don't know. I told them you'd probably seen the whole thing. The lieutenant wants to talk to you."

"Me?"

"You've been sitting right here, Jason. She was crammed right up against the doors, and you've been watching through the glass. Sure he wants to talk to you."

So, Grace introduced me to Lieutenant Linder from homicide, and I talked to him. I told him I had seen the protesters arrive, had seen them squinch themselves up against the doors, had watched them sitting there for almost an hour, and had then seen the police remove them.

"Anybody approach this woman?" He had a pale, middle-aged face with a long upper lip, pale lashes, and brows so high on his forehead they made him look like a surprised rabbit.

I explained that the protesters had been at least five rows deep, that nobody had moved once they were in position, because they couldn't, they were jammed in too tightly. Nobody stood up. Nobody came or went.

"How about when we cleared 'em out," asked the lieutenant. "Did you see that?"

I had. The row in front of the fat woman had been cleared. Then the people at each end of the back row. "The man to her left was skinny with crazy eyes, and he kept yelling obscenities at the cops. The woman on the other side . . ." I tried to think what it had been about her. "She wasn't dressed for the weather," I said at last. "She was wearing trousers, but she had on a light shirt, no jacket. An older woman, sort of full-bodied, with glasses and white curly hair. Maybe . . . oh, sixty."

"And this Fixe woman never moved?" asked the lieutenant.

"Who?" I said it louder than I meant to.

He gave me a quizzical look.

"I'm sorry," I said, recovering from the surprise. "What name did you say?"

"The dead woman," he said. "Simonetta Fixe." He watched for my reaction. When he didn't get one, he continued, "At least, that's what it says on her ID card." He turned his clipboard around so I could see it. He'd clipped the ID card by one corner so he could copy down the name and address, written below. Simonetta L. Fixe. An address in the northwest part of town. North Zuni Street. I memorized the number.

"No driver's license," he commented. "Just this card, her social security card, and a credit card. You know her?" He gave me the standard cop stare, but he didn't have the face for it. No menace. Grace does better than that.

"I ran across the name Fixe recently," I admitted. "But it wasn't anyone named Simonetta."

One pale eyebrow edged toward his hairline, but he didn't pursue the matter. "And you never saw her move?"

"Once they sat down, she never moved from that place," I said, running over various murder methods in my mind. "I didn't see anyone come up to her but the police. I didn't see anyone touch her except the people on either side of her. I didn't see anyone hand her anything. I didn't see her eat or drink anything, though she could have done that without my seeing it. If she'd had a candy bar in her pocket, for instance. I could only see her back, not what she might have been doing with her hands or mouth."

He shook his head, wrote down my name and phone number, and let me go. Police cars were moving away. Grace and I went back inside the clinic. We found Cynthia Adamson kneeling on the mat just inside the double glass doors, staring at them.

"Cynthia, what are you doing?" asked Grace.

"If she was killed, they're going to think it was one of us," she replied. "Aren't they?"

"So what are you doing?"

"Wondering if there was any way anyone could have done something to that woman from in here. Like, you know, shoot at her through the crack between the doors or something."

Grace pulled her to her feet. "Nobody said she was shot, Cynthia. Besides, no one from inside could have put that note on her. Jason was sitting here the whole time. He didn't see anyone do anything to the doors, or to the woman.''

I nodded wearily, wondering if Cynthia was right, if someone would suspect the clinic staff. On our way home, I said this to Grace.

She shook her head. ''There are fanatics on both sides of the issue, Jason, but they don't work at the clinic. The people there aren't zealots. That's one thing that kind of surprised me when I first started working down there. I was expecting to meet militant feminists who think abortion is more a duty than a right and try to sell it like crazy. But the people there aren't like that. They know how hard the choices are, and they don't push for one choice over the other. If you're looking for a pro-abortion fanatic, you'll have to look somewhere else.''

I had no intention of looking anywhere, not for Simonetta Fixe's murderer. Her death was not my concern. My only interest in her was that she might have a relative with the initial *H*. When we left, I talked Grace into coming with me to the Zuni Street address, just on the off chance H. Fixe might live there.

The house was tiny, set in a large plot of unkept lawn. There was nobody home. Next door we found Mrs. Walter Huggenmier, Vera, who came to the door in a light housedress and then stood bare-legged on her front porch, hugging herself to keep from freezing. We told her Mrs. Fixe was dead. She said that was a terrible shame, but the words were convention, not feeling, so I assumed she wouldn't mind being asked if Simonetta had a relative with the initial H. Simonetta's husband was named Herby, she said, but he'd been killed in an accident a couple of months ago.

She added, ''Of course, the way Herby drank, I always figured he'd end up killing himself.''

I, exulting at the discovery of an H. Fixe, even a dead one, asked her how he'd managed that.

During a blizzard in the middle of the night, she said, shortly before Christmas. He'd driven off Speer Boulevard into Cherry Creek, had landed upside down and drowned in about eight inches of water. Because of the snow, no one even saw the car until the next day.

We shook our heads over the vagaries of fate. "The Fixes aren't in the phone book," I commented.

"They had one of those unlissed nummers," Mrs. Huggenmier confided between shivers. "Simmy said there was people lookin for Herby, from somethin' he was mixed up in, a long time ago. She liked to be all mysserious about that, all the time sayin she could tell us stuff if she wanned to. Walt says it's a lot of crap. Walt says Herby was too old to be mixed up in anythin much, and besides, he was half drunk all the time."

"Your husband, Walt, knew him well?"

"Well, you know. A long time ago they worked at the same place. You wanna come back tonight, you can ask him. Walt'll be home about seven." Already frozen into inarticulation, she was convulsing from the cold and her lips were turning blue. I wondered what was inside that she'd rather freeze to death than invite us in to see.

We said we'd be back, told her to go in before she solidified, and went off to find something to eat. Grace's early breakfast had long since metabolized, as had the several doughnuts she'd consumed at the clinic, leaving her in danger of imminent collapse. She has a favorite Mexican place on Seventeenth Avenue, where she stuffed herself on chiles rellenos while enlightening me on the various types thereof. There were, she informed me, five basic types. First, the relleno auténtico: a whole, poblano pepper roasted and peeled, strips of cheese inserted, the whole dipped in beaten eggs (preferably with the whites whipped separately and folded in) and fried, then covered with green or red sauce. In the authentic relleno, the seeds aren't removed, the cheese is a white, farmer type, and the chile itself is barely coated with egg, just enough to seal it.

Second, says Grace, we have the tourist relleno, in which the stem and seeds are removed before cooking. Third is the bulk-manufactured restaurant relleno, which is made in a factory, and is covered with thick batter. The bulk relleno is very solid-looking and is usually stuffed with bright orange "cheese food," which neither looks nor tastes like cheese; it is shipped frozen and microwaved to order. Fourth, the yuppie relleno, in which cheddar and Monterey Jack cheese are shredded, mixed with chopped green chiles and sauteed onions, and (depending upon the ethnic background of the cook) rolled into A) a blintz, or B) a crepe, or C) an eggroll wrapper, or D) a tortilla, and then fried. Fifthly and finally, the relleno exótico, in which the stuffing may be most anything, including meat with raisins. My favorite place in Santa Fe serves them that way.

Grace finds four out of five of these acceptable. The place on Seventeenth Avenue serves the yuppie type. Grace had two and a half orders of two each, plus beans, rice, half a dozen buttered flour tortillas, and a basket of sopaipillas with honey. I had two stuffed chiles and nothing much else. Grace weighs one eighteen and does not vary by more than six ounces over a year. I weigh one eighty and can put on ten pounds by sniffing deeply outside a bakery. I need more exercise. I'm still not as mobile as I was before my leg got gunshot a year or so ago.

When Grace was topped up, we ordered coffee, then sat for a while, trying to figure out whether Jacob's interest in the clinic and Simonetta Fixe's death and H. Fixe showing up in Jacob's checks was all a coincidence. We thought it unlikely, but neither of us really believes in coincidences.

"Jacob's last check to Fixe was written shortly before Fixe died," I said. "It was dated late November."

"I wonder if Jacob knew Fixe was dead."

"I'm not sure how much Jacob really took in during those last few weeks. If they said Fixe's name on the TV news, Jacob may have heard it. Francis usually turns on the news around supper time, so Jacob could have known. Not that it makes any difference whether Jacob knew or not."

"Sure it makes a difference, Jason!" she said, reaching over to pat my hand. "You said yourself you were hurt because Jacob hadn't told you what this was about. Well, if he knew Fixe was dead, he wouldn't have bothered to tell you about it, would he? Not if it was something painful. Not if it was a threat that no longer existed. He probably never intended for you to see the checks, but he'd had that last stroke, and he wasn't able to destroy them or even tell Francis to do it for him.''

Since that last stroke, he'd been almost unable to communicate, but otherwise she was right. If the cause of his anxiety had been dead, he wouldn't have struggled to tell me about it.

We spent the afternoon at Grace's. I'd promised to help her lay tile in a new bathroom she was putting in, and we made good progress. That evening, we cleaned up and drove over to the Huggenmier house, dressed warmly in anticipation of another front porch conversation.

We didn't stand outside, however. Walt Huggenmier, a stocky, bowlegged bulldog of a man, invited us into a house so painfully clean and neat we hesitated to sit down. I decided we had not been invited in that morning because it had not been neat enough for guests. As I watched Mrs. Huggenmier moving about, tidying this and flicking at invisible bits of that, I knew she was one of those women who would have to clean the whole house before she could bring herself to call the fire department to report the kitchen was burning.

Walt was a salt-of-the-earth type, talky and jolly and interested in hearing all about his former neighbor. Vera Huggenmier, now that she wasn't freezing to death, was similarly interested. Grace and I had already decided we'd get further if the inquiry was official, so Grace identified herself as a cop and asked for anything they could tell her about the Fixes.

''Well, damn,'' said Walt. ''I'd knowed old Herb for a long time. Since we were kids. I should be able to tell you all about him, but you know, I can't. Herb got up to all kinds of stuff when he was a kid, and he'd brag on it all the time, but whatever he was up to lately, he only kinda dropped a hint, you know.''

''Illegal stuff?'' asked Grace.

''The way I knowed Herb, I'd hafta say yes.'' He didn't

seem saddened by the admission. "He was in with that North Denver crowd."

"Really? *The* North Denver crowd."

"Yeah, They was into gamblin, mostly. Started out boot-leggin, back in the twenties, then got into gamblin. Herby never tole me exactly what he did for them."

Vera said, "I'll tell you one thing. He drove that fancy car of his, so he had to have car payments, and insurance, and bills, you know, like we all do. But he didn' have a job. I said to Walt, I said, that tells you somethin', doesn' it? He had to have money coming from somewhere."

Walt nodded in agreement. "Right. That's what she said. And she's right, 'cause Herb sure wasn't like, what they say, innepennennly wealthy." He crowed with amusement. "Not old Herby."

"What did you think he was up to?" I asked.

Walt shrugged. "These days? I thought maybe dope. What else is there?"

"How about blackmail?" suggested Grace.

Walt thought about it. "That'd be good for ole Herb," he agreed. "He could talk tough. I guess he could scare some-body. Make somebody think he had somethin on 'em. He was sneaky." He nodded to himself happily, thinking how sneaky Herby had been. "He used to all the time leave things with me, you know, stuff to keep for him, letters to mail. Five, six years ago, he left me a letter to mail if he died. Said somebody might do him in, and the letter was his insurance policy."

"Did you mail it?"

"When he died? Sure, I told him I would."

"Couldn't remember where you put it!" his wife chal-lenged him. "Never would've gotten it mailed if I hadn't found it for you, and took you near a month as it was!"

"Yeah, well. It'd been a long time."

"Who was it addressed to?" Grace asked.

"Postmaster. It was addressed to Postmaster. There was another envelope inside, though. I could feel it."

"What about his wife? Did you know her?" I asked.

Vera didn't need to think about that one. "She was mostly by herself. He come here to see Walt oftener than he come to see her. Now here lately she got in with this antiabortion bunch from her church and turned kinda crazy. She ast me to go with her, and I tole her I didn' hole with interferin with people that way. People have to do what they think is right. I tole her that, but she'd just shake her head at me and talk about sin. I tole her, I said, 'Simmy, you're gonna wear yourself out! You're too ole and you're too fat for this runnin around.' She used to get real mad when I called her fat, but she was."

"Had they been married long?" I asked.

"Not all that long. She said ten years, I think. Course, that was a couple of years ago. We only moved in here about—what was it, Walt?"

He thought maybe '85, '86.

Vera went on, "I don't know why she ever married him, at her age."

"Did she ever talk about her childhood?" Grace asked. "About what she did before she got married?"

"Oh, she worked for people, doin housework. I know that. She worked for some big rich family for a long time. Some eye-talian name." Vera punched her forehead, as though she had a input key that needed manual operation. "Somethin happened to 'em, so she went to some other people and did cook-housekeepin for them. Even after her and Herby got married, she worked for somebody named Sinclaire. She was always talkin about 'em, Mrs. Sinclaire this and Mrs. Sinclaire that."

There were several wealthy Sinclaires in the Denver area; two of them had been clients of mine. I asked which family, but Vera didn't know.

I turned to Walt. "Your wife said you'd known him since he was young."

"Oh, sure. We both grew up on the north side. Lots of eye-talians on the north side. Well, Herby was always into somethin. Gamblin mostly. With the rest of the eye-talian families over there, you know," he winked at Grace. "You otta know. Herby's name wasn't Fixe, not to start with. It was Fitteli or Fissoli, somethin like that. They called him Herby the Fixer, that's how he got the name, an' he worked for the Leones. I guess that's how he got hooked up with Simmy. She was a Leone.''

"That's right!'' exclaimed Vera. "That's who she worked for before the Sinclaires! It was her uncle or somebody. The Leones.''

The name meant nothing to me. It meant something to Grace. She made a face.

"How about Herby,'' she asked. "Did he have any relatives?''

They shook their heads. They didn't know. There was nothing more the Huggenmiers could tell us. We thanked them for the information, refused an offered beer, and left.

"Who are the Leones?'' I asked Grace.

"There were three or four families named Leone. One of them used to be a crime family, starting in the twenties and up through the forties I think, maybe the fifties. It never amounted to much. Not like the east coast. Not like Chicago or Miami.''

"Crime? Drugs?''

"They were never into drugs much,'' she said. "Walt was right. They started in bootlegging. Then, mostly they went into gambling and protection, maybe prostitution, old-fashioned stuff like that. And there was only one biggish fish: Canello Leone. The rest were mostly small-time crooks. Everybody knew everybody, though. If there were any jobs going, one Leone would toss it to another Leone.''

"But it wasn't a godfather-type family, huh?''

"Not really that powerful. Just rather incestuous. Like a whole family of little fish, feeding on what the big ones left, swimming around under the big fish's protection. Kinfolk. A tribe. Quite a few of them, but except for Canello, they didn't have any connections with other places.''

"How do you know about them?''

"Lieutenant Hector Haymart gives us an organized crime briefing every now and then. Nice guy. He was telling us about crime history in Denver, and he mentioned Canello Leone. It was way back, though. Nothing recently. Hector says what few crime families we had are pretty well defunct. Lots of the old-time guys were racked up on tax charges. They never amounted to much in Denver and now they're like a footnote. Everything's drugs, now. Colombian. Peruvian.''

"I wonder if Herby Fixe really died accidentally." It was only a thought. The talk of organized crime had brought the question to mind.

Grace was way ahead of me. "According to the traffic report, yes. I called the station this afternoon and had them read it to me. According to the autopsy his blood alcohol was almost point two.''

"Skid marks and all?" I asked.

"No skid marks. He was so bombed he didn't even touch the brakes," she said. "He was flying long before he left the road.''

She seemed sure. Still, I wondered.

two

GRACE DID NOT stay at my place Saturday night. She said her Sunday was full of things to do and places to go, and she wanted an early start. Without the distractions of soft breathing and silky skin and a 6 A.M. demand for breakfast, I woke late, stretched largely, took an extra long shower, and went down with only Bela and Schnitz for company to get the Sunday paper from (I hoped) the front portico where the paperboy sometimes manages to put it. Even though I was well aware of Schnitz's proclivity for escape, I wasn't really alert yet, and as I picked up the paper and turned to close the door, he slipped between my legs onto the threshold. I practically fell over myself making a grab for him, and the report of the rifle and the crack of the bullet into the foyer paneling came almost as one. I must have fallen to the floor and rolled inside by pure reflex, with no thought behind it at all. When I came back to awareness, it was with a dry mouth, trip-hammer heart, sweaty hands, and laboring lungs, and me crouched in the corner where whoever it was couldn't get another shot at me. Schnitz stood halfway up the hall stairs, his tail fluffed out like a plume of pampas grass, back arched, eyes wild, growling. Or maybe it was Bela growling. Or me.

Somebody had goddamn tried to kill me. I could see the hole in the paneling, right where I would have been if I hadn't bent over to grab Schnitz. I heard myself making adjectives out of four-letter words, over and over in a raving somebody-else-not-me voice, so I shut up, embarrassed at the sound of it. By lying flat, I managed to stretch a leg and pull the door shut with minimum exposure. As it latched, I recalled hearing, as though on delayed replay, a car starting up and speeding away. Not from the street out front, somewhere farther than that. The alley of the block opposite, perhaps, where most of the old houses had been converted into offices. Certainly less than a minute had elapsed since the shot, but it felt like an hour or so.

When my knees quit shaking, I got up and looked at the bullet hole. A pencil inserted into the hole confirmed the trajectory was slightly upward and slightly to the left as I stood with my back to the front door. Whoever had shot at me had done so from ground level. Through a clear glass segment of the fancy window beside the front door I could see the driveway between the two conversions across the street. I knew it went through to the alley where the car had no doubt been. The rifleman could have shot from the corner of the nearest building.

I called Grace. She called Linder. He got there in about thirty minutes, which was twelve and a half minutes after she did. He brought two other guys with him who did what I'd done with the bullet hole, then dug out the bullet, put it in a sack, labeled it, and went across the street to see if the rifleman was perchance waiting around to answer questions.

"You think this has any connection to that woman's murder?" Linder asked me.

I told him I didn't know. It had no connection to anything, so far as I could see. Two persons had tried to kill me about a year before, but one of them was dead and the other one was still incarcerated somewhere at the pleasure of the FBI or the CIA or both. So far as I knew, and I think I'd have been informed if anything had changed.

"You were looking for somebody named Fixe," Linder reminded me, as though I might have forgotten.

"Herby Fixe," I affirmed. "He had had some dealings with my foster father, who died recently. I wanted to know the details. It turns out Herby was Simonetta's husband. And yes, Grace and I went over to their place yesterday and asked the neighbors some questions, but they didn't tell us anything that would warrant somebody taking a shot at me.''

He asked whys and wherefores, and I told him what I knew. No point in not. Whatever it had been about, it couldn't hurt Jacob. Jacob's H. Fixe had probably been the now-dead-and-no-longer-threatening Herby Fixe from Zuni Street. Even in the unlikely event that H. Fixe was not Herby but Harold or Horatio or even, God forbid, Hermione Fixe, Jacob was no longer around to be extorted from on my behalf, or Charlotte's. The previous night I'd decided not to worry about the matter anymore unless somebody came at Charlotte or me with malign intent. The decision had been premature. Somebody taking a shot at me definitely qualified as more than a little malign.

Lieutenant Linder put his notebook away and went off to help his men look for tire tracks or witnesses or whatever. Grace, after exhorting me to stay inside with the doors locked, took the bit in her teeth and went galloping off to talk to her friend, Lieutenant Hector Haymart of the organized crime unit. I didn't hear from her again until Monday noon.

When she called she sounded altogether too chipper and pleased with herself. ''I told Hector about Herby and the Leone connection and you getting shot at, Jason, so he got a warrant and went over to Zuni Street this morning. I went along. Hector hadn't found anything useful up to the time I left, but I got names and addresses of Simonetta's family. She's got a whole bunch of brothers and sisters—at least one sister and two brothers here in town. The brothers both have sheets on them, but the sister, Dorotea, evidently got out of the neighborhood and away from the family. She's married to a lawyer, Andrew Chapman. They live out in Cherry Hills, and the only place her name shows up is in the social pages.''

''Well,'' I said weakly. ''That gives us somewhere to start, doesn't it.''

Grace was way ahead of me. ''She says she'll talk to us this afternoon, if you've got time.''

I hadn't mentioned Sunday's events to either Mark or Eugenia. They'd come in the back and hadn't seen the bullet hole, and I hadn't quite decided whether I was a selected target or a random one. Now, when I called through the connecting door to ask Mark if he could get by without me for the afternoon, I halfway hoped he'd think of a reason my presence was essential, so I could stay inside for a while, out of range, so to speak. Mark, however, did not read my mind. Instead, he gave me a vague look and an affirmative grunt. I took it as an omen and stopped fighting the inevitable. "What time this afternoon?" I asked Grace.

"Mrs. Chapman said three. It'll take half an hour to get out there. I'll come by your place about two-twenty."

Which gave me time to enlighten the crew. The difference in their personalities was displayed fully when Eugenia went off immediately to call the painter while Mark was still asking me breathless questions. She, by God, knew that business came first and customers shouldn't be confronted by bullet holes! Mark was still shaking his head over me when Grace arrived, and he warned me to be careful as we went down the stairs. We were careful. Both of us scanned the neighborhood from the front windows before I went out to her car.

"Did Linder find anything?" I asked, looking nervously around myself.

She shook her head. "No empty case, no tracks, no witnesses, no nothing. On Sundays, Hyde Street is a tomb."

I knew the fourteen hundred block of Hyde Street was dead on Sundays. The restaurant on the corner doesn't open until noon. The next two buildings, 1487 and 1473, are office conversions. Then comes 1465, and south of my place are two more conversions before you get to the house on the corner, which has three apartments in it with the owner living on the ground floor. There are two owner-occupied homes across the street, but they too are at the far end of the block.

"How about across the alley?" I asked.

She shook her head at me. "Some people live there," she admitted. "But they were all sleeping off Saturday night or they'd already gone skiing."

Sunday morning was one time the shooter could almost have counted on not being seen. Denver's Capitol Hill, bracketed on the north by Colfax Avenue (Fifteenth) and on the south at about Sixth, on the west by Broadway and on the east by University, is the closest thing Denver has to a round-the-clock city. The rest of the town is dead by 9 P.M., with the sidewalks rolled up, the streets empty as a panhandler's pockets, and ninety percent of the families tidied away into the residential areas. Downtown Denver after nine looks like a model city somebody forgot to populate. Capitol Hill, however, still seethes at midnight, with hookers prowling Colfax and restaurants busy and fast-food stores spilling people and cars. By 3 A.M., even Colfax is quiet. On Sundays nothing opens much before noon and half the population heads for the mountains at dawn, those who hadn't already gone the day before. That's what too many people move here for: the skiing.

"No hope," I said to Grace with some gloom. "I wish we had a clue, something. Anything!"

"You made anybody mad at you lately?" she asked, giving me a worried look.

I couldn't think that I had. Except for some nut, maybe, who had seen me at the clinic and followed us when we left. I mentioned this.

"It's a thought," she said. "There are a couple of demonstrators who've made threats against the clinic personnel. Maybe one of them took a shot at you. We'll check, of course, as best we can." She sighed and cast me a sidelong look. "I wish we could provide protection, Jason, but you know as well as I do, the police can't sit on your doorstep. We don't have the manpower. We don't have the budget." She was pink, embarrassed for her profession.

I soothed her, telling her I didn't expect protection. I didn't. Nonetheless, the idea that I might need protection was intensely upsetting. I like to do something about problems. Nothing frustrates me more than getting into situations where I'm impotent, where I can't do anything. I don't like dealing with nuts. Logic won't work. Reason won't work.

And, worst of all, society conspires to prevent the average person from protecting himself against craziness. Crazy people can't be punished, because they're crazy. So they're sent to hospitals to be cured. Then they're let out because they're "Fine when they take their medication." Then they stop taking their medication, buy a gun, and kill a few innocent bystanders, but they still can't be punished for it because they're crazy.

Obviously, people who cannot control what they do are more dangerous than people who can. So, in a properly run world, craziness—along with drunkenness and drug use—would be an aggravating factor when considering guilt or innocence, not the other way around. If we could forget our Puritan obsession with punishment and decide that the only reason for locking people up is the safety of the population at large, we'd do better at law enforcement.

I said this, at length.

"Yes, Jason," said Grace. "You want to find the weather on the radio?"

I took the hint and shut up. Grace had heard it all before.

Cherry Hills is at the high-priced south end of the urban agglomeration. Ostentation is the norm. I fully expected the Chapman house to be yet another of the cheek-by-jowl multi-winged, many-gabled monsters that were hulked along both sides of the road in money-country. I have never been able to understand why anyone with the resources to build a house that size would put it on a skimpy acre or less with another monster house practically adjacent. Unless people live there *vide homolucrum*: to stare at people who have as much money as they do. Or to drive past even larger houses *vide supra-lucrum*: to stare at people who have more money than they do. Or to regard the homes of the *summa cum lucro*: as in the life-styles of the rich and famous.

I amused myself with such inanities during the ride so I wouldn't start shouting again, which I tend to do when I'm scared. If the truth be told, I found the idea of some nut gunning for me intensely disturbing. Not that I'd admit that to Grace. Not manly. Or something.

The Chapman house was not one of the side-by-side monsters. It was a French château with pure continuous lines, old brick walls with multi-paned windows, a copper roof patinaed the color of spruce buds, a matching flare of ribbed copper spread lily-wise over the front door, the whole set in sufficient grounds to give it gracious dignity. Inside were paneled doors and walls, well-proportioned rooms, beautifully furnished in French and English pieces, many of them genuine eighteenth century. I ran my fingers along the hall table and felt at home, among friends. I relaxed, feeling my frightened anger drain away. Nothing evil could happen in such a place.

We were shown into the sitting room by the uniformed maid who had answered the door. Grace had on her wary expression. She gets it in the presence of—what? Monied surroundings? Servants? It isn't awe and it isn't resentment. It is a kind of watchfulness that comes from not being sure whether she knows the acceptable thing to do—not that she'd necessarily do it, but she likes to know what the rule is when she breaks it.

Dorotea Chapman was waiting for us: lean, elegant, about fifty, gray-blond hair drawn smoothly back in a French twist, understated makeup, wearing the almost inevitable tweed and cashmere country clothes the house called for. We introduced ourselves.

"We don't want to take much of your time," I murmured in what Jacob had called the intimate-elect voice, one that says, I know how important you are, let's get this out of the way. It was the voice he had often used when asking a buyer, "And how will you be paying for this?"

"We need to know anything you can tell us about Simonetta Fixe," I said.

Dorotea Chapman turned her recently manicured right hand into the slanting light from a multi-paned window and examined the nails, which were quite perfect. The hand itself was smooth and ageless. "You're investigating her death?" she asked, almost as if she did not care.

"I am, yes," said Grace, surprising me. Simonetta's death

hadn't been her case the last I'd heard, and I'd supposed we'd have to skate over that question. "Lieutenant Linder has assigned me to certain aspects of the investigation."

"The doctor I spoke with told me she was stabbed," said Dorotea, closing her eyes briefly, as though to shut out some private vision. "Someone stabbed her with an ice pick. She bled to death internally, sitting there." Her voice was calm, but one eyelid twitched, over and over, fluttering, like a fly in a web.

Grace shook her head, for a moment shocked at this news. "I hadn't heard the results of the autopsy. I was told there was no wound on her body."

"There was no blood," Mrs. Chapman said. "The doctor I spoke with says there often isn't, in that kind of wound. Particularly if the person is . . . fleshy." She sighed and looked at us with a pained expression, no subterfuge in it at all. "Remembering Simonetta is painful. I don't like talking about the family, can you understand that?"

I looked around at the graceful, ageless room, a proper setting for the graceful, more or less ageless woman, and thought of that walrus-like form hunkered down at the clinic. Oh, yes, I understood. Grace did too. We nodded.

Dorotea took a deep breath. "I talked to my husband about this, and he said, if I could bring myself to be frank, it would probably all be over more quickly. I'd like it to be over. Remembering Simonetta isn't . . . well, dealing with her was always a frustration. What do you need to know?"

"Anything about her might help," I said. "We won't know until you tell us."

She marshaled her thoughts. "You know she was my sister. She was ten years older than I. The thing we always tried to remember about Simonetta was that she wasn't intelligent. We could get very annoyed with her when we didn't remember that. She wasn't exactly retarded, she just wasn't very bright, and we all had to keep it in mind. Mother had eight children who lived to grow up. Some of us are quite intelligent—intelligent enough to have left the old neighborhood and traditions and become . . . acculturated. Of course, some of us haven't done that.''

Grace gave me a significant look. "And Simonetta?"

Dorotea rose and stood at the window, thrusting a fall of brocade aside with one hand, staring out over her winter-dun lawn with her back to us, as though it was easier to talk if she didn't have to see who was listening. "Simmy wasn't in the family and she wasn't out of the family, if by 'family' one means the kind of things some of my brothers got up to. Papa was always very law-abiding, but some of my uncles were not. They had an unfortunate influence on some of us children. So did the toleration of them and their . . . lifestyle. We were always taught that blood was more important than the law. You can get trapped that way. . . .''

We nodded again, though she could have seen only our reflections in the glass.

"Two of my brothers and a sister and I decided—quite independently of one another—to get out of the trap. Three brothers liked things the way they were. One of them is dead now. Simmy wasn't on one side or the other. She was just always there, always around, the way a young child is, or an aged relative.'' She put her hands behind her, stretching her shoulders back. There was ache in that stretch, old pain.

"What was she like?" Grace asked. "Her personality?"

Dorotea made a ladylike snort. "Sometimes I felt Simmy had only instincts, or maybe habits. It was hard for her to learn things, but once she learned anything, it was set in concrete. She was intensely stubborn and intensely religious. We all went to St. Seraphia's school as children, but most of us were selective about what we believed, you know. Heaven but not hell. Baptism but not the ban on birth control. Simmy swallowed everything she was told, and everything was of equal importance. Once she'd learned to read a little, and enough arithmetic to count her change—practical things like that—the nuns took her over to their residence and taught her housekeeping. They were pragmatic about it. They knew she'd never be able to hold any other kind of job, and certainly none of us thought she'd ever marry. She worked for the nuns part-time while she was in school. They taught her to cook. She couldn't follow a recipe if it was at all complicated, but she cooked plain food very nicely. Italian foods, of course—she learned that at home—and fried chicken and pot roast and pies, things like that. She learned one way to do it, and she always did it that way. You could rely on each of Simmy's dishes tasting exactly the same, each time she made it.''

Her reminiscences had come haltingly, almost without expression, like a list of things she'd purposefully evoked, intentionally called up out of the past. A kind of inventory: Simonetta, who and what she was.

"She worked for families, did she?" I asked.

Dorotea turned to face us. "When she was eighteen, the nuns couldn't keep her any longer. Papa was worried about her being able to take care of herself, but he didn't want her at home where Mama would go on treating her like a child. He got her a job with Canello Leone. The Leone families in Denver are all related, of course."

Grace twitched, and Dorotea saw the movement. She shook her head resentfully. "I know. The Leones have had their occasional bad apples, but so far as I know, only Nello Leone ever had a genuinely evil reputation. One of those who tar all their countrymen with their brush, more greed than good sense, always stirring up trouble. Papa knew that, but he felt Simonetta wouldn't get mixed up in anything, that she'd be safe working there. . . .''

Her voice drifted off into silence. She took a moment to find her narrative again. "Nello Leone had two sons. Gabrielli and Geronimo. Nimo was oldest, he had recently married, and his wife was pregnant. Let me remember . . . her name was . . . Angelina? Something like that. At any rate, Canello didn't hire Simonetta to work in *his* house. He sent her to work for his daughter-in-law. She and Simonetta would have been about the same age, I suppose. Maybe Nello thought they'd be company for one another, or maybe he didn't know what else to do with Simonetta, or perhaps he just counted on his daughter-in-law being a kind person. I heard that about her, that she was a very warm, kind person.''

"What was the kinship between your family and Canello's, exactly?'' Grace wanted to know.

"I don't know, exactly,'' she replied, a bit impatiently. "We're some kind of cousins, I suppose.'' The idea did not please her; that showed clearly on her face.

She drew a deep breath and went on. "So, Simonetta worked for Nimo's wife as a maid: she cleaned and did laundry and was a kind of nursemaid after the baby came. Everyone in our family was pleased because Simmy was pleased. She loved the baby, she liked the work, and she worked hard enough that she didn't get monstrously fat. Big, but not monstrous. Simmy always had the tendency to put on weight.'' She paused, pressing the skin under her eyes with her fingertips, perhaps reassuring herself that she was not fleshy, not fat, not like her sister. Perhaps she was only pressing an ache away.

"How long did she work for Nimo's wife?'' Grace asked gently.

"She was with them three or four years, until there was some kind of accident. The wife and child died. I'm not sure exactly what happened, though I do remember going to the funeral. Papa insisted we all go, to show respect.''

"What did Simonetta do then?'' Grace asked.

"Well, by that time she had some experience. Nimo didn't keep her on, but he gave her references. She was really quite good at what she did—slow, but faithful. She moved about a bit after that, working for different families.''

"When did she marry Herby?'' I asked.

Mrs. Chapman flushed a deep and ugly red. She started to speak twice before she got the words out. "My father insisted that she and Herby get married about ten or twelve years ago. Papa claimed he'd found out Herby had been sleeping with her, when she worked for Nello Leone. Herby worked for Nello at that same time. Frankly, Papa's insistence didn't make much sense then, and I still don't understand it. I don't know if Papa really found out something

definite or someone just made an allegation. Mama and I
both tried to find out from Simonetta when this affair had
started, or if it was still going on, or . . .''

She made a gesture of frustration. ''Simonetta was never
able to talk about anything that might have been taboo when
we were children. Sex things and bathroom things were simply taboo! Whatever mama or the nuns might have shushed
her about when she was eight, she still couldn't speak of forty
years later! She would turn bright red and clamp her mouth
shut and turn away. Mama and I are still not sure that anything had ever happened between her and Herby, but Papa
gave Herby the choice of marrying her or . . .'' She blinked,
suddenly aware of what she was saying. ''. . . or leaving
town,'' she finished bleakly.

We waited. She obviously had more to say. It simply took
her a while to say it.

''Simonetta was almost fifty then. Mama and I tried to
talk some sense into Papa. She couldn't possibly have become pregnant, not at that age, and Herby wasn't the kind
of man who would ever make a good husband. Marriage
made no sense, but Papa was adamant. He said it was a
matter of honor.'' She made a little face and turned away,
hiding from us again. ''Lots of things were matters of honor
to Papa. To him, and to men of his generation. I remember
a great deal of talk about honor when I was a girl. One had
to be very sure not to do anything that would reflect on
someone's honor.''

We waited. When nothing more was forthcoming, I asked,
''What did you mean when you said your sister was religious?''

Dorotea sighed. ''I mean she was observant. Scrupulous.
After her marriage, she became even more so, if that's possible.''

Grace gave her a puzzled look. ''Yes, but what does 'being
religious' mean when you say it?''

Dorotea thought about this, turning to and fro on one foot,
a little swinging motion, as a child might do, comforting
herself by rocking. ''I mean she had always worried about

sin. Well, one can't go to parochial school without worrying about sin, though most of us took it with a grain of salt. Not Simonetta. She had to know exactly what a sin was and how bad it was and whether she'd done it or not. She had to know if she could commit a sin by mistake. She used to drive Mother crazy with questions like that. She wasn't bright enough to figure anything out, or make allowances for herself. We were always having to reassure her that she wouldn't go to hell. After she was married to Herby, she talked a lot about being a bad sinner. She thought she'd committed some mortal sin, and I blame Papa for that. She didn't understand Papa's insistence on that marriage any more than Mother and I did. She thought it was a punishment, but she didn't know what for. I'm sure Simonetta was a virgin until Herby got to her, if he got to her, and given Simonetta's prudery and religiosity, I still doubt he did. If he did, there was certainly no one else but him, and the sins of the flesh aren't all that damning. Try and tell that to Simmy! She was sure she was going straight to hell.''

"She was frightened?" asked Grace.

"Until about a year ago, when she got involved with these antiabortionists. She got the idea from something the priest said, that working with them would expiate whatever her sin was." Her tone was unsympathetic. "A lot of nonsense," she muttered. "Positively medieval!"

"You believe in freedom of choice?" I asked, curiously.

"Of course not," she snapped. "I was reared Catholic and remain so. But I don't believe in mobs harassing women who are not breaking the law, either. It doesn't demonstrate the compassion our religion teaches; it sets a bad example of public order; and it's in very bad taste!"

We gave her a moment to calm down. "Do you have any ideas who might have stabbed your sister?" Grace asked.

She shook her head, slowly. "Considering the tone of the message that was left on her body, I assumed it was someone connected with the abortion movement. Perhaps someone at the clinic itself."

"No," I said firmly. "I don't believe it was. Your sister

was where I could see her from the moment she arrived until her body was discovered. No one from the clinic went anywhere near her. In fact, no one except the people she arrived with went anywhere near her.''

She didn't contradict me, she just looked me up and down as though to say, "And who are you?" Nonetheless, she replied calmly enough, "If *that* is the case, then who else would have done it? Canello Leone comes immediately to mind, but he's been dead for years. If she had interfered with *him*, he might have murdered her, but he would have done it then, not later. They say one should always suspect the spouse, and I'm not such a fool as to think Herby incapable of murder, but Herby drove himself off a road and killed himself before Christmas. So who?''

I didn't know. "Am I right that you have very little contact with your family?" I asked.

She shook her head at me, giving me a slight, very ladylike sneer. "To the contrary, Mr. Lynx. I see my mother every week. She's in a nursing home, but she looks forward to my visits and we enjoy the time together. When Papa was alive, I saw him at least once a week. I talk with two of my brothers frequently: one is in Los Angeles and the other in Chicago. I see my sister Veronica whenever I get the chance. I left the family environment, not the family itself. My conscience, in case you are wondering, is quite comfortable in that regard.''

I think I flushed. "I meant, you don't see your brothers here in Denver. You didn't often see Simonetta?''

She shook her head, bleakness descending once more. "No,'' she said with the same little sneer, only this time I knew it was at herself. "I have not seen either of my convict brothers in some time. And I rarely saw Simmy. Of all the family, only Mama kept in close touch with them, particularly with Simmy, and since Mama's been in the nursing home, she's been unable to do that.''

We thanked her and left.

"What's this about your investigating Simonetta's murder?'' I asked Grace, once we were in her car, headed down the curving drive.

"I asked for the assignment this morning," she said. "I told Linder I had the inside track, with you being there at the clinic and me working there sometimes. Also, he thinks maybe Simonetta's murder has something to do with whoever took a shot at you or vice versa, whatever. So, I'm on the case. I have to share everything with Lieutenant Haymart in organized crime, but that's okay. He's not even all that interested. Nello Leone died twenty years ago, and since he's been gone, the family hasn't been up to much."

"What about his son, Nimo? And what did she say Nimo was short for?"

"Geronimo. Nimo'd be in his sixties now. You know, I don't think I've ever seen his name on an arrest report. Our last organized crime briefing didn't even mention him."

"That branch of the family must be defunct."

"I'd think so. Except for what happened to Simonetta. And even that may have nothing to do with the family."

"You know," I commented, returning to my earlier frame of mind, "except for that shot at me yesterday, I'd be tempted to drop this. I was after somebody who had bothered Jacob. Since I'm ninety percent sure that was Herby, and Herby's dead, should I really be much concerned with the rest of this?"

She gave me a look. "You might not be concerned, but I would be," she said in a firm, no-nonsense voice. "Forget somebody shooting at you. Jacob cared about that clinic, and right now everyone who works there is under a cloud. They're all worried. Dorotea isn't the only one talking as though the clinic people did it."

"I told the police it's unlikely anyone associated with the clinic could have done it!" I exclaimed in irritation.

"So who are you? Mother Teresa? The Archbishop of Canterbury? The Chief Rabbi of Jerusalem? Who appointed you the last word on truth? All you can say is you didn't see anybody do it. Until we know who did do it, the clinic people will be under suspicion. And believe me, the antiabortionists will do everything they can to make them suffer. Making false accusations fits right in with their usual pattern."

I humphed and snarled at her when she said it, but the Tuesday morning papers proved she was right. One inflammatory quote followed another, both from those who had been arrested and those who supported those who had been arrested. All the rhetoric gave more heat than light. The words of the police lieutenant to the effect that the clinic personnel were not under investigation at this time were buried in the second column of a long overview story, and most people wouldn't read that far. I searched all the coverage for anything about Simonetta I didn't already know, but there wasn't anything.

I sat and stewed about being shot at for a while. I get this thing, sometimes, this hubristic conviction that if I concentrate hard enough I can find the answer to anything. Since I only do this when I'm not finding the answer to anything, it is invariably self-limiting. After thirty minutes of fume and glower, I still had no idea who was trying to kill me. So, I went around my apartment, making sure the curtains were pulled so that nobody could get a clear sight on me, then tried to give it a rest.

The sight of the scattered newspapers reminded me of the clinic, and my conscience started bothering me. I'd been so wrapped up in my own problems, I'd forgotten Cynthia Adamson and her problems. I called the clinic and left a message. When Cynthia called me back, I suggested additional security, saying I'd make some money available now if she needed it.

"We've already hired guards," she said. "We've been through these storms before, nothing quite this bad, but the pattern's the same. Over the next few weeks, someone will probably try to burn us out, or the staff will be harassed and threatened, or all of the above. There are a few real nut cases who hang around on the fringe of this issue. Any public spectacle sets them off, and they're unpredictable. Quite frankly, they worry us a hell of a lot more than the organized opposition does. The organized groups help incite these nuts, but the organizations themselves usually stop just short of committing a serious crime."

"Are the nuts someones in particular?" I asked.

"Two someones in particular," she said. "Both male, both with histories of mental illness. Both very much into machismo. The kind of guys who would consider it honorable to pick up a semiautomatic weapon and knock off a dozen female staff and patients before you could say 'gun control.' Like the guy who killed all those female students at the college in Canada a few years back."

"I can't understand that," I said helplessly.

She laughed angrily. "Try real hard," she said. "They're the same kind of people who put on robes and murdered civil rights marchers in the 60's. The same people who threw rocks at kids who were bussed to their schools in the 70's. It's all about dominance. You know, you've got to keep those black folks and those women folks where they belong!"

"What about saving babies?"

"Saving babies, hell! Once the children are born, they don't care what happens to them. You think it's an accident that the U.S. has one of the highest infant mortality rates in the developed world? Men who vote against abortions for poor women also routinely vote against the programs which would allow poor women to have healthy, well-fed children. Antiabortionists by and large aren't pro-baby, they're anti-female!"

I thought she was overstating the case and said so, as gently as possible.

"I'm not making it up," she said angrily. "Look at what they do—or don't do—instead of what they say. They scream 'Adoption, not abortion,' but they don't adopt kids who need homes. They scream 'Don't kill your baby,' but they elect representatives who cut the food and shelter programs that keep those same babies alive. The people who picket us aren't interested in healthy children, they're interested in dominance. Didn't you watch their faces when you were here?"

I had watched their faces. Remembering those faces, I stopped arguing with her, admitting to myself that I couldn't look at those faces on a weekly basis, as she did, and disbelieve what she was saying. "I'm sorry you all have to go through this," I said inadequately.

"Me too," she said in a calmer voice. "I get upset sometimes."

I let her get back to dealing with her problems, wondering whether I could have stayed calm under the same pressures. She was stressed and fractious, but she was keeping it together. She knew what she was doing.

Which was more than I did, at the moment. I had no idea what was going on. Though some famous person had once remarked that being sentenced to die remarkably focuses one's mind, being shot at hadn't had that effect on me. I was not focused. I felt irritable and decidedly scattered. I didn't really want to attract the further attentions of the gunman, whoever it may have been, who'd taken a shot at me. This meant, in turn, that it might be smart to stay away from further involvement with the clinic. Which meant, stay uninvolved in the matter of Simonetta's murder.

Grace, however, was not going to let me get away with that. Besides which, she'd been right in saying Jacob would have cared, about the clinic at least. So, for their sakes if not my own, it was up to me to stay involved, like it or not. I sat staring at my desktop while I made the conscious switch from the former question of "Who is H. Fixe?" to the newer ones, "Who killed Simonetta? What has it to do with the clinic? Has it anything to do with me?"

Stating the problem was as far as I got just then. The rest of the day was eaten up with odds and ends, most of them boring and none of them profitable. I didn't even think about Simonetta until Grace dropped by late that afternoon, bringing with her a fat envelope bulging with the records and photographs of all the people who had been arrested on Saturday. "I need you to look at these," she said, shoving them in front of me. "Simonetta must have talked to some of them on Saturday, and I need to know which ones."

"You want me to help with them?"

"No, it's official police business. Besides, I don't think

they'd talk to you. Your face was all over TV. I think they mentioned your name, too.''

I hadn't known that. ''When?'' I asked.

''Saturday night,'' she said. ''The anti's always call the TV stations before they stage a demonstration. They want publicity. You just didn't notice the cameras. Anyhow, if any of these people watched the news, they'll know you were on the other side, so to speak, so they won't talk to you.''

I was considering whether the person who had shot at me Sunday morning might have been someone who'd watched the Saturday news. Pleasant thought. Only included a million or so people in the metropolitan area, excluding very young kids, very sick people, and those in jail. I tried to bring my mind back to the issue at hand.

''You're going to interview all these people? Alone?''

''No, not all of them. I told you, Jason. I'm going to find out from you who was next to her or who talked to her.'' She waved a finger at me. ''Pay attention. That's why I brought the arrest records. I have to take them back as soon as you've looked at them. I only bought them over to save time!''

''Too much to hope any of them are still in jail, I suppose,'' I remarked as I turned the sheets over one by one.

''Oh, they were out that afternoon, most of them. On their own recognizance. Except a couple of people who weren't from around here. They had to post bail. Anyhow, tell me which ones were next to the victim.''

I'd already found the man with the crazy eyes. He had a diagonal scar above the left eyebrow, and seeing it made my hand go to my neck where my own scars had been. I could still feel them there, under the bristly bits of new hair. The transplants would never grow like normal cranial hair, but they already covered the scars.

Grace saw my unconscious movement and asked, ''Does your hair hurt?''

I laughed. My hair had hurt, a good deal, when it was being planted. So had the ear when it was being rounded off and reconstructed. The pain was over. The man in the mirror looked normal, though he still came as a surprise each time I saw him. I always expected someone else.

Grace hugged me and directed my attention back to the arrest reports. "Anybody else?"

A few other people had been in the row in front of Simonetta. They hadn't sat facing me, but there'd been a certain amount of squirming around and talking to one another over their shoulders. I sorted them out and went on looking for the woman who had sat on Simonetta's right. After going through the sheets twice, however, I still couldn't find her.

"She's not here," I said.

"I have a report here on everyone who got arrested," said Grace, being patient with me.

"The woman to Simonetta's right had glasses and curly white hair. There is no woman here with curly white hair."

She shuffled through the pictures finding no woman with curly white hair.

"Look," I said indicating the man with the scarred face. "Ask this guy. He was on Simonetta's left. He should know who was on her right. Don't these people all know one another?"

"More or less," she admitted. "However, I understand people come in from out of town to take part, sometimes. People sent from another church or another group. They'd be vouched for, but not necessarily known to one another."

"They were all arrested," I said stubbornly, "and she had white, curly hair. It was cut short. And she didn't have a jacket." I thought for a moment and then asked what I should have asked long ago. "Where was the wound?"

"In front. Slanting in from the right."

"You're saying . . ."

"The doctor says she might have been stabbed even before she sat down. Maybe she didn't die right away. People were milling around. We've subpoenaed the unedited TV tapes, just in case the camera saw anything."

"Would that mean the murderer was left-handed?" I was holding an imaginary ice pick, jabbing with each hand in turn, trying to decide which hand could more easily stab to the right.

She shook her head. "The doctor says from the front, easier with the left hand. From the side, easier with the right hand. From the back, reaching around her, easier with the right hand."

"Hell," I said. "You couldn't reach around her."

"Well, if you could. Anyhow, I think you're right, I should talk to the people nearest her. This guy with the scar isn't local, so it may take me a while to catch up to him. Tomorrow morning. Now I have to go. I got these records out by promising to file them when I brought them back." She kissed me and trotted off, focused as a cat with mouse on her mind.

I sat there stubbornly reviewing my recollections. The woman to the right of Simonetta had had white, curly hair. I could see her in my mind. A stocky woman, past middle age. Fairly tall. Five-seven, maybe. Dark trousers. A long-sleeved shirt. A considerable bosom. Glasses. And white, curly hair.

I realized I was stroking the new hair at the back of my head, and with the realization came the thought that hair was not always attached to the person. When I'd looked at the pictures, I'd been looking for hair, not clothes or shape. The hair could have been a wig, but the woman wouldn't have had time to change clothes. I should have looked at the clothes!

I made a mental note, thinking that we still hadn't come up with any motive for someone killing Simonetta. Assuming there had been a motive, and the murder hadn't been an arbitrary act by one of the nuts Cynthia Adamson had mentioned.

I needed more information about Simonetta. Who might have known her? Dorotea saw her seldom if it all. Her neighbors had told us what they could, but they obviously hadn't been intimates. Grace said her colleague hadn't found anything of interest at Simonetta's house, and Grace herself had been looking only for names of the family. My interest was perhaps more general than either of theirs had been. I sat in colloquy with my conscience for some little time, staring out the north window of my office as the sky darkened. The neighboring building was unlit. Above its roof a bare branch flexed its muscle against the glow from a streetlight over on Colfax. A good time of day for burgling. People busy with their suppers. Too dark to see clearly.

My conscience gave up. I put out some food for the animals, then went to change into jeans, a navy sweater, and a dark down vest. My burglar clothes.

Jacob taught me to pick locks years ago. One sometimes buys pieces of furniture that turn out to be locked. One does not wish to smash them to get them open, so one learns to pick locks. I do it now and then, just to keep in practice. I did it that evening, on the Fixe back porch, while people moved up and down the alley and dogs barked and a brazen voice down the block yelled for Roger, Roger, Roger to come in for dinner. I wondered briefly if Roger was boy or dog. Or maybe husband.

The lock wasn't much. Once inside, I closed all the curtains that would close and drew all the blinds that would draw. The place smelled of dust and closed rooms, small rooms with too much in them and too little space for air. I listened to the sounds of the house, deciding Herby hadn't been big on household maintenance. Doors rattled on their latches. Faucets dripped. A loose windowpane clattered in a sudden breeze. No people sounds. Only the sounds of a lonely house, suddenly untenanted, relaxing into continuing decay.

I switched on the flash and began to make my way through the clutter of Simonetta's life, Herby's life, wall by wall, drawer by drawer, closet by closet.

A typed list of numbers was posted by the kitchen phone: family names (including Dorotea Chapman's), the doctor, the public service company, the police. The paper was ocher with age, so brittle the edges had split and curled like dried leaves. Someone had prepared the list for Simonetta. Someone had posted it here years ago. It had never been moved or replaced. It was undoubtedly the source of the names and addresses Grace had found.

Aside from that one discolored list, there were no address books, no phone numbers written in the back of the phone book, no orderly setting down of known people or places. There were scraps of paper stuffed in corners and between canisters and stuck to the side of the refrigerator with fruit-shaped magnets. There were piles of unsorted mail, catalogues and letters, piled in tottery heaps. There were boxes of junk on top of drawers and in closets.

One bedroom was obviously hers, one his. His was almost totally empty. Nothing in the drawers to speak of, a few bills, a few sheets of paper, two sets of underwear and as many socks. One fairly good jacket hanging in an otherwise empty closet. Why had he left it? He hadn't lived here. Was the marriage ever anything but a fiction?

Her room was a different matter. Here were all the stockings Simonetta had ever owned, neatly rolled into beige tennis balls and stuffed tightly in dresser drawers. Ditto underwear. Ditto shirts and blouses, the sizes decreasing as one burrowed down. The ones on the top were 3X.

Everywhere were rubber bands and string; pieces of aluminum foil, folded and flattened and stored; those little plastic envelopes of soy sauce and ketchup and mustard they pass out at fast-food places, several hundred of them filling one drawer, along with plastic stirrers and paper packets of sweetener.

Simonetta had been a keeper. I cursed all keepers, everywhere. As I went on digging, I caught on. The drawers and boxes had been filled years ago. When they would hold nothing more, they became a geological stratum upon which later strata were laid down. Recent stuff was nearest the top. Recent stuff included articles of clothing and shoes and mail and little gift boxes with the ribbons put back around them, and Christmas cards standing in an accordion-pleated row along the mantel, their envelopes stacked neatly to one side. Almost all of them had returns. No Christmas tree. What had Simonetta done at Christmas time? Who had she been with? With her husband dead, the fiction of a marriage couldn't be sustained. Or could it? Was it easier for her family to sustain the fiction than to remember Simonetta was alone?

I came back to the Christmas cards. Considering the contents of the house, I was unlikely to do better. All the cards fit nicely in a paper sack, one of a stack of perhaps five hundred paper sacks I found on the back porch, neatly arranged by size, folded, and stacked. I snapped off the flash, opened the curtains, raised the dusty blinds, and went out the way I had come, feeling I'd been in those claustrophobic, airless rooms for hours while down the street a tireless voice still called Roger, Roger, Roger. Maybe it was taped on a continuous loop.

Back at home, sitting at the kitchen table drinking coffee and trying to forget the hopeless, lifeless smell of Simonetta's house, I matched up as many envelopes and cards as I could on the basis of color or size or names. Most of the cards were religious. There were a lot of Madonna and Child ones, a lot of Three Wise Men, a lot of Stars Over Bethlehem, and only a few on which holly or robins or reindeer made a generic reference to the season. It made me hopeful that these were cards from people Simonetta had known when she was young, in school. Perhaps I could hope for a few from people she had once worked for. Perhaps, just perhaps, one or more of them had known her well enough to have kept in touch over the years.

When I had as many matched up as I could manage, I made a list of names and addresses. Most of the cards were not personalized and many of them were the same size, which meant I was at a loss to connect ''Betty and Joe'' who signed the card with ''The Williams'' or ''The Bentleys'' named on little stickers on envelopes. Sometimes the envelopes gave only the return address with no name at all. Where there was no match, I listed them separately.

It was only when I was a quarter way through and encountered the same little sticker for ''The Williams'' for the third time that I realized this wasn't one year's harvest. Postmarks verified it, making me feel like a fool. I should have noticed the changes of postal stamps from year to year. Simonetta had never thrown out Christmas cards any more than she had disposed of anything else. There were at least five years represented here, maybe twice that. The same people might be represented every year, or by four or five different addresses. My great number of possibles shrank suddenly to an entirely manageable and perhaps inadequate number. How many different people had sent cards?

Ah, well. I knew who to put on this particular job. I finished up the list, including the year dates on the postmarks, and sacked the cards, ready for return to their dusty mantel. Were Betty and Joe the same persons as Elizabeth and J.B.? Were the L. Smiths on Baker Street the same as the L. Smiths on Lilac Way? Myra Sharp would find out for me. I was sure of it.

Myra is one of those extremely competent and ambitious young women who will turn their hand to anything at all, so long as it pays reasonably well and doesn't keep them from proceeding toward their well-thought-out goals. Myra has been studying accounting, and her goal is to become a very high-priced tax attorney. Myra pays attention to detail. She gets things done.

Except when she isn't available.

Mark made the call for me on Tuesday morning and came back apologetically. "Her mother says she'll be back Thursday," he said. "She's on some kind of an educational tour, looking at law schools. Her mother also says that her final semester leaves her some free time, so she can probably fit us in."

I grumped, not sure I liked being fitted in.

"It's a slow Tuesday. Is it something I could do?" Mark wanted to know.

Well, of course, it was something either of us could do. Or Eugenia Lowe, for that matter. Or possibly some office help hired by the hour. It's just that I had my mind set on Myra Sharp.

"I'm trying to find someone who knew Simonetta," I explained, showing Mark the Christmas card list. "I wanted Myra to find phone numbers for these people, getting the right last names with the right first names, you know. Then I thought she could call them and weed the list down to the few who might have had some contact with Simonetta. . . ."

"If you're determined to wait for Myra, you could try the nuns in the meantime."

I looked at Mark blankly.

"You said Dorotea Chapman mentioned they all went to parochial school."

"Sure. St. Seraphia's. Possibly thirty-five, forty years ago."

"Well, St. Seraphia's is still in business and they undoubtedly keep records," he said patiently. "Maybe there'll be some old nun still there, someone who not only remembers Simonetta but can tell you who her friends were. Of course, you may not find any old nuns at all. There's a shortage these days." He was no doubt quoting his former friend, Rudy, who had been reared in an Italian Catholic family and had endlessly described the glories of the heritage while eschewing involvement in it. Mark had inevitably picked up a bit of the cultural esoterica.

In this case, I already knew something about the subject because the history of some art *is* the history of monasticism. Many forms of medieval art originated in monasteries, where there was no shortage of nuns or monks because monastic life was often longer and healthier than life on the outside. In medieval times, women died in childbirth and men died in wars, fates generally avoided by the religious. Daughters with no dowries and younger sons with no land often had no future worth mentioning outside the convents and monasteries. There, they'd get at least two meals a day and a roof over their heads while they engaged in peaceful pursuits such as gardening, carving, making lace, embroidering vestments, or illuminating manuscripts. Of course, that was during a time when both birth rates and death rates were high. When families are smaller and starvation is rarer, monasticism is not so attractive. Creating, as Mark said, a shortage of nuns.

Shortage or not, I found one.

She was Sister John Lorraine. When I called, I asked for anyone who had been at the school forty-five years ago, and Sister John was the name I was given. She was at the school still, seventy-five years old, clear of eye and mind, and she remembered Simonetta.

"They keep me around as a relic," she told me when I arrived posthaste, eager to pick her brain. "I'm too old to change my habit, so I'm a historical exhibit." Sister John wore the wide white headdress I remembered seeing in my youth, one that made her look as though she had wings. "I'm used to it, so they let me wear it." She touched her wimple with affection and pride, like a little girl with a new dress.

I had introduced myself only as someone involved in investigating Simonetta's death. Sister John hadn't asked for identification, and I hadn't offered any. We sat in her office, a cluttered little room at the end of a side corridor on the ground floor of a school that looked and smelled like all schools, no holier than the one I'd attended as a child, for all its parochiality. Sister John said she no longer taught. All of the teachers were lay teachers now. She was an administrator, she said, kind of a superior-type clerk, and she would go on doing that until she grew too old to do anything. She lived as she had for the past fifty years, at the Sisters' residence next door, just behind the church.

And she, too, spoke of a shortage of nuns. "There are only three of us over there. Used to be a dozen or more. Sometimes I wonder what's going to happen next."

I sympathized. We spoke of the difficulties with education in a secular age. We spoke of the weather. Then we got around to Simonetta.

"She was a trial," said Sister John. "I suppose that's why I remember her." She nodded to herself, then to me. "What do you want to know?"

"Everything you can tell me. Anything might help."

"Well, she was a great lump of a girl," said Sister John.

"In all the time I've been here, there've only been two or three the size of Simonetta. Sister Julian and I tried to keep her busy so she wouldn't eat all the time. Any time she could, you'd find her stuffing candy, or sweet rolls, or cookies. That was her mother's fault. Mrs. Leone felt sorry for Simonetta, so she always sent a sack of food with the girl when she came to school. I tried talking to Mrs. Leone myself, but I didn't get anywhere. All she could say was poor girl, poor girl, she has to keep her spirits up." Sister John looked away then back at me with a sly grin. "It was my idea to teach Simonetta about the sin of gluttony. That got her, I'll tell you."

"Sin?" I asked, remembering what Dorotea had said about Simonetta's concern with sin.

"Oh, sin, yes indeed. More than three moderate meals a day is gluttony, I told her. I had a talk with Father Waring, and he backed me up. He was a dear man. We got her down to a hundred fifty pounds, among the three of us, Father Waring, Sister Julian, and me. Kept her there, too, right up until she left us."

"I should think she'd have appreciated that. It must have made her a lot more attractive."

"You couldn't make Simonetta attractive. Being thinner made her a little less lumpish, that's all. Sister Julian and I used to trade her off as penance. She was very difficult to love. It was like loving a great chunk of . . . oh, I don't know. Clay, I guess. No. Something harder than clay. She was just . . . like a chunk of wood." Sister John smiled ruefully at a memory. "Sister Julian and I both thought that Simonetta was living evidence of God's inscrutability. We could not find any purpose for someone like her. It was a sin, of course, and I don't know how many times we confessed feeling that way and listened to Father lecture us about the sin of arrogance. I remember I'd do my penance, and then the very next week, I'd find myself sinning again. Sister Julian felt just the same. Poor Simmy. She wasn't helpless enough to move us to holy pity. She was just . . . lumpish!

"Sister Julian and I, we'd talk and talk and talk to her, and she'd look at us, and we'd be sure none of it was getting through. Then, later, she'd come back at us with something we'd said, but it would always be whatever we'd said that hadn't mattered.''

I know I looked puzzled. I didn't know what she was trying to tell me.

She tried to help me. "If I said to you. 'When we add numbers, two and two always make four,' what would I be trying to tell you?''

"That two and two always make four.''

"Not to Simonetta. She would come back at me, oh, maybe weeks later, and say, 'Sister, when is it we're supposed to add numbers?' ''

I thought about that. "You mean, she thought you were giving her rules for living?''

The sister nodded, her headdress fanning the air, the breeze brushing my face. "Exactly. *Everything* was a rule for life. And all rules were unbreakable.''

"She made rules out of things that didn't matter?''

"Exactly. That's exactly it. She was always at me with questions about things that didn't matter. She thought there had to be one right way to do everything!''

I had seen the inside of Simonetta's house. Now, I started to understand it. Someone had told her to roll stockings. Someone had told her to stack paper bags. That was the rule for doing it. There was no rule for un-doing it, no rule for throwing things away. "Strange." I shook my head in wonder. "She had no sense of humor, then.''

"She was completely literal-minded. I'll never forget the time Father preached on the text, if thine eye offend thee . . .''

That one I knew. "If thine eye offend thee, pluck it out.''

"Simonetta thought he meant her. Her weight, you know. She went on and on about plucking it out! Sister Julian and I had to talk like parrots for over a week to get that idea out of her head. We were frightened to death she'd start carving pieces of herself off. With most children, you can joke a little or poke fun, or tease. Not with Simonetta. She didn't think anything was funny except things the rest of us didn't.''

"As for example?"

"When one of our occasional parishioners tripped on the front steps and broke his hip, Simonetta laughed until she cried. She thought God had done it to him because he was sinful and didn't often attend mass."

"She thought it was funny when God brought people up short?"

"She thought the miraculous conception was hysterical."

I must have looked blank.

"The virgin birth," she said gently. "Jesus. Simonetta thought it was very amusing that God had arranged it, no matter what Mary might have thought about it."

"I've always felt it would have been nice if He had asked her rather than just announcing His intentions," I said.

I had been trying to be amusing, but Sister John gave me a look. I was sure she had perfected that look on whole generations of young Catholics. I felt the heat of it all the way to my coccyx.

"Is this conversation about Simonetta leading somewhere?" she asked me sternly.

"I was hoping it would lead to her friends. Did she have any? Did she talk to anyone? Would anyone she knew at school have stayed in touch with her?"

"Why?"

"We want to know who killed her," I said. "Innocent people are being suspected. We need to know more about Simonetta."

When I said "innocent people," her face shut down like a garage door.

"The news said there was a note on her body. The note said, 'She interfered; she's dead.' And you don't think it meant she interfered with that slaughterhouse?" She gave me a glare, daring me to contradict. "You don't think it means they killed her? Why wouldn't they? They kill babies all the time!"

She was going to put us on opposite sides; she was going to make us both angry; and then I'd go stalking out, or she would, relieving herself of any further responsibility. I wouldn't let her get away with it.

I smiled as I said, "If you mean the clinic, no, I don't think that's what was meant at all. I was inside that morning, as an observer. I saw Simonetta sit down outside the doors. I was there the whole time. No one came near her except the people she arrived with. And the note doesn't say she interfered with the clinic. It may have been something else entirely. It's in the interest of justice that we find the truth. We need to talk with her friends."

I could see her trying to decide her Christian duty. Part of her wanted to send me, an obvious heretic, packing. Part wanted to help. Neither side emerged winner.

"I'll think about it," she said. "If I think of anyone, I'll let you know."

I had to be satisfied with that. Once more, I wished for Myra Sharp.

three

IMMEDIATELY AFTER JACOB'S death, Charlotte had offered to have his ashes scattered at her ranch near the little town of Elizabeth. Since the ranch stretches over the better part of two square miles, she didn't think the neighbors would object—not that she had any intention of asking them.

"Daddy's and Mother's ashes are here, too," she said. "They felt pretty much the way Uncle Jacob did about things like this."

Grace and I drove out late Wednesday, getting there just before dark. The weather was clear and cold. Though there'd been no snow for several weeks, we both wore heavy jackets and boots, more to keep warm than dry. I took with me the photo Jacob had shot years before, the one of the pine grove on the rounded hill. We could see that same hill from the front windows of Charlotte's house, a gentle slope in the middle distance, tree-fringed against the pale sky.

Charlotte exclaimed over the snapshot, then stumped off to get the jeep. She bumped us across the frozen pastures with experienced nonchalance, getting us halfway up the hill before we were stopped by the terrain. We climbed from there. Jacob's ashes melted invisibly into the winter grasses among wind-curved eyebrows of lingering snow. Anemones would bloom there in April, Charlotte said. I remembered them as pale and ethereal, like the spirits of flowers. Pasqueflowers, they're called. Jacob told me once that though "Pasque" means "Easter," it comes from a root which means "to pass," so the pasqueflower is also a Passover flower.

Both holidays celebrate life triumphant, so it's suitable, one might say.

As we walked down the hill toward the car, the dusk gathered around us, sending the daytime landscape into another country. This world was shadowed and mysterious. I stopped to look back at the darkening grove, the treetops still sunlit, the wind sighing through the branches, moving them like waving hands. One ought to say good-bye, I thought. How does one say good-bye?

Charlotte asked us to stay to supper, and when we demurred for politeness' sake, she demanded we stay because she felt all alone and abandoned and sad and besides, she had already cooked for us.

"Where's Richard?" I wanted to know. Charlotte's husband is usually more uxorious than otherwise. I'd been a little surprised at his absence.

"Richard is in Alamosa buying hay," she said. "It was so dry last year the pasture gave out, and we started feeding hay six weeks earlier than we usually do. We don't have nearly enough to last through March, much less April, or even May. God knows, the way things are going, we'll probably have no snow for months, then a freezing blizzard in late May, and drought all summer again. Anyhow, Richard went down to the San Luis Valley to see what kind of a deal he can make on forty tons or so. I told him just to call down there and see who has any, because we've pretty well got to take whatever they've got, but you know Richard. He won't buy anything without looking at it.

"Besides," Charlotte went on, as though she'd been reading my mind. "You were asking about Jacob. You wanted to know about him when he was young? Well, I've found some stuff. Last time you called, when you asked about Jacob's girlfriend, it made me remember there was still an old trunk of Dad's in the cellar."

We got back into the jeep, and Charlotte drove us to the ranch house, explaining as we went.

"The trunk was full of pictures and papers. I kept it because I thought my kids might want it someday. These days everyone seems to be into finding their roots. Jennifer and Jeremy haven't shown much interest in who Richard and I are, much less who *our* parents were, but I thought someday they might.''

From what I had seen of Charlotte's offspring, I doubted it. They were far too poised and secure to need ancestrification.

She went on, "I'd forgotten all about the trunk until you began talking about Jacob, and then I remembered they were twins, Jacob and Daddy, so anything Dad had kept from his school days would probably have been about Jacob, too.''

I didn't often remember that Jacob had been a twin. He had never made much of the fact. He and Harry had looked nothing alike, and of course Harry had been gone for over fifteen years.

"Anyhow," Charlotte continued, "I dragged out the trunk and sorted through the newspapers and letters and yearbooks from when they were young, before Dad got married to Mother.''

When we had divested ourselves of coats and boots, Charlotte took us into the kitchen where we found the table ready with three place settings, a large bowl of salad, and a pile of yellowing documents and newspapers. When we were seated, Charlotte thrust the salad bowl toward Grace and the papers toward me, then turned to the oven to bring out a casserole of chicken, a mixed vegetable dish, and a pan of au gratin potatoes. Charlotte had met Grace before. There was enough food for ten.

We looked through the papers as we ate. Under the newspapers was an envelope containing a duplicate of the photo I'd found among Jacob's things, the one of the young people and the fancy car. On the back of this one, however, someone had written, "Left to right: Jake, Livvy Cerraverdes, me, Peggy Penrose, Vangie Curtis, Vangie's car. May, 1931.''

The "me" had been Charlotte's father. "Livvy" was the same girl as the one in the studio portrait among Jacob's things. Olivia. Her face shone from the dim old photograph like a moon reflected in murky water. "Beautiful," I murmured, echoing Mark.

Charlotte took the car picture and traced her father's features. "Daddy looks so young. Half my age. I've seen pictures of him as a baby, but I don't think I'd seen one of him this age before. So young."

They all looked young to me. Mere kids in love. The expression on Jacob's face as he looked at Livvy Cerraverdes left no doubt of that, though Harry's slight leer at Peggy Penrose was perhaps more lecherous than amatory.

"This is Olivia," I said, pointing with my fork.

"Livvy. Not a pretty nickname," Charlotte commented. "Sounds like a bruise."

"Mark says her family probably broke up the love affair because of religion," I commented.

"Oh, Daddy knew that was the reason!" Charlotte shuffled through the papers to pounce on an envelope with a foreign stamp. "Read this!" She pulled out the folded letter and handed it to me.

Blue ink, in a round, childlike hand.

"Dear Harry, I couldn't bear to write to Jacob but I couldn't bear his not knowing, either, so I'm writing to you. Please tell him for me. Tell him I don't take back anything I ever said to him. Not one word. Tell him I'm getting married because Mother and Daddy want me to. He's very nice. He isn't Jacob, but no one will ever be Jacob. His name is Octavio Desquintas y Alvarez. He's a little older than I am. He's related to Daddy's family here, and he's a Don, and he speaks English, which is a good thing because I'm hopeless with Spanish. Most important, I guess, he's the right religion, and Jacob knows what I mean about that.

"We're going to live here in Spain. Mother wants me to have maids and jewels and all the things Octavio can give me. They don't matter to me. Jacob knows that. Mother wants me to be married in the church. That matters. Jacob knows.

"Tell Jacob good-bye for me. Tell him I'll never forget him as long as I live. Tell him I will love him always."

It was signed, Olivia. Dated October 14, 1932. Saragossa, Spain.

"Oh, that is sad," said Grace, tears in her eyes. "Poor Jacob."

"She didn't get to stay there, though," Charlotte said. "Don Octavio got run out." She sorted through the newspapers to find pages from the *Denver Post*, dated August, 1935. The social page reported the arrival from Spain of Don Octavio and Señora Olivia Desquintas y Alvarez, together with their infant daughter. Because the Desquintas estates in Spain had recently been overrun by the forces of General Franco, the "titled refugees," so gushed the reporter, would make their home temporarily with Señora Desquintas's parents, Mr. and Mrs. R. J. Cerraverdes, of Cerraverdes Imports.

"She didn't get her maids and her jewels, after all," breathed Grace. "Or at least, not for long."

"So she came back to Denver," said Charlotte. "Right here where Jacob was. I wonder if they saw one another."

I had picked up another newspaper, one from 1942, folded to display a story on page five: "Local Men Join Armed Forces." Paragraphs of names followed under the headings of army, navy, marines, air force. I searched for Buchnam on the alphabetized list, finding it almost at once under the "army" heading. Harry and Jacob Buchnam. As I was putting the paper back on the pile, a name two lines below caught my eye. Octavio Desquintas. One name only. He had probably found Americans unsympathetic to his double-barreled patronymic, so he had truncated it.

I found the article a little puzzling. "They weren't drafting fathers that early in the war, were they? As a matter of fact, if he wasn't a citizen, would they have drafted him at all?"

"He could have volunteered," Grace offered. "Even if he wasn't a citizen. The Cerraverdes were probably taking care of Olivia and the little girl. Maybe Octavio had nothing else to do. He might have been eager to join up and get back at the Fascists, since they're the ones who ran him out of Spain.''

Both their names appearing on the same list was a bit of irony. Buchnam and Desquintas. I wondered if anyone else had noted that contiguity. Olivia's parents, perhaps? Olivia herself? Perhaps no one had remarked upon it until now.

"Coincidence," said Grace, disbelievingly.

"Coincidences have to happen sometimes," I said. "The laws of probability strongly favor that point." Not that I believed what I was saying. When two related things show up together, it's because they're related, right? Common sense tells us that, and the hell with the laws of probability.

We found no more new information, though there were interesting pictures of the young Jacob, Olivia, Harry, and Peggy playing tennis, of Jacob and Harry on a fishing trip, of Jacob and Olivia at a bridge tournament, smiling over a silver cup. I asked Charlotte's permission to take the papers back to my place so I could make copies, and on the way back to town I ruminated on what we'd found.

History has always fascinated me, but this was unlike the attraction of ancient history. Ancient history is mysterious, strange, like science fiction, a world in which we have no part, among people who were not personally connected to any of us. This was different, close, a time when people I knew were alive. I could see the faces and read the words and think, *I was almost there, like a character standing in the wings, waiting for my cue*. It almost seemed I should be able to remember that backstage existence. My real parents were alive then. Jacob had been born and gone to school then. He had fallen in love and seen his love taken away from him then, and I'd been almost there.

Jacob's remaining a bachelor all his life had been a mystery to me, but perhaps he'd never wanted anyone but Olivia. I wondered what had happened to her, and to Octavio. Women live longer than men, on the average, so she might still be alive. And according to the newspaper account, she'd had at least one child, a daughter.

I had told Mark that Jacob would have paid extortion to protect only me or Charlotte, because he'd had no one else. But perhaps there was someone else. If Olivia was alive, perhaps he had been trying to protect her, or her child.

The possibility was intriguing enough to keep me entertained during the drive home while Grace slept beside me, her breath making a little warm spot on my shoulder. I decided to add Olivia's name to the list I would give Myra. How many Desquintas y Alvarezes—or even just Desquintas—could there be?

Myra came over Thursday afternoon, full of bubbling comments about the universities she'd visited and which ones she might attend. She had not changed at all since I'd first met her, three or four years before. She was still skinny and eager, with a little boy's freckled face, snub nose, and haircut. She still sat in any chair balanced on her coccyx and the back of her head. She still talked to herself—I'd heard her chatting all the way up the stairs on the way in.

She still brought enormous enthusiasm and keen attention to every task she took on, as she did when I gave her the list I'd prepared, the picture of Olivia and the other young people, and photocopies of the two newspaper articles.

"We've got two separate things going here," I told her. "One of them pertains to the murder of Simonetta Leone. We want to find anyone who may have stayed in touch with her over the years, anyone who may have seen or talked with her recently. This other thing is personal. I want to find Jacob's old girlfriend. We know nothing about her except what's here, in these papers, and there's no Desquintas y Alvarez in the current phone book." I'd looked the night before, just on the off chance.

"Myra Sharp," she entoned in a dignified voice, "Tracer of Lost Persons!" She giggled. "Mom says there used to be a radio show about a tracer of lost persons. She'll flip." She simmered over the photo, memorizing it.

"Olivia may not be lost at all," I told her. "The fact that

there's no Desquintas in the phone book doesn't mean much.''

"City directories." Myra gave me a crafty look. "Old city directories. Old phone books.''

"More power to you. I'm hardly in any hurry at all. How about tomorrow?''

"Monday," she said firmly. "Don't count on anything until Monday at the soonest, and you pay all expenses, right?''

Right. We shook hands on it and Myra left, reading the list aloud to herself as she went down the stairs and out the front door.

"Jason," Mark said from the door.

"Umm.''

"Do you think you might bring yourself to do a little business today or tomorrow? You've got a stack of messages on your desk you haven't answered, and one of them is from Lucinda Hooper.''

I bowed contritely toward the god of making-a-living and called Lucinda Hooper. Last year the Hoopers had bought a Chippendale oxbow-front chest of drawers from me for fourteen thou. Lucinda wanted to know if I'd take it back as a credit (full value) on the Federal sofa. We talked about that at exhaustive length. I finally told her I'd ship it to New York for her, sell it there, and she could give me the money toward the sofa, but I would not take it back in trade for the retail price.

"I can sell that sofa tomorrow for the asking price in cash, Lucinda. When you're in business, you buy at dealer prices and sell at retail, that's how you stay in business. If I take that chest back from you at fourteen thousand, I can't make a dime on it here in Denver. I'll have to ship it to the east coast.''

"Well, maybe we'll keep it," she said.

Which is what I wanted her to do anyhow.

The next phone slip had Sister John Lorraine's name on it. I called Sister and received from her the names of two women: Cecily Brent and Yaggie Costermyer.

"Yaggie?" I asked.

"Don't ask me what it stood for," she said. "People give their children very strange names these days. When I was a child, you couldn't go to parochial school unless you had a Christian name. Come to think of it, she probably did have a Christian name that I've forgotten. Yaggie is what she was called."

"Yaggie," I confirmed, writing it down.

"Neither of those girls may be around anymore," she said. "They knew Simonetta when she was in school, mostly because their families were neighbors. They weren't friends, but they were reasonably kind. You know what I mean."

I did know what she meant. I thanked her effusively, and she told me she was praying for my enlightenment. I thanked her for that as well. She had evidently decided my eternal fate was still undecided and a little enlightenment might help. I called Myra, who had just arrived home, and added Yaggie and Cecily to the list she was already working on.

"Yaggie?" she asked. "My God!"

The third phone slip down was a decorator I'd dealt with before. She was what one might call a hobbyist. She "did decor" when she wasn't flying off to Europe with her husband or flying down to Tucson for the winter or flying somewhere else for something else. I didn't bother to return that call.

I did call Charles Nutting, a client I'd done a house for the year before. His boss at the brokerage firm (about whom I'd heard much, none of it good) had bought a big house which he wanted to refurnish. Charles had given him my name (Thanks awfully, Charles) but he wanted me to know I should get everything in writing because the old bastard would try to cheat me.

The last call was to Kansas City, to Orvie Spender, an old friend of Jacob's who wanted to offer condolences. I'd met Orvie a time or two, a colleague in the antique trade, a warm and friendly guy whom Jacob had much liked.

"How did you learn Jacob had died?" I asked when I reached him at last.

"I was through Denver last week. I called Jacob's place, and that man of his told me about it."

Francis was staying on in Jacob's apartment until we could get everything packed and into storage, and until Frances himself decided where he was going next.

Orvie went on, "I was real eager to tell Jacob about the table, but I guess I was just too late with it."

"What table?" I asked.

"The one Jacob wanted."

"I'm sorry. You've lost me, Orvie. What table did Jacob want, and why?"

"Oh, well, I thought maybe you'd know. Last time I saw him, he asked me to keep an eye out for an antique card table, a really good one. He wanted to give it to someone for a birthday present. Eightieth birthday, he said."

"When did you see him last?"

"Oh, October, I guess. About the middle. I was on my way back from San Francisco, and I stopped over."

"When did you say this birthday was?"

"Didn't say. Just told me to keep my eye out. I found the table before Christmas, but I've been so busy . . ."

"It wouldn't have made any difference. Jacob had a final stroke in November, and he wasn't able to communicate with us much after that."

He made sympathetic sounds. "You wouldn't want it, would you? The table?"

"Is it good?"

"This is a very nice piece, Jason. Jacob said it had to be special, and this is. Chippendale, five-legged, pre-revolutionary. New York manufacture, I'm pretty sure. Mahogany, maple, and some poplar. Fancy top, inlaid with felt, and the felt's not even worn. I doubt the tabletop has been opened out more than half a dozen times. I could have got it for ten, but I paid twenty-five because the family was struggling and, even though they'd had this piece forever, they had no idea what it was. I figured I'd let Jacob have it for thirty. Or you, of course. I suppose you know who he wanted it for?"

I made a noncommittal noise and asked, "Can you send pictures and provenance?"

He could. He would. Thank you and sorry about Jacob and talk to you soon again.

And I sat there with my mouth open. Jacob had wanted a present for an eightieth birthday!

Mark asked me, "What's the matter with you? Your mouth's open."

I shut it, then opened it again. "Olivia's alive," I said.

"Olivia? How do you know?"

"It has to be her. She."

"Her, she, who?"

I explained, not too coherently. "Who else would Jacob want to give an eightieth birthday present to?" All kinds of possibilities and incredibilities were opening up. There had been that picture of Jacob and Olivia with the bridge trophy. Jacob had been a bridge fanatic. I'd disappointed him by remaining vulgarly addicted to poker. Right up to the time of his first stroke, Jacob had played bridge. Perhaps he had played with Olivia. Perhaps they had been lovers. If they could have been, honorably . . .

Though what was honorable, when love was concerned? When Olivia turned her back on Jacob's love to marry the Spanish Don, was that honorable? Her parents and priest no doubt believed so. Jacob was, after all, a Jew. The holocaust had not yet happened. The Nazis had not yet made anti-Semitism revoltingly unacceptable for any civilized person. So Olivia had gone off to Spain, and both of them had no doubt wept at the unfairness of it all.

But what about when she came back? There were seven years from the time she returned until Jacob went off to war. What happened then? And what happened after the war?

Was it any of my business?

I had the feeling—though it was only a feeling—that Jacob would have said no. If this were purely personal, I should perhaps back off, grant privacy where privacy was due, re-member that Jacob had never introduced me to the lady and, therefore, he had probably wanted to keep her to himself. Or such of her as he had.

However, there was the possibility that Olivia could be connected to the H. Fixe puzzle. If the extortion business had nothing to do with me or Charlotte (and I didn't, quite frankly, see how it could), then perhaps it had something to do with Olivia. I had to keep reminding myself, as I had reminded Mark, that it was "extortion" Jacob had written on the envelope, not "Blackmail." Blackmail would have been easier to understand. From what I knew of the early decades of the century, there had been many rather common shortcomings which were thought too shameful for public acknowledgment. That two people had been lovers, for example. I could imagine blackmail over that. Extortion was something else. Extortion did not mean that Herby Fixe would reveal something. It meant that something bad would happen. A threat. Though it seemed unlikely that anyone would threaten an eighty-year-old woman, the fact remained that Jacob had not gone to the police about this matter. He'd paid.

Mark and I talked it over, inventing scenarios: this had happened, that had happened. I offered as a hypothesis that Jacob and Olivia had not, in fact, been in touch, because if Jacob had been, he would have introduced me to her.

Mark considered this presumptuous.

"Why would Jacob have introduced you to her?"

"Because he loved us both," I said, astonished at the question. "Of course."

"Oh, of course," he replied. "I always introduce my family to people I love."

Well, maybe not. Jacob had loved me like a father. "I suppose fathers don't tell their sons everything."

"You've got that right," said Mark. "And vice versa."

Mark went home. I wandered around the place, checking windows, turning down thermostats. Bela padded behind me, wagging his tail and whining softly. He wanted some attention. He wanted to go for a run. Schnitz did not want to run. He hid under a couch and growled at me, like a tiger. All

right, cat, stay home and sulk. I got Bela's leash and we
started for the park, stopping across the alley for a moment
to visit our friend Nellie Arpels. Nellie's daughter and son-
in-law, the Fetterlings, had recently remodeled their attached
garage into a ground-floor suite for Nellie. After twenty years
confined to a wheelchair on the second floor, Nellie had
spent the past several months reveling in unaccustomed ac-
cessibility. In the summer, she would be able to wheel herself
out into the garden. Still, she had confessed she missed being
able to see all up and down the block.

Bela and I slipped in through the back gate and knocked
on Nellie's outside door, three and two, which means Jason
and friend. I could hear Nellie's chair as it rolled up to the
door, then the lock snicked and it rolled away. I waited until
she had time to get out of the way, then pushed open the door
and stuck my head around it. Nellie's cat, Perky, retreated
to the closet when she saw Bela, though the dog only sat
beside me quietly as Nellie and I chatted. Since Nellie enjoyed what she called "real soap opera," I told her about
our recent discoveries.

"This old girlfriend might be alive," she opined, nodding
firmly at me, as though she had to convince me. "If I'm
alive, she could be alive. Do you suppose she knows Jacob
is gone?"

I hadn't thought about that. "There was an obituary in the
paper."

"If she reads obituaries." Nellie wrinkled her lips and
nose. "I don't. Too depressing. She might not know."

Bela whuffed to announce the arrival of Nellie's daughter,
bringing her mother's supper. Nellie preferred to eat alone,
at her own pace, which was slow, rather than attempting the
family dinner table. She said hurrying her meals made her
gassy. After promising to come back soon, Bela and I left by
the alley, jogged across Fourteenth and Thirteenth to the
park, and did a slow, lolloping circuit as the light faded. It
was dark when we got back to the shop.

There's no logical explanation for what happened then. I
was pleasantly tired, quite hungry, and not thinking of any-

thing much except supper. As I came up the back stairs, I got a whiff of something, an unpleasant frisson, the merest hint of smell, or perhaps part scent, part recollection. I was suddenly possessed by old dust, by curtains left hanging, carpets left lying too long. I was lost in claustrophobic airlessness, as though packed away in some ancient trunk or box, sealed against life, saved . . .

Imprisoned.

Fourteen sixty-five Hyde had never smelled that way. Not when Agatha was alive, not since. The cleaners came every week and bustled about in a flurry of dusters and a slosh of lemon-scented oil. What I smelled was something else. The smell of old attics, old basement storerooms. The quintessential fragrance of Simonetta's house. A stored-away odor, the smell of old clothes in the bottoms of old sorrowful trunks. Renunciation of life. Habit and custom and routine.

Some rather long time later I found myself sitting at the kitchen table, the animals busy with their supper and I with no memory of having fed them. I with no memory of anything except loss and the revelation it had brought with it.

I didn't have to stay here.

The thought wasn't welcome or unwelcome, though it was chillingly unfamiliar. I didn't have to stay here. This had been Jacob's house. This had been Jacob's business. He had asked me to come back and take it over when he was too ill to go on with it, but I didn't have to go on with it now. Agatha and Jerry and I had been happy here, but they were gone, and Jacob was gone, and I didn't have to stay.

I didn't have to spend my life dickering with an endless series of Lucinda Hoopers—not that I disliked Lucinda, I didn't—or going to auctions or scuffling for inventory. I did those things because Jacob had done them, but it didn't matter to him anymore whether I stayed or not. As long as he had been alive, yes, I'd owed him that. Loyalty. Security. Affection. But now he was gone, and I'd made no such commitment to anyone else.

I thought of Grace. Well, what about Grace? We'd considered the question. Or perhaps we'd only danced around it, like a couple of courting cranes who weren't sure about the nesting season, going through the motions of an uncertain gavotte. She had a career and was intent on taking it further. She had made no promises. And, perhaps, she had simply told me the truth, unflattering as that was. Perhaps I was not quite what she envisioned as a husband, being too sedate, too set in my ways, too quiet, too moody, too sad . . .

And perhaps I was that way because I had not only stepped into Jacob's business but also into his emotional shoes, into his life, his mold, his style, his habits. Like him, alone. Like him, devoted to someone I couldn't have, or didn't have any longer.

Now . . . now what? I wasn't required to stay in the mold, the rut. How did the old question go? What is a rut but a grave open at the ends? And what is a grave but the end of a rut?

There was no compelling reason I couldn't do something else. Anything I liked. Inside myself I could feel shiftings and rearrangements. Hard internal chunks pushed past one another, making momentary discomforts as they rubbed corners. Perhaps this was what a religious experience is supposed to be, though there was nothing ecstatic or beatific in it. Spaces were opening around me. Veils were lifted. Somewhere in my psyche, stagehands were shifting the scenery. I could almost hear the grunting and heaving.

When they had finished, they left a vast and twilit moor with roads leading in all directions and the air so clear I could see almost to the horizon along all of them. Jacob's words were upon every signpost. *You can be whatever you want to be. You are whoever you choose to be.* Almost as though he had come back to paint them, to focus my attention once more.

Well, who, at this late date, did Jason Lynx choose to be? Forty years old, still in reasonably good shape, still (so I'm informed) attractive to women, some women; well educated—though only in the fields of art and the history thereof. Not gregarious. Not a man for crowds, team sports, or locker-room bonhomie. Not a man for sexual sniggers. A romantic, perhaps. Not a true expert on anything, lacking the experience to be an expert, but full of snippets and bits of disparate knowledge and irrelevant skills, nonetheless. A lock picker, target shooter (out of practice at the moment), navy-trained demolitions man, antique dealer, puzzle solver.

Who would do what, given the opportunity to do anything at all? Who would live where? With whom? Who would earn his bread how?

The questions bubbled and fulminated, and then, as suddenly as they had come, they drained away, leaving behind a feeling of empty repose. No need to decide now, I told myself. No need to do anything at this moment, so long as I kept in mind that decisions needed to be made.

Bela pawed at my leg. He'd had his head on my knee, and I'd been ignoring him. Schnitz sat on the table before me, at eye level, staring into my face. I'd been out of it, and they knew it. Where are you, Jason? Come back, person. Come back and pay attention to us, your creatures.

I wondered if God ever became distracted. Perhaps that is the purpose of prayer. Come back, Lord. Pay attention to us, your creatures.

I came back to my own creatures, tussling Bela and rumpling Schnitz and giving them both treats while I fixed myself a sandwich of leftover meatloaf. The mind-moor was still inside my head, placid and empty, all roads waiting. Anytime, Jason. Anytime at all.

Clearly, whatever else I did, I would have to take time to solve the twin puzzles of Olivia and Simonetta. They were not unlike other puzzles I'd solved for other people. I would finish them up for Jacob, just as I would finish up the rest of Jacob's business. So there would be no untidiness left behind to haunt me if I later chose to go away.

Grace was busy for the next three days. She called me once or twice, but she had no time for us to get together. On Friday, the Hoopers decided to buy the Federal sofa. On Saturday, I took Bela and Schnitz, by invitation, to visit my friends Marge and Silas Beebe on their farm outside of Littleton, where they introduced me to Celia and Bill Boniface, who had recently moved into a "turn-of-the-century farmhouse" nearby. Marge had decided they should meet me. When they left, they gave me directions and asked me to stop by on my way back to town.

They'd described it correctly. It was a farmhouse, a sizeable one, vaguely Queen Anne, with a wraparound porch and a semi-tower on the southeast corner. It had a homely charm, though no particular elegance. The worst feature was a poorly built, tacked-on one-story extension at the back, and it could come off without problems. I told them a good landscape plan would offset some of the architectural deficiencies, especially, in my opinion, the fact that the place looked slightly "tilted," needing mass at the north corner to balance the apparent weight of the tower. I thought a terrace garden would do the job.

The rooms were of good size, not chopped up with multiple doors or odd windows, and the ceilings were high. The Bonifaces intended to insulate the house, and to redo the wiring, plumbing, and heating, which immediately told me they were amateurs. Anyone familiar with such major renovation would have waited to move in until it was done. I suggested they rent a place in town or park a trailer on the property temporarily.

"Don't try to live in it while they're working on it," I advised. "You'll hate it. You may end up divorced." It had happened to more than a few couples I knew. Living in constant mess and annoyance carries over into personal relationships.

I suggested replacing windows with double pane, to cut down the heat loss, and recommended a couple of architects and builders I knew to be reliable. The furniture in the house had come from the townhome they'd moved from, slick contemporary stuff in the still popular southwest pastels. I agreed with Celia that it didn't do much for the house. She wanted to know what the original furniture might have looked like, but she shuddered when I told her that turn-of-the-century farmhouse furniture, bought new then, had probably been either mission style or arts and crafts, which I have always considered fairly crate-like and not terribly comfortable.

"You could do it country," I suggested.

"With churns and things?" She wrinkled her nose.

"That's country-cute," I said.

"What's the difference?" Bill asked.

"In country, you leave the farm implements in the barn, where they belong. In country, you make your parlor and dining room a little formal, with nice window treatments and carpets, because that's where company is entertained, and one wants to show off a little for company. In country-cute you go for lamps made out of butter churns and chandeliers made out of wagon wheels, both with ruffled gingham shades. In country-cute, you put ruffled curtains on every window, with ruffled tiebacks and valances, and you put down 'rag-rugs,' made in Italy out of new fabrics, at forty bucks a square foot, and you go in for fireplaces which won't heat your rooms. In country, you might use woodstoves or coal stoves, sitting right out in the room because they can heat a room, and you use functional, well-designed lamps. You get the idea."

They laughed and said they got the idea. "But I don't want it severe," said Celia.

"It doesn't have to be severe. It can be serene and practical and a little utilitarian, the way well-kept farms were. And are."

They made an appointment to come in during the week and look at some Shaker things I had in stock. On the way back to town it occurred to me I'd gone through this whole exercise out of habit, paying very little attention, as though the revelations of Thursday night had never happened. I hadn't once stopped to think that I might not be around to do a job for the Bonifaces.

Sunday I took Nellie some chocolates and spent an hour with her before going on to dinner with Trish and Greg Steinwale. Greg is a very well-known artist. I'd met them both about a year before, and we'd become friendly. Trish tells me Greg likes me because I don't drool and grovel over his

paintings, and it's true that I've tried to act sensible around
him. When he shows me something, I try to see what he's
aiming for, then I comment as briefly and intelligently as I
can, after which I shut up.

At any rate, Greg's invited me on several occasions to
showings or family meals at the studio, like tonight. Trish's
preschool daughter, Frosty, was with us, and we all sat on
the floor slurping spaghetti and drinking red wine—or fruit
juice for Frosty and for Trish, who was eight months pregnant.

Later in the evening Frosty fell asleep on the couch, and
we three adults were chatting pleasantly over coffee when we
were interrupted by the arrival of Greg's mother, Harriet
Steinwale, and her friend, Dr. Lycia Foret. I wished immediately for a cloak of invisibility. I'd been avoiding them both
for a year, ever since what Grace and I called "the dogwalker
matter." It wasn't that I disliked either of them, I was fascinated by Lycia, and had been since I first laid eyes on her.
It was just that I'd come out of that affair knowing things
they'd rather no one had known. I'd chosen avoidance in
order not to embarrass them or me, in spite of my inexpli-
cable fascination with Lycia.

There was no avoidance possible under the circumstances.
The studio is all one big room with only a tiny bath and
kitchenette arrangement on the balcony. So, I smiled and
said how do you do, so nice to see you again, and then faded
as gracefully as possible into the wall surfaces. As it turned
out, Harriet and Lycia had stopped by to pick up a small
painting Lycia had bought from Greg as a birthday gift for
her mother. I admired the picture; it was marvelous. Greg
wrapped it carefully in bubble-wrap, and the two women left.

"Quite a nice gift," I commented, relieved they were
gone.

"Lycia's mom's a great old gal," said Greg. "She's going
to be eighty in a couple of weeks."

Everyone seemed to be turning eighty. I launched into the
story of Jacob and his planned gift for someone's eightieth
birthday.

"Oh, what a pity!" cried Trish. "And you don't know who?"

"There's the possibility it could be Jacob's childhood sweetheart," I confessed. "But we don't know for sure, and so far we haven't located Olivia."

Trish laughed, then Greg. I hadn't said anything funny.

"That's old Mrs. Meyer's name, Lycia's Mom. Olivia."

My heart pounded. "Olivia was married to a man named Desquintas y Alvarez. She had a daughter in about 1929 or 1930. Does Lycia Foret have an older sister?"

Trish said thoughtfully, "I don't think Lycia's mom was ever married to anyone but Mr. Meyer. Besides, Lycia's an only child. She was saying just the other day it's too bad there aren't brothers and sisters to help her arrange her mother's party. Sorry."

I was sorry, too. It would have been a wonderful coincidence to confound Grace with.

Celia Boniface jumped her appointment and came in Monday morning to look at the Shaker furniture. We also looked at pictures of farmhouses, English style, American style. We talked about reupholstering some of her pieces. We talked about using leather instead. I gave her photocopies of things she wanted to think about. I didn't push. If they wanted me to do the job for them, they'd let me know.

About the time Celia departed, Myra arrived, her mouth turned down in a discontented curve.

"No luck?" I asked, feeling hollow.

"Oh, some," she muttered. "Just not as much as I'd like." She sat on her tailbone, slid down in the chair until the top of her head was against the back, paged through her notes, and began:

"These people who sent Christmas cards. I called a great number of these people, some of them gave me the names of other people, and I have to say that none of them knew Simonetta worth diddly."

"No result."

"Not diddly," she said with gloomy satisfaction. "They

were friends of her mother, and they sent cards to Simonetta because her mother had asked them to . . .

"However, I did get this Yaggie person. It turns out the Cecily person is in Brazil for the nonce . . ."

"For the nonce?"

"That's literary for a few weeks. You know, if you look like me, you've got to sound like you went to a liberal arts college, even if you are majoring in accounting. It's kind of hard to bring Principles and Techniques of Inventory Management into general conversation. Anyhow, this Yaggie, she used to live on the same block as Simonetta's family. She doesn't remember all that much about Simonetta except for one episode that happened when the woman she worked for died. Simonetta had a fit."

Myra looked up at me to see if I cared, and when I nodded encouragingly, she shuffled her notes, settled more slantingly into the chair, and said, "Hokay! Now, here's how that went:

"Yaggie Costermyer was home from college, her junior year. She thinks it was spring break. Simonetta's family lived on the same block, though not Simonetta herself. She lived with the family she worked for. On this particular morning, a cab pulls up in front of Simonetta's family's house and Simonetta practically falls out. She pounds on the door, which is locked, because her mother is off shopping or something. Yaggie is outside getting the mail out of the mailbox, so she sees all this.

"So then Simonetta starts up and down the block, knocking on everybody's door, telling everybody the woman she worked for is dead, she committed suicide, she committed this terrible sin, and stuff about the baby, and this thing and that thing. So, Yaggie corrals Simonetta and takes her over to Cecily's house, and everything settles down. Later, Yaggie reads in the paper the woman died of a gas leak, accidentally. From what Yaggie says, Simonetta had a real crush on her, the woman who died."

"What year would that have been?" I wondered.

Myra pursed her lips and fiddled with a strand of hair. "Yaggie said something about ages. What was it? She said she felt sorry for the woman who died, because she was only three years older than Yaggie was. That doesn't help, does it?''

"Sure it does," I said. "Yaggie was a junior in college, so she was around twenty. The woman was three years older, so she was around twenty-three. Simonetta was the same age as the woman she worked for, so Dorotea Chapman said, and she was sixty-two when she died. So, we're talking about 1953, give or take a year, right?''

Myra nodded, ticking off on her fingers.

"Have you got anything else?" I asked.

"Not yet. We need that other person, Cecily Brent. Yaggie says Cees—that's Cecily's nickname—Cees knew Simonetta better than anyone. According to Yaggie, Cecily aspired to sainthood. She planned on being a nun, and she spent a lot of time trying to be holy. One of her holiness kicks was being very sweet to Simonetta, listening to her, talking with her, explaining things to her. Yaggie said this was a real pain, because it was no fun for Cecily to be a saint all by herself, she had to do total recall at anyone who'd listen.''

"And Cees is now a nun in Brazil?"

"Cees is now a housing expert, currently in Brazil. She gave up on the nun business when she moved to California with her folks. She finished college and became an architect, and now she lives in Santa Fe, New Mexico, married to another architect, and the two of them design what Yaggie calls 'technologically appropriate dwellings' for developing countries because, Cees told Yaggie, it's a more practical way of doing good.''

"When did Cees move to California?"

"Not long after this thing with Simonetta. Yaggie was talking with her, commiserating, saying it was too bad Cees had to leave all her friends, and Cees said there were some things she wouldn't mind leaving, like Simonetta Leone, because you could get in over your head with people like that.''

"And that's all?"

"One more thing. When Cees moved, Simonetta had another hysterical fit. Showed up again and screamed the neighborhood down." Myra sighed. "That's all I've got on her. It isn't much, but I haven't given up yet."

I thought she had a lot. "How'd you find Yaggie?"

"She still lives there. Her real name is Amy Agnes Costermyer. She'd been married and widowed twice, but she took back her maiden name when she moved into the old family home when her folks died. She's a funny old dame. She cracked me up."

"And she's still in touch with Cecily."

"Still in touch. She and Cecily talk on the phone all the time. Cecily's name is Stephens now, and when she gets back to New Mexico, we can follow up with her."

"Okay. Now what about Olivia?"

Myra shuffled papers, putting the top on the bottom. "Nothing, Jason. Zippo. The Cerraverdes family is in the city directory up until 1954, and so is the Cerraverdes Import Company. Olive oil, cork, wine, that kind of stuff. After 1954, they're not there anymore. Instead, there's somebody named Ralph Burnam at that address, and he's listed there for eighteen years, then somebody tore the house down and built a parking garage. I can't find Burnam after that, and there's nothing listed at the former address of the Import Company . . ." Her voice trailed off as she searched her notes.

"No Desquintas y Alvarez shows up in any directory. There are lots of Alvarezes, but no Octavio or Olivia. I called all the Alvarezes with initial O. Some of them, I didn't get, so I'll keep trying. So far as the city and the phone company are concerned, there wasn't any Olivia."

"Ahh," I said, realizing for the first time how much I'd really wanted to find Olivia. I'd wanted to follow through on Jacob's plan to buy the table and present it, from him, as a sign of undying love.

Which she might have found, of course, intensely embarrassing!

Myra was plowing on. "Since I wasn't getting anywhere, I decided to work on the neighbors of the Cerraverdes. I made a list of the names in the neighborhood, up and down the blocks on either side, from the years after Olivia came back. Then I looked them up in this year's phone book, looking for anyone with the same names." She preened a little, waiting for the question.

"And you found?"

"I found a man named Daniel Brockman. He was a teenager in the 50's, and he had a terrible crush on Olivia's daughter. Maybe he'll talk to you."

"To me?"

"Not to me. He doesn't talk to women. He's now Brother Daniel."

"A monk?" I told myself it wasn't surprising. The Cerraverdes had probably lived in a Catholic neighborhood, near their parish church. "Catholic?"

"Don't ask me. All I know is what his sister-in-law told me when she gave me his name and the phone number you call to get hold of him. I found her because her husband is Arthur P. Brockman, Jr., and his father was Arthur P. Brockman who lived down the block from the Cerraverdes. His wife says A.P. never paid much attention to the Cerraverdes family, but his little brother was so crazy about Olivia's daughter it became a family legend. Daniel became a monk because his heart was broken. She said it was Romeo and Juliet all over again."

"Jesus, Myra. What is this? Lost Loves season? Incredible Romances? We've got Jacob and Olivia. Brother Daniel and the Desquintas girl. Simonetta and the woman she worked for."

Myra smiled understandingly. "I know it. I feel like I've been up to my neck in that TV show about the unsolved mysteries. You're going to scream when you get my phone bill. I did the best I could with weekend rates, but I'm not finished yet."

I nodded absently. All these spiderwebs spinning off in various directions produced no pattern at all. I approve of pattern. The lack thereof makes me itchy!

So, all right. There seemed to be nothing more Myra could do to locate Olivia, not at the moment. I would talk to Brother Daniel and Myra could concentrate on Simonetta.

"When is Cecily returning from Brazil?" I asked.

"In the next few weeks sometime. Yaggie said she'd let me know."

We left it at that. She went away down the stairs, talking earnestly to herself, leaving me to stare at Brother Daniel's phone number, considering what I might say to him, what questions I might ask.

Any decision on the matter was forestalled by Mark, who came in waving an envelope, grinning widely. "We did get it," he cried. "The bid on the Stanley job."

I couldn't think what he was going on about. Then it came to me. Six months before we'd bid on an office furnishing and decoration scheme for a law firm: Stanley, Seeley, Meyer, Huffnagle and Wirtz.

"Damn!" I exploded.

Mark stared at me as though I'd lost my mind.

"Wasn't the thing due months ago?" I asked him.

He read the letter, his smile fading, then went out to dig through his files. He came back flapping several documents. "You're right. It was due for award in November. At the time, I assumed they'd given it to someone else and neglected to inform us."

"So did I. So, in the meantime we've sold a lot of the specific items we'd included in the bid."

Mark flipped through our bid copy again. "Of course we have. You're right. Damn."

"I suppose we could renegotiate. We could offer to meet the bid price on everything except the items we don't have anymore. We could supply replacements at cost plus."

"You don't sound eager," he said.

I wasn't. But then, recently I hadn't been eager about much. "Well, the fact they're three months late on the award doesn't augur well for the job, does it? You can call them and set up an appointment. It won't hurt to talk."

It never hurts to talk. While Mark went off to make the appointment, I went downstairs to check inventory with Eugenia, leaving Brother Daniel's number on top of my desk where it was covered by the inventory sheets when I brought them up. I knew the number was there. I just didn't think about it for a while.

Our relationship with Stanley et al. had been entirely through Elbert Stanley, son of the original and late Mr. Stanley. I'd been told that Seeley and Meyer were also dead, and I hadn't met either Huffnagle or Wirtz or, needless to say, any of the other personnel except the receptionist and Elbert's secretary, whom he had not bothered to introduce. I have an aversion to businessmen who refer to competent staff members as "the girl" or "my girl," which Elbert habitually did.

The firm had obtained an extremely favorable long-term lease on space in one of the high-rise office buildings with which Denver is greatly oversupplied. (During the oil boom, buildings sprouted like corn; since the oil bust they stand largely vacant.) According to Elbert, the money saved on the lease was to have gone into decor. During our meeting late Tuesday, however, Elbert did not carry the matter forward. Instead, he chose to be purposefully obtuse about the consequences of his own dalliance.

"Surely you can obtain other pieces at the same price."

I explained yet again there was no surely about it. The original pieces had been authentic period furnishings, and antiques do not come available on order.

"Well, if you don't want the job," he whined.

"If you'd wanted the job done," I said in a not particularly ingratiating tone, "you'd have awarded the bid as per your original terms. Since you didn't bother to do that, you can hardly expect us to turn handsprings for you now. I've told you what we can do. You can accept that or not."

Someone came in behind me while I was talking, but I didn't turn. I was too interested in watching Elbert's face turn purple.

"Elby, why are you being an idiot?" a voice asked.

Then I turned. She was formidable, dressed in a fuchsia suit, iron-gray hair drawn back in a complicated knot, massive jaw thrust forward, coming into the room like the U.S.S.

Indomitable. I almost expected to hear her say, "Damn the torpedoes!" Luckily, she wasn't aimed at me.

Mark, meantime, had risen to his feet with every evidence of delight. "Amelia," he cried. "I didn't know you were the Wirtz in this firm! Jason, I'd like you to meet a very dear friend of my mother's. Amelia Wirtz, Jason Lynx."

"How do you do," she said, giving my hand a single, hearty pump stroke before turning back to her luckless partner. "Elby, why are you being obtuse?"

She didn't wait for an answer, but turned to me, saying, "My colleagues outvoted me and gave the bid to someone else who was a lot cheaper, only to find the low bidder had more or less vanished along with his defunct business. Didn't Elby get in touch with you then?"

"We heard nothing from Mr. Elbert until yesterday," I said in my most dignified tone.

She trained her guns on Elbert, who attempted an exculpatory explanation to do with our not meeting the terms.

"Well, you didn't, dear; why should they? My God, Elbert, do you want this firm cleaned up or are you content to go on looking like the shabby butt end of World War I?" She shook her head at him, part pity, part contempt.

"Come into my office," she bellowed. "We'll settle this once and for all." She snatched the papers from Elbert's desk and sailed out under full steam.

Mark grinned at me behind her back, and we went after her.

"How's your mother?" she asked him. "I haven't seen her in months. Business has been far too good. Lots of people mad at each other. Lovely for lawyers, having people mad at each other. Nothing like the frustrations of a rotten economy to increase litigation. Are you and your father still not speaking?"

"We speak on occasion," said Mark, trying not to laugh. Or maybe, trying not to cry. It was hard to tell.

"So difficult, I've always thought, having a gay child. Though not nearly as difficult as having a criminal one, or a drug addict, or something like that. And no more difficult than having one's child married to someone impossible. I have a daughter-in-law you would not believe. Not one brain in her pretty little head, but my son will nonetheless be aghast when his children turn out to need remedial reading classes. I'd far rather he were gay than married to her. I told your father so. I told him to count his blessings. He told me to mind my own business, of course.''

She settled into her moorings and let her eyes skim the agreement she'd swiped from Elbert's desk. ''From what I overheard, I take it you can do everything on the original terms except provide a few things you no longer own, correct?''

I nodded. She seemed to need no more than that. She leafed through to the schedule of specific items, where I'd listed each piece together with its provenance. ''You can find us similar items at cost plus. Cost plus what?''

''Shop overhead, which is eighteen percent, plus profit, which is twenty.''

''Ten,'' she said.

''Fifteen,'' I countered, carried away.

''Done,'' she said, pressing a button on her desk. ''We'll stick in a not-to-exceed figure, just so you don't go hog-wild.''

A person came in, was introduced, and went out again after receiving instructions. The same person returned in two minutes bearing a bucket of ice. Amelia opened the cabinet behind her and asked what we would have. Every liquid made by man appeared to be available.

''I understand you have a new companion,'' she said to Mark as she handed him an ice-filled glass. ''Has Rudy really married?''

Mark nodded, sipping. ''Yes, Amelia, Rudy has married. He went back to California and wed himself to a nice, convent-educated Italian Catholic thirty-year-old virgin with a little mustache. Rudy no doubt approached his marriage bed with his eyes shut while concentrating upon his duty to the family.''

''Meow,'' she commented. ''Don't be a little cat, dear.

Who's your current friend?'' She gave me a drink and sat back with every evidence of having limitless time to bedevil us.

"His name is Bryan Langton. He's a professor of mathematics at C.U. Denver. He's thirty-nine. He rides to hounds.''

The hunt clubs in Colorado chase coyotes, not foxes, but aside from never catching anything, the sport is much the same as it is elsewhere.

"To hounds? That displays a certain level of social grace if not of good sense. I'll tell your mother. She's been worried he may be unworthy of you.''

"That isn't what Mother's worried about, Amelia. Tell her he checks out medically and I'm not into chance encounters. That's what's worrying her.''

"And what about you?'' she demanded, swiveling her head in my direction.

"I'm forty, heterosexual, neither married nor engaged, not into chance encounters, and have no mother to worry about me.''

"Pity,'' she said. "Overcoming parents builds character. Like overcoming a stutter, or being left-handed.''

Mark choked on his ice. I sipped and kept a serene countenance, trading her stare for stare.

"I thought you might be related to someone I know,'' she said. "You have a familiar look about you.''

"I'm not related to anyone I know,'' I said. "I was a foundling.''

"Really! Tell me!'' She folded her hands beneath her chin and gave me her complete attention.

I told her briefly about my life, and about Jacob.

"What a good man,'' she said. "I like hearing about good men. In my business, you sometimes believe they are extinct, like the dodo or the moa. A marvel, created by God, but unable to sustain itself in the face of human depravity and natural selection.''

The person tapped at the door and came in, bearing documents, which we all signed. We shook hands. She looked at her watch.

"I have to run. The firm is giving a dinner for the widow of our late partner, in honor of her eightieth birthday in a few days."

"Would that be Lycia Meyer's mother?" I asked. "Olivia Meyer?"

"You know her?"

"I've met Lycia. She and I have a mutual friend in Greg Steinwale."

She smiled widely. "Harriet's son, of course. Harriet and I are old adversaries. We do battle here and there. Well, small world, and other such clichés . . .

"Here's your copy. You'll get a check for the advance within a few days. I, personally, would appreciate your doing this as quickly as possible, though I know we've no right to ask. I'm heartily tired of the rest rooms in this building, as well as the slow elevators and the drab Edwardian look we've settled into. All fust and worn leather."

"As soon as possible," I promised.

"And we'd better do it, too," said Mark on the way down in the slow elevator. "Or she'll eat us alive."

four

WE SPENT THE following few days in the kinds of activity any large job involves. One good thing about Law Firm Jobs (Eugenia calls them that—we've done several) is that only busy lawyers can afford us, and busy lawyers have no time to get involved in details. Aside from getting a list of color preferences from the partners, we had a free hand to get on with the work. Amelia had stressed that they wanted a solidly traditional look with some sparkle to it, and that's what they were going to get, with authentic period furniture used wherever it made sense and was not too expensive.

Desks are always a problem in period offices. Most desks made before the 1900's are simply inadequate for today's use, they're too small, they have too little knee room. Originally, desks were simply boxes in which paper and ink could be stored, often with a slanted lid, hinged at the top, which could be used for a writing surface. The occasional literate individual strapped up the box, lugged it about, and set it up on any convenient bench or table. Later on, carpenters began putting drawers in the boxes and building stands to hold them; still later the French began putting drawers in the stand, all the way to the floor, and covering the writing surface with a fabric called *bure*, thus "bureau" for any chest of drawers. By this time, the hinge had been moved to the bottom of the slanted top, giving us the so-called "fall-front" desk where the lid hinges down to make a level writing surface.

Eventually, the drawers in the base were split to yield a little knee room, and this was increased over the years until we had something looking very much like today's pedestal desk, with two sets of drawers and a large, flat top. Women workers with short skirts led to the invention of the so-called "modesty screen" between the pedestals, but otherwise the basic design remains unchanged since the nineteenth century. We planned to use good, but large, period reproductions for Amelia's job.

Chairs always have to be idiosyncratic: people have to choose their own chairs. No two rear ends are built alike, and even if they were identical, people have varying ideas of what constitutes comfort. The clerical workers would have contemporary chairs with every adjustment of back, hip, and thigh known to man, as well as very modern work stations for their word processors, printers, and so forth, but their work space wouldn't be visible to most people visiting the offices.

We'd ordered conference tables built to order. Any genuine period table that size would cost a fortune. The genuine pieces we were using would appear in the halls and reception areas and the partners' offices. Mark spent all day Wednesday and Thursday plus Friday morning at the fabric houses and the carpet wholesalers. Eugenia called dealers, asking if they had anything we could use, while I conferred with our currently favored general contractor. One problem with doing period styles in modern space is that the surfaces themselves are inappropriate. Glass areas are too large for traditional window treatments; walls are too flat and ceilings are boring. It's necessary to break up windows and walls with columns or panels, then treat the parts individually. The resultant surfaces, if well done, are more interesting; they look warmer. The dropped ceilings found in most offices—if there aren't heating or air conditioning ducts in the way—can sometimes be raised wholly or in part by eliminating fluorescent fixtures.

Of course, there are purists who believe all this is heresy, that buildings and rooms should be structural and unadorned. I prefer rooms and buildings that make people feel good, no matter how the buildings are constructed.

The contractor said he could start in ten days. Friday afternoon I talked to Myron Burstein in New York, read him my list of things we hadn't found locally, and asked him to do his best. That concluded the preliminaries. We estimated the job should take no more than three months. Mark phoned Amelia and told her so.

By four o'clock we were ready for a TGIF party, so after Mark reconnoitered, the three of us sneaked down the alley to the Painted Cow. I left a message for Grace, telling her where we'd be. Mark phoned his roommate. Eugenia said she could have one drink and then had to run because she had theater tickets.

We sat in the bar. Grace showed up. Eugenia left. Bryan Langton, Mark's friend, showed up. The four of us became convivial and went elsewhere to dinner. Grace took repeated advantage of the salad bar, then ate all her dinner and half of mine. Throughout the evening—drinks, food, conversation, laughter—I was aware that the days just past had not occasioned any great excitement or sense of accomplishment. A year ago they would have. Even six months ago I'd have been patting myself on the back at how well everything was fitting together and how clever we all were to have thought of this or that or the other thing. This past week, I'd done more or less the right things without thinking much about them. The job would turn out well. The lawyers would be happy—at least, Amelia would be. And I, when all was said and done, would be glad their money was in my bank, but I wouldn't care much otherwise.

I was a little disconcerted by the feeling, but I thought I'd hidden it from everyone else. Grace, as she often does, surprised me. When we arrived back at 1465 Hyde, she asked me, "Is something wrong, Jason? You're not happy about the new job. You're preoccupied."

I started to say something evasive, but then decided not to. Grace has a way of zeroing in on evasions that's most uncomfortable. I told her nothing was really wrong, but I'd been sort of preoccupied with the thought that with Jacob gone, I didn't need to go on with the business unless I wanted to. I said it in a casual voice, not making much of it. I was prepared for any reaction except the one I got.

"Well of course you don't," she said in an exasperated tone. "Hadn't that occurred to you before now?"

Considerably piqued, I confessed it had not.

"It should have," she assured me. "I mean, we both know you came back here to Denver because of Jacob. If he hadn't asked you, you'd still be at the Smithsonian or somewhere like it. Now, if Agatha were still alive and you had children, you'd probably stay, because Denver's a pretty good family town. But since there's just you, I can't see why you haven't thought about leaving before now."

"Maybe I didn't want to," I offered, stung at the implication. I didn't want to think about the implication.

"It would be easier just to go on doing the same old thing," she agreed. "Changing your life is really hard. I know. I've been trying to change just a few things about mine."

"Like?"

"Like not running every time Ron gets himself in trouble."

Ron was her brother. He lived in San Francisco, being part of a casually gay and feckless life-style that was virtually guaranteed to get him either jailed or prematurely dead. Not, Grace assured me, out of malice or wickedness, but simply because he was both lazy and sensuous. It was easier for him to go along with people than it was to do anything requiring will or determination. Easier to get drunk than stay sober. Easier to get involved with druggies than to stay away from them. Easier just to have sex when he or someone else felt like it than to plan ahead and protect himself.

"How're you doing?" I asked.

"He called three times this week, and I said no each time. No, I wouldn't come out. No, I wouldn't send money. No, I wouldn't pay his lawyer."

"Tough."

"Really. I feel guilty all the time. I wake up feeling guilty. I go to bed feeling guilty. I cry a lot."

"What was it you told me? You either do it your whole life, or you don't do it?"

"That's right. Only, if he dies, if he ends up in jail, then what?"

"Only, if you die, what happens to him if he's never learned to stand on his own two feet?" It was a question she had asked me. I suppose it is a question every parent asks about every child. What happens to this child if he hasn't grown up by the time I'm gone?

"Some people never do learn," she said, shaking her head angrily. "Why are we talking about me? We were talking about you! I'll tell you one thing, Jason. This business isn't enough for you. Otherwise you wouldn't get all involved in these puzzles of yours. Maybe you do that because you're kind of bored. Did you ever think about that?"

I shook my head at her, warningly. "I haven't thought about that, no. And I don't intend to think about it today. You may be right, but I'm not prepared to deal with the larger issues just yet. There's no hurry. That's one thing I know for sure. There's no hurry."

"Just so you don't get in a rut," she warned. "If you do, you'll ossify."

I shrugged again. "If I do, it means I didn't want anything else badly enough to go after it. Or, maybe, what was here was what I wanted."

She gave me one of those deep looks she occasionally pulls off, as though she had x-ray eyes and could see into places I'm not even sure are there. "Maybe," she said at last. "Maybe, Jason."

We made love that night, and there was a kind of carefulness in it, as though one of us—or maybe both—was fragile. It was sweet but painful, a reluctant engagement, a tender touching, careful not to hurt. Careful not to bruise.

Afterward we lay close with her head next to mine on the pillow, her mouth next to my ear. I said to the ceiling, "I am not going away. Not anytime soon!"

"Hmm," she murmured. "I'm not either."

"We have to figure out who killed Simonetta," I argued. "I can't do anything before that."

"And where's Olivia," she whispered.

"And where's Olivia," I agreed. "And who's trying to kill me."

"That's right."

"Well then," I demanded. "Well then! What's all this parting lovers' ambience. All this melancholy."

"Well, we don't know," she whispered, half asleep. "That's it, Jason. We just don't know."

Then she was asleep, all the soft length of her against me, warm. All of Grace was warm, even her feet. She had no cold, bony places. Everything about Grace was comfortable except her habit of seeing things I didn't see.

It was a long time before I got to sleep.

At the breakfast table, Saturday morning, we avoided any recap of the previous evening's discussion. Instead, Grace filled me in on her attempts to find witnesses to Simonetta's death.

"The picture you picked out, the man with the scar on his face, he's from Utah. He posted bail and went back to Salt Lake City. Linder got him on the phone. He says he didn't know any of the other people, so he didn't know who the woman on the other side of Simonetta was. I went through the pictures again, and I double-checked to be sure I had them all, and none of them have curly white hair."

I told her about my wig idea, and she promised to bring the arrest photographs back, so I could look at them again.

"The lieutenant says if it wasn't anybody at the clinic who killed Simonetta, it must be somebody from her past. So, Hector's been digging into Nello Leone. Turns out, he died in a mental hospital back in '60. Hector no sooner found that out than somebody told him Nimo died the same way. Some kind of inherited disease, father and son, both."

It rang a faint bell. "Yaggie told Myra that back in '53 or thereabouts, the woman who Simonetta worked for was accidentally killed—a gas leak, the papers said. That'd have been Nimo's wife, right? The one Dorotea told us about.''

Grace looked up from her English muffins and ginger marmalade, two furrows between her eyes, remembering. ''Right. Nimo's wife and the baby. An accident, she said.''

''The thing is, Simonetta said suicide. The papers said an accident, but Simonetta said suicide. Why would a young mother commit suicide?''

Grace snorted. ''Married to Nello Leone's son? I can think of a dozen reasons.''

''Yeah, but when you mentioned an inherited disease, it occurred to me she could have discovered her husband had this disease. Which could have meant maybe her child had it.'' I thought about it. ''Though I can't see how Simonetta could have interfered in that.''

''Well, suppose the wife died by accident. But Simonetta thought it was suicide, so she went around saying so. That would have been interference, for a Catholic family.''

There was a more convincing explanation. ''Suppose the young wife *did* commit suicide,'' I offered, ''but the family tried to hush it up. Tried to claim it was an accident. And then Simonetta went to her family and said it was suicide. That would upset the family some.''

''But the baby died too, so it wasn't . . .'' She looked down at her plate. I knew what she was thinking.

''We don't know how the baby died,'' I said. ''All we know is Dorotea said the mother and child died, but she didn't really remember.''

''It could have been murder-suicide,'' Grace offered. ''The mother finds out the baby has this genetic disease, so she kills the baby and then herself.''

''Even if that happened and Simonetta knew about it, why would that get her killed almost forty years later? I could see somebody trying to shut her up then, but now?''

Grace wiped marmalade off her lips and made a rueful face. ''I think we're clutching at straws.''

I had to admit she was probably right. The idea of murder-suicide was an interesting if rather repulsive idea. Parents killing their children to protect them from life happened now and then, but it always came as a shock. If and when we spoke with the peripatetic Cecily, maybe we'd find out.

"If she did, I know how she felt," said Grace.

"If who did what?"

"If the mother killed her baby, thinking it had a horrible disease. She couldn't face the pain. Not her pain, not the baby's pain. She thought it would be easier. I know how she felt."

I put my arms around her and held her, her and the muffin and the marmalade. She was thinking of brother Ron again, of his constant hysterical demands on her, of his inevitable pain and of her own. He kept on doing stupid things, and hurting himself, and passing the pain to her by asking her to make everything all right. Let Gracie kiss it and make it well. Let Gracie come up with the bail money, the rent money, the whatever. She knew she couldn't go on doing it, but it hurt to say no. There wasn't anything I could do to make it better, so I just sat there and held her, and after a long time she took a deep breath and said she was all right, so we got dressed and went to the Natural History Museum in City Park to see the Aztec exhibit, the way we'd planned.

Rather, not quite the way we planned.

I'd wanted to see the exhibit. Grace had agreed to go along if we could go to a movie after.

"Doesn't gold fascinate you?" I'd asked her.

"Not other people's," she'd told me soberly. "If I had some of my own, it might."

So, I was going for the art and she was going to keep me company, and after that, we'd go to the movie. That was what was planned. We got as far as the parking lot. It was packed with cars near the museum, so we went all the way to the extreme northern end of the lot. We locked the car, then walked through the intervening lanes of parked cars and driveways, stopping under some bare oaks on a strip of ice-coated grass to allow two or three cars to cross in front of us. A few hundred yards west of us was the giraffe enclosure at the zoo. Whenever I'm anywhere near the giraffe enclosure, I look for giraffes, so I was staring in that direction, paying no attention to the traffic. Suddenly Grace threw herself into me, and we both slipped on the ice and went down in a heap. The car that had been in front of us screeched its tires, bumped over two or three concrete curbs, slammed through a planted area, and shimmied northward, over the frozen grass toward the golf course.

Then I realized there'd been a bang. A gunshot. Somebody had shot at somebody, and from the sound of the words coming from Grace's mouth, the somebody had been one or both of us.

"Did you see what kind of car that was?" she demanded, dragging me to my feet.

I shook my head mutely. I hadn't really noticed it until it started cross country. "Dark blue," I said. "Four door. That's all."

"Damn!" she said. "Come on. I have to get to a phone."

"What did you see?"

"I saw a *gun*, Jason. What do you think I saw? Lions and tigers and bears?"

She was headed back toward the car, yelling at me over her shoulder, and I was limping after her. The fall had done my damaged leg no good. On the other hand, remaining upright would probably have done it no good either, since it was attached to the rest of me. "Which one of us was he shooting at?"

"I didn't have time to ask," she said. "The key, Jason. The key."

I came up with the key, we drove across Colorado Boulevard to a 7-Eleven where there was a public phone, and Grace phoned her colleagues at the station. We waited until a car showed up.

"He was fifty-five, sixty, pasty-faced, half bald, and he had on a beige down vest," she told them when she'd explained what had happened.

"Been throwin your weight around, Grace?" one of them asked her.

She glanced in my direction and said something baleful.

The glance was enough. She hadn't said so, but she knew the gunman had been aiming at me. That was twice. Even after the shot outside my door that Sunday morning, I'd been only marginally careful because I hadn't really believed it was meant for me. I'd convinced myself it was random. Some kid, maybe, playing lethal games. Now I had to admit to myself that it was a real threat. There really was a gunman and he'd really been aiming at me, and he'd missed once because of Grace and once because of luck. If I hadn't been lucky, I'd have been dead.

Somehow I no longer cared about the Aztecs. Grace and I went back to Hyde Street, and I limped upstairs to find an Ace bandage for my leg while she chivied me from behind, like a sheepdog.

"So why me?" I asked her as she strode jerkily to and fro, her forehead furrowed in thought.

"The same damn reasons we talked about last time. You were on TV," she said. "Maybe. In connection with the clinic. Remember what Cynthia said about those nuts. Maybe one of them has decided you're the devil incarnate."

"It's an idea," I admitted. "You ought to tell Linder."

"I already did. On the other hand, it could be something else."

"Like what?"

"Like your looking into who killed Simonetta."

"Nobody knows I'm doing that!"

"Anybody who's watched you knows you're doing that! You went to Zuni Street and talked to her neighbors twice. You talked to her sister. You've had Myra calling all the old neighbors. And there's Yaggie. Myra talked to Yaggie, and from what you say, it sounds like Yaggie probably talks to the world at large."

Grace was angry. When Grace gets angry, she gets very pale and pinched-looking.

"You went with me to Zuni Street," I pointed out. "Both of us went out to talk to Dorotea."

"I'm just one cop. Kill me and the department gets mad, then somebody else asks the same questions, only more so.

Killing a cop doesn't make sense. Kill you, though, maybe after a while the department get distracted, loses interest in Simonetta, and nobody gets anywhere."

"Then whoever is doing this must think I'm getting somewhere, right?"

She shrugged. It was the weak point in her argument, because I wasn't getting anywhere. Not yet. Unless I was getting somewhere without knowing it.

"If they get me, promise me you'll talk to Cecily," I said, trying to be funny.

"Oh, Jason, shut up. This is serious. That guy really meant to kill you." She clenched her fists and squinched her eyes and threatened me.

"Maybe it was just a warning shot."

"He was looking right at you."

"Well, if it's a nut, there's nothing I can do about it. But if it's because of Simonetta, then we have to find out who killed her."

"That would help, yes," she cried, giving me an accusing look.

"I have been a bit busy with other things," I yelled. "Like earning a living."

"I know." She shrugged apologetically and hugged me with tears in her eyes. I melted.

"I could set my mind to it."

"Do that. Do that while I make a snack of something."

So I set my mind to it and came up with nothing much. Until Cecily returned from Brazil, we were at a dead end. Except for the death which had set Simonetta off . . . the death of the woman she'd worked for, in 1953.

"Library," I said, when we'd had Grace's snack. "Let's go to the library."

The Denver Public Library has a file of Denver newspapers going back to the turn of the century, all on microfilm. We wanted the spring of 1953 or, failing that, 1952 or 1954. Grace took one machine and I another, and we scanned away, she working on April, and I on March. I found the reference in the third week of March.

Gas Leak Fatality. Young Mother Dies. The story told how Mrs. G. R. Leone, 21, was overcome by gas during the night. The leak had been traced to an old gas log in the fireplace, one which was thought to have been sealed off. Comments from the Public Service Company. Funeral Friday at St. Mary's.

I read it. Grace read it. Grace said, "There's nothing about a child! I thought the child died!"

I read it again. She was right. The only reference to a child was the implication made by the headline, where Mrs. G. R. Leone was identified as a young mother.

"Dorotea Chapman was rather indefinite about it," I mused. "She said she didn't remember what had happened except that it had been a tragedy and she'd gone to the funeral. She was still a child herself at the time."

"But, according to Myra, Simonetta was yelling about a baby."

"So Yaggie said. But if the woman had been pregnant again, perhaps it was another baby, in utero, who died. If Simonetta thought the woman had committed suicide, and if she'd been pregnant . . ." None of it seemed to mean much, quite frankly.

"Damn," said Grace feelingly. "We don't have diddly." She continued to inventory what we didn't have all the way home and then stalked off up the stairs.

Before I followed her, I gathered the small pile of Saturday mail from the hall floor. Mark had filed all the stuff pertaining to the law firm job on Friday, so when I dumped the mail on my desk I found it empty except for Brother Daniel's phone number. Which had nothing at all to do with Simonetta. Still, Grace had vanished into the bathroom, and while she was in there, maybe I could make an appointment. I called and got hold of someone with a Brooklyn accent. I explained I was attempting to trace a friend of my foster father and had been told Brother Daniel might have useful information. The voice told me I could see Brother Daniel on Sunday afternoon and advised me in a singsong voice that women who were not family members were not allowed entry. I mentioned this to Grace when she returned from the bathroom, but she only shrugged.

"Silly," she said. "If I wanted entry, I'd get it."

"You want to go to the movie?" I asked.

"Probably safe enough, if you slip across the alley and go through the Fetterlings' and I drive my car and pick you up out front of there and nobody follows us."

"Shit!" The idea was intensely annoying. "We went to the library!"

"He didn't have time to regroup before we went to the library," she said. "Maybe we could stay home and pull all the curtains and watch a movie on the VCR? We never watched *Little Dorrit* and you've had it for ages."

"Ten hours' worth of Dickens?"

"Well, until we get tired or run out of food or find something better to do."

We didn't get tired, and we didn't run out of food, but we only watched about an hour of *Little Dorrit* before we found something better to do.

My predicament was not susceptible to easy solution. If an unknown man is coming after you with a gun, and if he's patient, he'll get you sooner or later. Even a rotten shot like the guy who'd tried for me twice will get the job done if he's given enough time. The Secret Service knows this. All those guys who guard the President spend their lives sweating and praying it won't happen on their shift. The truth is, if somebody is reasonably careful and absolutely determined, he can get to anybody. Guns are easy to get, and high-powered automatics are lethal even in the hands of idiots who can't tell east from west. Just point one of those in the general direction of the victim and he'll end up dead along with half a dozen innocent bystanders.

Figuring this out took very little time after Grace left on Sunday morning. Maybe the guy out to kill me hated antique dealers and had picked me at random by sticking a pin through the yellow pages. Maybe he had mistaken me for somebody else. The why's didn't matter. There were only two ways I could see to get at him. I could figure out why he wanted to kill me and therefore who he probably was, or I could catch him and then figure out why he wanted to kill me. Grace and Lieutenant Linder had already kicked that idea around. She'd suggested having me followed in an attempt to catch the guy. The trouble was the same old thing: the department had a limited budget, nobody knew how long it might take, and if they caught the guy, it might be *after* he'd shot me rather than before.

If he was following me, I might be able to lead him into a trap. If he wasn't following me but just taking a stab at me every now and then, when he thought of it, trapping him would be difficult. Though, come to think of it, both attempts had been on weekends. The first time early Sunday morning, then again the following Saturday.

Which meant what?

Coincidence. Or, maybe, somebody who only had time off to go gunning on the weekends. Or somebody who was only in town on the weekends. Somebody from out of town. Which made no damned sense at all! However, if true, it made today more dangerous than tomorrow.

Though, as a boy, I was as much a show-off as any of my peers, I am no longer into feckless nonchalance. I do not like horror stories where the heroine goes off in her chiffon nightgown to see what's making the strange noises in the middle of the night. I do not like adventure epics where the hero walks around in enemy territory ignoring the most elementary precautions for protecting himself—like keeping his back against a wall—and lets people come up behind him and whop him over the head, escaping later only because someone else is even stupider than he is. I am disturbed at the low level of intelligence displayed by these characters, also at the amount of alcohol they consume, the number of times they fall into bed with high-risk sex partners (asking no questions), and the number of times they end up in the hospital. If they were flesh and blood, they would have died of liver disease, AIDS, and trauma-related problems long before they reached volume four of the series.

In my book, hero(ines) should be at least a tiny fraction smarter than the lowlifes they so consistently encounter!

Thus ruminating, I decided I'd been living in a fool's paradise, just like the characters I despised. It was my duty to stop blundering around and outthink whoever was after me. Whatever the reason, twice was sufficient warning. I was not about to walk into another bullet!

First I went down to the basement, opened Jacob's old iron safe, and got out my four target handguns that had been in there for years. I took them upstairs, got out the fifth one, the one I keep in my desk, then cleaned, checked, and loaded all five. One went in my bedside table, one back in the desk, one in the kitchen. The fourth one went downstairs, inside a Chinese vase in the main showroom. The fifth one went in the basement, in its holster, which I strapped to the leg of an old square piano with duct tape. Just in case, I told myself. If I'd had that gun down there a year before, I might not have been shot.

Then I sneaked across the alley to Nellie's place and begged the use of her phone. This took care of the remote possibility my phone was bugged, as it had been on one previous occasion. "Man who stumbles over same rock twice deserves to break fool neck," Jacob had often said, claiming to quote Confucius. I called Mark, who, fortuitously, was home and asked him to pick me up outside the Fetterling house at twelve-thirty. I ordered a cab for one o'clock at Mark's apartment house, because he has a drive-in basement garage with entrances on two separate streets. When the cab got there, I'd ask Mark to meet it, bring it into the garage, and I'd take it out the other way.

All of which worked pretty much the way I'd planned, up to and including the use of a few props I'd taken along.

"Laugh all you like," I said, pulling down the brim of my slouch hat over a pair of Jacob's horn-rimmed glasses I'd knocked the lenses out of. I'd also found an old raincoat down in the basement, the kind nobody has worn for thirty years. "I was the one who got shot at, not you."

Mark sobered. "What can we do to help, Jason? We've

got nothing planned. I could pick up a wig and false beard for you. Maybe a pair of elevator shoes?"

"If you really want to help, meet me outside this abbey I'm going to," I told him. "Either or both of you. I should be finished there about three. If I haven't lost whoever's gunning for me by now, he's too smart and I might as well give up!"

When the cab arrived, Mark brought it into the basement, I scrunched down in the back, and the driver took us up and out. After half a dozen blocks he mumbled, "If there's anybody following us, buddy, he's invisible. There's nobody on the streets but us."

So I got up, feeling only a little like a fool, and we talked about the Broncos all the way to the abbey. Or rather, he talked, and I said "Right" and "You said it" and "You just never know, do you?"

When I tipped him, he winked and said, "I never saw you, right?"

"Right," I said.

"You runnin away to become a monk?" he asked me. "I thought of doin that once. Kind of nice life. Quiet."

I shook my head. "I'm not patient enough," I confided. "Besides, I like women. And good coffee."

"Me, it's beer," he said. "Beer and sports. What you gonna do, right?"

"Right."

"Nothin like beer."

"You said it."

"When you're a kid, you think everything's gonna be a big deal. You never think much about the little stuff. Like havin a few guys over for a beer. And a little bet on the game, just to make things interestin. Life's not such a big deal. It's just, you know, kinda nice." He smiled and stretched, the perfect picture of contentment. I envied him.

"You just never know, do you," I said.

"You have a nice day," he said, looking around to see that we hadn't been observed before he drove away. I took off the raincoat, the Indiana Jones hat, and the glasses before ringing the bell at the gate.

Until my phone call to the place, I hadn't known there was an abbey on the grounds of the Catholic seminary, which sits on a hundred acres or so of prime residential land southeast of downtown. As we'd turned onto the approach street, I'd noticed for the first time that one corner of the property was set off behind its own wall, making it a separate enclosure. The separateness of it was much in evidence from inside, for I was led down a brick-paved cloister beside a walled garden. I was left in a small room containing a few straight chairs and another door across from the one I'd entered by.

The silent man who came through that door didn't offer to shake hands. He was sixty, perhaps, with a pale, quiet face. He looked serene, but not well, like a man with a chronic illness who's gotten used to it.

"Mr. Lynx?" he asked, as he seated himself on a straight chair across from me. He wore a brown robe and stout shoes. I'd expected sandals, but Denver's winter would be a little severe for sandals. He looked like a monk. "You are Jason Lynx?"

I nodded, realizing I'd been staring.

"How can I help you?"

I sat down and told him about Jacob. I said Jacob had ordered a birthday gift for someone's eightieth birthday, and we believed that someone to be Olivia Cerraverdes, or Olivia Desquintas y Alvarez, but we couldn't locate her.

He nodded, letting a tiny smile move one corner of his mouth. "That was a long time ago. How did you come to connect me with the Cerraverdes?"

I told him about Myra and her research.

"My brother," he said, letting the smile broaden into something real. "Yes, of course. We were neighbors of the Cerraverdes. I'm not sure I have any information that will help you. I've been here since I was eighteen."

"Anything you can tell us about the family. Even if you don't know where Olivia may be, some other member of her family might help us find her."

"You believe this is important?"

He asked it rather sadly, like a man who found very little of importance. I supposed from his point of view, such worldly things were rather picayune. I'd said nothing about Jacob's lifelong love. I didn't want to. I simply said yes, I thought it was very important because Jacob had thought so and I felt morally responsible for carrying out his last wishes.

Moral responsibility seemed to set well with him. "Well then, let me tell you what I can remember, though I didn't know Mrs. Alvarez well. Only the way a schoolboy would know the parent of a schoolmate. It was her daughter I knew."

He seemed unable to get past that point. "Your sister-in-law mentioned you were childhood sweethearts," I said carefully, hoping I wasn't venturing on forbidden ground.

He looked surprised, then almost relieved, as though I had given him permission to say or feel something he'd been wary of saying or feeling. "Yes. We were . . . we were childhood sweethearts. We loved each other very much." He dropped his eyes, examined the hands knotted quietly in his lap, as though he had never seen them before.

"But you decided to enter a religious order," I said politely, when he didn't go on.

He looked up, eyes blazing. "No!"

I waited, dismayed at having evoked that fiery negation.

"No," he said more calmly. "She and I had decided to be married. We were both eighteen. She had just turned eighteen. We were old enough. Her father . . . her father was a very . . . strange person. That is, strange to me. He was Spanish. He had been, I believe, very wealthy, very important in his own country. That was before the war. He was driven out, forced to accept the charity of his wife's parents. It was very hard for him. He was very proud."

Brother Daniel used words carefully and individually, each one placed neatly, precisely, in the formal manner of a man perhaps unaccustomed to narrative. Certainly in the manner of a man avoiding emotion. Except for that blazing "no," there was no warmth in his words.

"You knew him?" I prompted.

"She told me about him. My angel told me." Suddenly there were tears in his eyes.

"I'm sorry," I said, starting to get up. "Perhaps I shouldn't have . . ."

He waved me down. "No. It's all right. It's a relief to talk about it, actually. If you have the time, I'll tell you the whole story."

He waited. I nodded.

"His name was Octavio Desquintas y Alvarez. She used to say it that way. 'My father is Don Octavio Desquintas y Alvarez.' When America entered the war, he volunteered to fight in Europe. He was not a citizen, but he volunteered to fight against those who had driven him from his home. He was badly wounded, and his life was saved by a fellow soldier. They became friends." He stood up and turned, grimacing a little, as though in pain.

"Mr. Lynx, even now it's hard for me to tell this, because I've never been able to explain it, not even to myself. Even now, after all these years, I can only imagine these things. I have never been in a war, never been wounded, never made such a friend. Here . . . here we are warned against making close friends, you understand?"

"I've read something . . . a little."

"Too close a human friendship distracts us from God. We swear our deepest friendship to God. But Don Octavio swore an oath of a different kind, an oath of friendship with this man who had saved his life. In his oath, I do not believe he even considered God. His oath was that their two families should be united. His daughter should marry this man's son."

"Your . . . sweetheart? Olivia's daughter?"

"Yes. At the time he swore this oath, she was only a child. Ten. Eleven, perhaps. He didn't tell her then, not when he first returned from the war. He was an invalid. He didn't talk to her much, and he never mentioned this oath until she told him about me, about us. Only then did he tell her she couldn't marry me because he had promised her to someone else."

"Told her she was to marry someone she didn't know?"

It seemed barbaric to me, like something out of the Middle Ages.

"It was on her eighteenth birthday. He told her that day. Less than a month later they were married. The bans were waived. It was all in a great hurry. The day she married, I came here and asked to be admitted. They did not take me then, but soon they did. It was my way of being faithful to her . . . then. Later it became my way of being faithful to God."

"I can't imagine a father doing that to his daughter!" I exclaimed. "This is the twentieth century, the United States, not . . ."

"Not medieval Spain?" he asked me gently, seating himself with a grimace of pain. "No, this country is not medieval Spain. But Octavio Desquintas y Alvarez was not from this country. He was only its unwilling guest. And he was a medieval man in many ways, a man who had been wounded in the war and never regained good health, who had been treated for years as we treat sick men, dutifully, gently. A very arrogant man who saw his honor as the only important issue. He lived only long enough to see her married. It was a matter of honor. Not only for him, for the boy's father as well. A matter of honor."

"But she agreed!"

He looked past me, out the window at the sky, his eyes empty. "Her father was ill. She was dutiful. She took seriously the commandment about honoring her father. She had that much honor of her own."

I shook my head, trying to get myself back on track, finding it hard to put aside my outrage for Olivia's daughter. "If you came here when you were only eighteen or nineteen, then you probably don't know what happened to Olivia."

"Oh, I wasn't cut off from the world. My parents visited me regularly. They told me when Don Octavio died." He shook his head slowly. "They told me the Cerraverdes had moved away, to St. Louis, I think. They took their granddaughter, Olivia's younger daughter, with them. Olivia left the neighborhood, too. Later she married again. I can't remember her second husband's name, if they ever told me.''

"Meyer," I said, suddenly sure of it. "And the younger daughter's name was . . ."

"Alicia," he said, surprised. "They called her Lycia. She was ten years younger than my angel."

Everything fell into place. Lycia Foret was Olivia's daughter! She had always seemed familiar to me. Now it was clear why. She resembled the picture of her mother, the picture Jacob had always kept by him, hanging above the walnut cabinet beside his bed, lost among a clutter of other photographs, of his parents, of his brother, of places he had traveled in his youth. I'd seen the photographs there every day of my growing up, but they had been like the pattern in the wallpaper. He had never called my attention to them, never told me they were important.

I looked at the quiet man in the brown robe almost absently, my mind aswirl with sudden plans. I would buy the table Jacob had meant for Olivia. I would tell Lycia Foret about her mother and my foster father. I would . . .

I would do nothing at the moment. I warned myself. Nothing. Not until I knew I could do it without hurting anyone. Jacob had known details I didn't know. I couldn't go trampling in, like some mad elephant . . .

"Is that all you wanted to know?" he asked me.

"Yes. Thank you. I'm very grateful."

"Remember me in your prayers," he said. He stood up and was gone, silently.

The same person who had let me in let me out. Mark and Bryan were waiting in Mark's car. I got into the back seat.

"You look like you've found the Holy Grail," Mark said.

"I found Olivia," I told him.

"Jason, that's wonderful!" He turned to Bryan and filled him in on Jacob's lost love, evidently a topic they had already discussed. They wanted all the details. Even after I'd recited them exhaustively, Mark wasn't satisfied. "What's the matter with you?" he demanded. "I should think you'd be excited and you're all gloomy. Where is she? Olivia?"

"She must be here in town, somewhere. Her family are planning a birthday party for her sometime soon."

"So why the gloom?"

"Well, for one thing, I'm not sure how Olivia may react to hearing from Jacob's foster son. I'd like to talk to her daughter Lycia first, but since that matter a year ago, I don't really feel comfortable doing that." Mark didn't know the whole truth of that matter, but he knew enough to explain my discomfort to Bryan.

"Oh, hell, go ahead," said Bryan. "If she's like my mother, she'll love anything that will make her Mama happy or interested. Mother goes crazy trying to interest Gram in anything at all."

There was a certain amount of sense to that. No matter how Lycia Foret felt about me, she wouldn't deprive her mother of pleasure—assuming it would be pleasure. Besides, it had just occurred to me I could ask Trish Steinwale to explore the situation for me. That way, nobody would be made uncomfortable, at least not face to face. If they'd rather not, they could tell Trish and Trish could tell me.

Mark and Bryan dropped me off at the Fetterlings' house and I went home via the alley. Once inside I called Trish, asking if I could see her sometime Monday. She and Greg had recently bought a pleasant old house in Park Hill, which they were renovating slightly before moving in. Trish said she'd be at the new house in the morning and could drop by my place on her way down to Greg's studio at noon. I thanked her profusely, got myself a beer out of the refrigerator, and sat down to watch TV and think about things—such as how Olivia Meyer might have somehow attracted the attention of an extortioner. Or how her daughter might have done so.

Though perhaps it had been the other daughter, Brother Daniel's love, the one he called his angel. I realized suddenly that the information about Olivia had come as such a welcome surprise that I'd neglected to ask Brother Daniel what had happened to his childhood sweetheart, Olivia's older daughter. On further consideration I decided that even if I'd thought about it, I would not have asked. The subject was obviously painful for him.

Besides, he might not even know. Lycia had commented that she had no brothers or sisters to help throw the party for Olivia, which might mean her sister had died or that she lived far away. Her sister could have ended up in some remote place, some foreign country. The family into which the girl married could have been European, like Octavio himself, or perhaps Latin American. I hated to think what the girl's life must have been like, married to a man she'd never seen, taken to an unfamiliar place, perhaps to an unfamiliar culture, leaving her childhood sweetheart behind, knowing she'd probably never see him again. Doing all that to fulfill her father's sense of honor, only to see him die very shortly after the wedding.

Had she ever come home to visit her mother and sister? Had she ever driven to the walled enclosure I'd visited that afternoon, to sit outside, wishing she could go in? Had she lived a long time with her stranger husband? Had she grown old with him?

In a way, it was Olivia's story all over again. She, too, had married to please her family. Perhaps, having done so, she had felt she could not interfere in what her husband had arranged for their daughter. More likely, she'd simply felt impotent in the face of her husband's Mediterranean ideas of honor.

Myra and I had been right when we'd said it was like an episode of Lost Loves. Pure melodrama, except for the reality of the people involved. If the same situation had presented itself now, the daughter would tell her father he was out of his mind, and then she'd run off with her boyfriend to California or New York, they'd spend a few years finding themselves before settling down to middle-class obscurity and one point three children in a suburb somewhere. Daddy might die without his honor satisfied, but every year on the anniversary of his death, his daughter would go to his grave and tell him how well everything had worked out. I could see the final screen credits.

It was infinitely more gothic the way it had actually happened. I knew Grace would think so. When she called about eight, I told her everything, and she remarked that it read like a miniseries, but she'd missed the final episode. I said the final episode might be yet to come.

"Did you check your windows and doors, Jason?" she asked when we had finished with Jacob's tale.

I told her I had, and that the alarm was on. I had also checked the three upstairs handguns, but I didn't mention that.

"And Bela's feeling alert, right? How about the dog door?"

I had both latched the dog door and inserted the panel on the inside which made it burglar proof. If Bela needed to go outside during the night, he'd just have to tell me so.

This met with her approval. "Good night, Jason," she said. "Be careful in the morning."

I was immediately careful, not waiting for morning. I did not walk in front of uncurtained windows with the lights on. I had a long soak in the big tub and went to bed. Despite the fact that someone seemed to be trying to kill me, I slept soundly. If I dreamed of anything at all, I didn't remember it when I woke.

Amelia Wirtz dropped by on Monday morning. She wanted to look at the drapery fabrics Mark had chosen for her office. Because she was a family friend, he was going out of his way to be sure she was happy. Because she was Amelia Wirtz, I thought that was a damned good idea.

"What's new in your life?" she demanded, plunking herself down in the chair across from my desk, thus forcing Mark to bring the samples into my office, though he'd had them nicely arranged in his own. "Did you find out who your foster father ordered the table for?"

I didn't remember having told her about that. I glanced at Mark and saw him flush dark red. So, he'd told her—a kind of addendum to what I had told her about Jacob.

"As a matter of fact, yes." I said. "However, for the time

being at least, this must be a professional confidence. We've found that Jacob's old sweetheart was the wife of your former partner, Theo Meyer.''

"Olivia Meyer? I'll be damned. Come to think of it, Theo mentioned she was a widow when he married her.''

"Her affair with Jacob was before her first marriage,'' I said. "When they were in school together. As a matter of fact, knowing Jacob, he probably respected her too much to have allowed it to be anything more than a very chaste relationship. Girls were into virginity in those days, weren't they?''

I hadn't meant the question to sound personal.

"Honey, how the hell would I know?'' she bellowed. "That was my mother's generation, not mine.'' Then she laughed. "So what are you going to do? Are you going to give her the table?''

"I haven't bought the table yet. It would be a fairly expensive gift, and I don't want to present something that would embarrass her or that she wouldn't treasure as Jacob intended.''

"Why a card table?'' she demanded of Mark, who only shrugged and left it to me to explain Jacob's fondness for bridge. In the end I dug out the pictures I'd brought home from Charlotte's, and we looked at them together, including the one of the young people with the tournament trophy, eternally youthful, smiling into the camera.

"So what're you going to do?'' She was intensely, vitally interested, and she carried me along, getting me to tell things I hadn't necessarily planned to tell. No doubt an appropriate talent for a lawyer. No doubt an excellent technique for questioning witnesses in court.

"I shall be silent on the matter,'' she said when she'd wrung the last detail from me, taking a moment to glare at Mark. "As your flunky here, who has blabbed, should also be!''

"I only blabbed because I counted on your discretion,'' said Mark, weakly. "Which is, of course, legendary.''

She laughed and stalked out to Mark's office, making him move the fabric samples a second time.

She'd not been gone long before Trish appeared, and I told the same story again, this time with the doors closed to give at least an appearance of discretion. She listened and commented and even cried a little, burrowing in her coat pocket for a tissue to blot her eyes. "That's so sweet," she said. "Honestly. Sure, I'll tell Lycia and she can decide whether to tell her mom. Wouldn't it be great if you could give her Jacob's present during the party."

I grimaced. "Great if she knows Jacob is dead and won't be offended by receiving a gift from beyond the grave. Not so great if she a) doesn't know he's dead and finds out then, or b) either knows or doesn't know but doesn't care much either way."

"I can't imagine Olivia not caring," Trish objected. "I've only met her a couple of times, but she's . . . she's sweet. She's got a kind of lovingness about her."

"If she still cared about Jacob, why didn't she marry him when her first husband died, I wonder?"

She took time to think about this. "Probably because her parents were still alive. They wouldn't have liked her marrying someone Jewish any better then than they did when she was twenty. Maybe she wanted to bring Lycia up in a religious household."

It sounded dumb but likely. Trish promised me she'd let me know what Lycia said. The birthday party was the following week. I called Orvie in Kansas City and asked him where the heck the pictures and provenance were, and he said he'd fax them to me.

"Can you get the table here by next week?" I asked him.

"If I have to," he said. "Did you find out who it was for?"

"I think so," I told him. The only thing that remained was to find out whether Jacob's old love would enjoy being reminded of him.

When Trish left, about noon, Mark and I went out (carefully) and lunched over a couple of sale catalogues. There were some auctions coming up in New York that Mark wanted to attend. An old friend of his was getting married in Connecticut; Mark thought he could go to the wedding, then go down to New York City for the auctions and to see a few shows. Bryan, it turned out, had some time off, plus a sister on Long Island. So, we went over the catalogues, deciding what we could use and how much we could afford to spend.

"Buying the table Jacob had in mind will leave us a little short of cash, won't it?" he asked.

I shrugged. "It amounts to what I'd have paid Jacob in three months. So, it'll take us another three months to be in the black. We won't be any shorter than usual, and if it was something he wanted . . ."

"Sure. Well. I doubt we'll pick up many of these items, anyway. The local bidders will go higher than we can."

"You're going to be there, so go to the auctions! Take the trip off your income tax. Half, anyway. If you're lucky enough to get something we need at a reasonable price, great. You've got vacation coming, so use some of it. Also, while you're in New York, take the Bursteins to dinner."

He subsided happily into the catalogues.

We got back to the shop about two. At two-thirty, to my enormous surprise, Lycia Foret came wandering in, very casually, as though she did it every day. Aside from that brief encounter at Greg's and Trish's, I hadn't seen her in a year. I hadn't expected to see her at all, but she greeted me like an old friend.

"Trish came by," she said. "I'm taking off this week, getting caught up on some domestic things and arranging Mama's birthday party. Trish says you're of a mind to give Mama a present."

"Not me," I smiled at her. "Jacob."

"Mama's mystery love," she said. "Do you know, I have heard about Jacob since I was about two, though she has never once mentioned his name. She still says things like, 'No matter who you marry, there'll always be someone you think of, wondering what might have been.' "

"You think she meant Jacob?"

"Well, she didn't mean my real father. There was no 'might have been' about him. He was very real, always in a chair by the window with a blanket over his knees, always throwing terrible tantrums to prove who was boss, always yelling for Mama to come do this, do that. He'd been badly wounded in the war, but it wasn't just his body that was wrong. Mama never had time for anything else with Don Octavio there. Including me. My sister almost raised me, at least until I was about nine . . ." Her voice trailed away. She flushed, aware she'd raised her voice. Don Octavio was evidently an old pain that still hurt to touch.

"How'd you find Mama, anyhow?" she asked, changing the subject.

I explained about Myra's finding the son of a former neighbor. Something kept me from mentioning Brother Daniel. Perhaps the feeling that I'd intruded on him painfully and should try to keep him out of it.

"The neighbor spoke of your older sister," I said.

She paled. "Jason, please, if you come to Mama's party, don't mention her. Don Octavio rode roughshod over her, just as he did Mama. She died tragically. Mama still can't think of her without a good deal of pain. I don't want Mama upset!"

Speaking of it obviously upset Lycia as well. "I'm sorry," I said. "I know nothing about it except the mere mention."

"That's just as well. Just pretend I'm Mama's only child. I was the only child for a long time, hers and Theo's. He adopted me when he and Mama were married, even though I spent a lot of my time with Grandma in St. Louis."

"Didn't they want you with them?" I asked, surprised.

"It wasn't them, it was me. Everything here reminded me of things I needed to forget. I had nightmares all the time. I was better in St. Louis . . ."

Seeing her consternation, I resolved not to ask her anything more about it.

She pulled herself together and said in a brisk voice, "So, do you want to come to the party and bring this present Jacob got for her? She'd be pleased, I think."

"Does she still play cards?"

"Does she! She still wins tournaments! Very little ones, of course."

"Then she'll be pleased. Jacob's gift is an eighteenth-century card table, a very fine piece." I reached into the bottom drawer and pulled out the envelope of photos and papers I'd shown to Amelia only that morning. "I thought I might have this old photo of your mother and Jacob duplicated as a kind of gift card." I showed her the tournament photo, then the portrait.

Lycia did what Mark had done, touching the young face gently and saying, "Beautiful." Then she went back to the other photo, smiling down at it and saying, "So this was Jacob?"

I said yes, that was Jacob.

"He was a handsome man. You're his foster son. No blood relation?"

"Right."

"He told you about Mama."

"In a manner of speaking. There were . . . instructions left among his things." The instructions were only implied. Charlotte and Grace and I had read the young Olivia's letter. Her daughter didn't need to see it.

"Ah," she said. "Well, if you make a copy of this one, with the two of them at the tournament, she'll understand."

"Small problem."

"What?"

"Does she know he's dead. I'd hate to bring her a gift from him and have her find out only then that he's gone."

"I'm sure she knows, but just to make doubly sure, I'll tell her you're invited, and who you are, and how you came to know of her. If that makes any problem, I'll let you know."

We left it at that. She told me the party would be held in Harriet Steinwale's penthouse apartment, Tuesday a week, at six-thirty. "Mama has quite a small apartment," she said. "Mine isn't what you'd call huge, and Harriet offered. You know where it is."

I said yes, I knew where Harriet's apartment was. Neither

of us reminded the other how I knew or what had taken me there before. It seemed we were to ignore that. By mutual consent.

I had a final thing to tell her. "When I first met you, Lycia, I thought you looked familiar. I never knew why until I found this picture of your mother. I recall that it hung beside Jacob's bed when I was a boy. You look very much like her."

"Do you think so?" she seemed honestly surprised. "I'm flattered." She looked at the portrait again, searching for the resemblance. She smiled, gave me her hand, and took herself away with a final stroke of the back of the carved chair she'd been sitting in. She'd done that the last time she'd sat in that chair. I watched her go, feeling satisfied and pleased and almost familial toward her. It was a good feeling.

I phoned Orvie and told him to ship the blasted table ASAP as it had to be here by the following Monday. With the party on Tuesday, that would give me a day to clean it up, if it needed cleaning up, and arrange delivery to—to where?

Mark came in when I howled.

"What is it?"

"Damn it," I said. "Where do I take the table? The party's at Harriet Steinwale's place. But that's not where Olivia lives. Lycia said she had quite a small apartment."

"Shush," he said. "Don't make mountains out of molehills, Jason. You'll give the gift at Harriet's, of course, because that's where the party is. You'll include in the card a note saying you'll have it delivered wherever she wants. If she wants to make room for it in her rather small apartment, she will. If not, she'll say so."

Sensible Mark.

I gathered up the photos to tuck them away with the other pending matters. When I opened the bottom drawer I saw the large manila envelope which had been festering away in there for the past year and a half. With some half-formed idea of getting rid of the contents, I took it out and dumped the half-dozen letters it contained onto my desk. Mark's eyebrows went up at the sight of the cut-out words and letters.

I passed them across the desk to him, and he sat down in the chair Lycia had recently vacated.

"My God," he breathed when he'd been through them once. "When did you get these?"

"Not recently. The first one was postmarked about eighteen months ago, I think. The last one came in October or November."

"You didn't pay . . ."

"No. I didn't pay."

He ran his fingers across the glued-on words. "Somebody went to a lot of trouble to hide their handwriting."

"I've thought that. I've wondered if it's someone I know, someone whose handwriting I might recognize."

"But you're not going to pay?"

"I haven't had one for a while, maybe the offer's no longer available. Even if it were, I tell myself I don't care that much—a kind of homage to Jacob. He always said it didn't matter."

"It doesn't matter," he said soberly. "I know exactly who my parents are, Jason, and I'm no better off than you are because of it. Often I wish I were like you, without all that familial baggage. It gets very heavy sometimes."

He made a face at the letters, gave them back to me, and returned to his work. I put them back in the envelope. If ignoring this temptation was really a homage to Jacob, next time I went down to the basement, I'd take this along and burn it in the vast old furnace. Burnt offering. And about time.

five

CONTINUED CAREFUL, and busy, during the following week. Grace had one final weekend off before her schedule changed. We chose recreation in lieu of valor and on Friday afternoon drove down to New Mexico for the weekend, taking Grace's car, and going through a few well-thought-out gyrations to be sure we weren't followed. The first part of the drive is always sheer boredom getting out of Denver, and then getting through the clutter and fume of Colorado Springs, which has twelve square miles of new and used cars along the highway. Once past the cars, we saw hilly, lunar landscapes runneled with spaghetti-like tangles of motorcycle trails, pastures dotted with dispirited horses, winter-dun fields stretching away to mud-dun hills, bristly with yucca, lined with drooping fences and speckled with bored-looking cows either in the last stages of parturition or being butted in the udders by hungry calves. A dull fur of bare cottonwood twigs marked every watercourse, every gully.

I pounded a fist upon the steering wheel and confessed a hatred for March, and February, and perhaps even January when it didn't snow. Grace yawned and stretched but otherwise ignored me. She had heard this opinion before. Grace has, without doubt, heard most of my opinions before.

The mountains were blue and snowcapped, but I longed for grass. There was no grass. Instead, tan succeeded dun succeeded greige succeeded a vile ocherous tinge betraying some kind of weed infestation. Yucca was reinforced by chamiza and choya, each trying to out-bristle the other. The

University of Southern Colorado appeared on the southern horizon, arranged along the treeless bluff to the east of the road, like a set of children's blocks set in a row, sun glinting from the squat cylindrical water tanks. Smokeless blast furnace chimneys jabbed upward at the southern edge of Pueblo, one of only two steel towns west of the Mississippi. Traffic increased for a few miles, the mills themselves came up on the right,. were succeeded by miles of slag heaps, barren as Mars, heading into an infinity of dun prairie and long, stone-edged, sky-seeking diagonals rimmed with juniper.

At Walsenburg we turned west, over La Veta Pass and down into the San Luis valley, miles on miles of flat as we drove south out of Ft. Garland, mountains gathering in from either horizon. I started to yawn. Grace and I traded seats, and I fell asleep before she'd driven a mile. I didn't wake up until we were just north of Taos.

As we drove through Taos, we decried this sign of growth and that. We both remembered it as a historic core with a small shopping area to the south and a long bare stretch between Taos proper and Ranchos de Taos, the first town south. Now the built-up area stretched along both sides of the highway, joining the two towns with a miles-long clutter offering goods and services.

Beyond Ranchos de Taos the road led more or less along the Rio Grande, past small orchards, up and down juniper-speckled hills, through Española—we stopped to pick up a few groceries—and on down to Nambe, where I turned onto the side road that led east toward my friends' place, Los Vientos. The Wilsons, who owned the place, were in Hawaii until April, but the caretaker had been told I was invited to occupy the guest house. I'd earned the privilege by helping Mike furnish the place. I'd saved him a lot of money, and he'd reciprocated.

The weekend went by in the scent of piñon smoke and long nights full of unimaginable stars. When you live in a city, you forget there are such things.

While there, I tried to call Cecily Stephens. None of the firms listed under "contractors" had the name Stephens attached, though there was a residential number listed for a C. Stephens that yielded only an answering machine. I did not feel like explaining to a machine.

We drove back on Monday, arriving about two in the afternoon. Grace dropped me off in the alley behind the shop. The sight of the Fetterling back gate provoked an attack of conscience at having neglected Nellie recently, so I set my overnight bag in the garage and went to say hello to her.

"Some man was watching your house," she told me. "I saw him through the gate. He even stuck his face in here a time or two, but my son-in-law ran him off."

"When, Nellie?" The sinking feeling I'd subdued over the weekend was suddenly back.

"Saturday and Sunday both. Jeannie was here Sunday when he showed up." She was speaking of Jeannie Rudolph, a teenaged girl who came in a few times a week to sit with Nellie and her cat so Janice, Nellie's daughter, could get out. "When the man went off down the alley, I told Jeannie to walk along the sidewalk out front, kind of see if she could see where he went. He went around in front, walked right past her, got in a car and drove off. He never even noticed her."

"What kind of car, Nellie?"

"It was blue, that's all she could tell."

I sighed. Too much to hope for, that Jeannie had been able to come up with anything really useful.

"Of course, she got the license number," said Nellie, digging into the bag that always hung on the arm of her wheelchair. "If that'll help." She handed me a scrap of brown paper bag with the number scribbled in Jeannie's schoolgirl hand. "Colo," it said, then three letters, three numbers.

"You and Jeannie," I said admiringly, giving her a hug. "You're some team."

A little further conversation elicited a description which wasn't unlike the one Grace had given the last time I'd been shot at. Pasty face, sixtyish, half bald.

I gave Nellie another hug and a promise of a longer visit

soon, then hurried across the alley and up to the office. Grace wouldn't be home yet, so I called Linder direct and gave him the license number.

"If you want to talk to Nellie Arpels, send Grace," I told him. "Nellie knows Grace." I gave him Jeannie's number, as well.

Mark was standing at my elbow. "What's this about a license?" he asked.

I told him about the man and the car.

"I thought there was someone hanging around!" he said. "When Bryan and I came over Saturday morning to feed the animals and let Bela out, I saw him! After I put Bela's food out in the kitchen, I went into your bedroom to be sure the windows were locked, and when I pulled back the curtains, I saw somebody duck away down the alley. By the time Bryan and I got downstairs and out the back door, he was gone, but Bela was sniffing and growling all over the backyard, as though some stranger had been in there."

My unknown enemy hadn't given up. He'd shown up on the weekend, just as before. After worrying at that fact for twenty minutes or so, I called Linder again and pointed out that the assailant, whoever he was, seemed to prefer Saturdays and Sundays.

"That license number is from Trinidad," he said. "Maybe the guy can only get up here on weekends."

The town of Trinidad lies almost on the Colorado-New Mexico border, a hundred eighty some odd miles from Denver. It had been (perhaps still was for all I knew) a mining town that had recruited a number of Italian workers to add to the original Mexican inhabitants. The miners sent for their families, then their relatives, then their more distant kin, and the town became an interesting Mexican-Italian mix.

"Whose license number is it?" I asked Linder.

"Some roofing company. Snowy Peaks Roofing ring a bell with you?"

It didn't so much as tinkle. I said so profanely and at length.

My frustration must have come across, because Linder

said, "Relax. There'll only be so many people who drive that car. I've already asked the local police to get us the names, and just in case the car's still in the Denver area, we've put out a pickup on it. We've got the bullet we took out of your front hall, and if the guy's in the car and the gun's with the guy . . ."

"It's Monday," I complained. "He'll be back in Trinidad by now. He fired a rifle at me the first time, a handgun the second. The rifle bullet is the one we have, but he'll have put the rifle away somewhere already, and when he knows we're on to him, he'll drive some other car and dispose of both firearms!" I was fairly hostile about it, but my anger wasn't directed at Linder, particularly, just at the frustration of the circumstances.

"Calm down," he said again. "Don't worry, Jason. I won't let him get away. If I did, Grace'd kill me! We've got an idea who the guy is, and we've probable cause to search for the gun."

Probable cause! I had no idea as to probable cause. Some person from a smallish town on the Colorado border, someone I didn't know, had never met, had no reason to like or dislike, was trying to kill me for a totally unknown reason! Probable cause!

I took several deep breaths, got myself some coffee, and was summoned downstairs by Eugenia to admire Orvie Spender's card table, soon to be Olivia's card table, which had arrived Friday afternoon after I'd left. In a private van, no less. Special delivery. It was, thank God, every bit as good a piece as Orvie had said it was, and Eugenia had already gone over it with cleaning oil and a soft brush followed by buffing cloths. The delicate curved corners shone like cabochon gems.

The rest of the day went by doing this and that, none of it very rewarding. The long drive had made my leg ache, so when everyone left, I gave it a long soak in the big tub and stretched out early with *Foucault's Pendulum*, which I'd been trying to read for a year. Everyone I knew claimed to have read it back when it was first published, but I kept losing my place or falling asleep or trying to figure out why the characters were bothering to do what they were doing. Of course, Jacob brought me up to be a skeptic, which made me not entirely sympathetic to their metaphysical obsession.

The phone rang in the middle of the night, or rather about two o'clock Tuesday morning. The heavy book was still on my chest, though I seemed to have turned out the light. I fumbled the switch and dropped the phone twice before I got it to my ear. Grace.

"The station just called," she said. "Linder wasn't available and it was sort of my case."

"What?" I mumbled stupidly, trying to get myself focused.

"That license number Nellie came up with. They located the car on a street out in Aurora. The patrol car tried to pull it over, and the car took off south on Gun Club Road. I guess the driver got it up around ninety. He hit a gravel curve southeast of Buckley Air Base somewhere, skidded off the road, went through somebody's fence, and ended up out in the middle of a pasture. The car rolled and burned."

"Who was driving?" I asked stupidly.

"Hell, Jason, wake up! I said the car burned. One guy was driving, but he'd bailed out before it crashed. It's black as a coal miner's neck out there, and they haven't found him. Maybe tomorrow we'll find out who it was. I thought you'd like to know we've got a line on him, that's all."

She too had been awakened in the middle of the night. She too was grumpy about it. She hung up. I lay back on the disarranged pillows, provoking a baffled half-growl from Schnitz, who had inserted himself beneath one of them. He clawed his way out and stalked frowning to the foot of the bed, his tail fluffed out in annoyance. Not many cats can actually frown, but Schnitz shares that ability with his father. Bela whuffed from his basket. Phones aren't supposed to ring this time of night. It made us all edgy, even though the news was, from my point of view, good. Given the car and the description, my mysterious assailant was, presumably, identifiable.

If that had been he, driving the car, and not someone else. Of course, the man in the car might not have been alone; he could have had an accomplice or been an accomplice. If the driver had gone south on Gun Club Road, he might have started somewhere near Motel Row on east Colfax, where the rooms rent by the hour as often as they do by the night. Along there, nobody really paid much attention to who came and who went. Some other, unidentifiable person could be in a motel, just waiting for morning to take another shot. Or in my backyard. Or my basement.

I decided I was being paranoid and tried to think of something else. The town of Trinidad. Possibly a largely Catholic town. I didn't know that for sure, but it seemed logical. Catholic, therefore probably antiabortion, therefore, someone from there could have participated in the clinic blockade. Someone inclined to fanatical enmities or explosions of religious fervor. I told myself it could be true, but I didn't believe it. No one would drive almost four hundred miles every week, roundtrip, to shoot someone they'd only seen on television, out of mere fervor!

Schnitz growled again and blinked his amber eyes. I turned off the light. It made no sense in darkness either. I gave up and went back to sleep.

Tuesday. Party day. Mark called Harriet Steinwale and arranged to deliver the table. He'd put a huge red velvet bow on it and made an oversized card of the enlarged photo. Before he delivered it, I double-checked with Lycia to be sure her mother knew about Jacob.

"She knew, Jason. When I mentioned his name, she was surprised at first, then she cried a little and said how much she missed him. They used to talk on the phone every few days. Did you know that?"

I hadn't known that. It seemed I had been wrong in thinking Jacob would have introduced me to her. He had kept her a secret, even from me. I had thought I shared deeply in Jacob's life, and this secretive bit hurt a little. Why hadn't he told me?

Lycia went on, "Mama was seventy when Theo died. She says she and Jacob talked about getting together then, but they decided what they really wanted from one another was the companionship they'd have had if they'd been together always. So, they met once in a while but mostly just talked by phone."

I heard her sniffling. "A friend of mine remarked that this whole business was like a romance novel," I commented lamely.

"Well, it is, in a way. Anyhow, Mama read his obituary when it came out. You know, there was a time there a few weeks ago when I knew something was bothering her. She was very quiet and seemed not to hear when I spoke. She didn't say at the time, but it must have been Jacob's death."

I murmured in agreement.

"Mama's looking forward to meeting you. Jacob often mentioned you to her."

Well, at least he'd shared me with her, even if he hadn't shared her with me. That was helpful. I wouldn't have to explain.

While Mark was delivering the table, I took an hour to visit the one and only barber who knows how to cut the transplanted hair on the back of my head so it looks like hair and not Spanish moss. He also manages to cover my odd ear (though it's not nearly as odd as it used to be before surgery). When evening came, I put on my most elegant and conservative gray suit, one I'd had custom-made and only worn three times. White on white shirt, charcoal tie with little red diamonds in it, black dress shoes so new the soles were still slick. Seeing as how Olivia had heard such nice things about me, I couldn't let Jacob down. Confronting myself in the mirror, noting the new touch of gray at the temples, I told myself I was thoroughly acceptable.

I took a cab, thinking of another plot cliché I dislike, the one in which the hero, after exerting due caution for sixty percent of the book, gets stranded through his own stupidity and becomes prey. Driving my own car in Capitol Hill would lead me down that road very nicely, since the area's packed

with apartment buildings and short on parking space. I had
no intention of having to park a dozen blocks away and making a target of myself. The cab let me out twenty feet from
the front door of Harriet's building, and I made it inside
unscathed.

Harriet Steinwale owns all or part of the building, in ad-
dition to living there. As I passed through the foyer, I resolved to mention the furnishings to her. Just because the
place was called "The Louvre" didn't mean it had to be quite
so fakey-French. Next time it was redone, maybe I could get
her something a little more classy. That is, if the tenants
didn't prefer the bad fakes.

Harriet's elegant and spacious penthouse was on the top
floor. Nothing fakey about that, at least. The affair was being
catered. A black-jacketed attendant took my coat, another
one offered me a glass of champagne, a third directed me to
the buffet. Lycia saw me come in. She took me by the arm
and led me through the crowded living room to the enclosed
lanai where the gifts had been assembled.

I would have known her anywhere. She was ensconced in
a high-backed chair with the lights of the city spread behind
her. Despite the fluff of white hair and the fine patina of
wrinkles, she looked like the girl in the portrait. It was there
in the hairline, in the curve of the brows, in the sweet set of
the lips and the delicately rounded chin. The fine bone structure was still there, the shape beneath the years.

"Olivia," I said. "I'm so very happy to meet you."

"You're Jason," she responded. "Jacob showed me pictures of you, such a handsome boy. He spoke of you all the
time. He was so proud of you."

I may have blushed. Jacob had never told me I was handsome, and I'd stopped thinking of myself as a boy about
fifteen years ago. I sat down beside her and we talked. She
had already seen Jacob's gift and read the card. She wiped
her eyes, crying and laughing at the same time as she re-
counted occasions when she and Jacob had had great tri-
umphs at the bridge tables. She didn't get technical about it,
for which I was grateful, since I'd never been able to work

up any interest in the game. Poker was, perhaps lamentably, a sturdy relic of my misapplied childhood.

Other guests came in to offer best wishes, and I retreated to the buffet table, wishing for Grace. She'd have loved both the food and the fact there was so much of it. I filled a plate and circulated and acted the part of a social animal, chatting with Keith Foret, Lycia's son, and with Ross Whitfield, her companion, roommate, lover, what have you. We talked mostly about local politics. Then I spoke with Harriet, mentioning, in passing, her lobby furniture.

She glared at me. "Every article of furniture in that lobby is stolen on the average of once each six months."

I gaped, uncomfortably aware I'd hit a nerve.

"We've fastened chairs with steel chains through holes in the floor. We've bolted the legs through the floor into the garage ceiling below. We've attached alarms. The last time someone cleaned us out, I said the hell with it and bought a dozen replacements for everything, the cheapest I could find, and put them in the storeroom with my name sprayed on the bottom. They get stolen, I replace them. If they don't get stolen, they fall apart in a year, but they're usually stolen before that. One of these days, we'll catch somebody taking them."

I expressed astonishment, and she snorted at me.

"You're naive, Jason. People who rent apartments have the idea they're being exploited by the landlord. Some of them come from the East where they have rent control, and since there's no rent control here, that makes stealing from the landlord seem somehow cute and acceptable. After all, here they are, paying this enormous rent, three or four hundred a month, or maybe even more, and all they can see is this greedy old person just raking it in. So, they keep pets without paying the pet deposit; then their animals ruin the carpets; and they move out leaving a thousand-dollar repair bill which all the other tenants end up paying." She pointed a long, bony forefinger at me, stabbing me repeatedly on the shoulder.

"If the heat's included in their rent, they leave their heat on and their windows open. If you put meters on their apartments, they turn their heat off and let the people on either side heat them through the walls. They never see the mortgage payments, or the fuel bills, or the electric bills, or the insurance bills, or the elevator repair bills, or the janitorial bills, *or* the taxes. Last year, I made less than four percent on my investment in this building. I could do better tearing it down and building a parking garage!''

Someone across the room waved to her, and she strode off in high dudgeon, leaving me gasping but rather glad she'd found something to harangue me about. If she'd felt at all uncomfortable with my being invited to the party, her discomfort had been well sublimated.

Seeing that Olivia's well-wishers had dispersed somewhat, I went to say good night.

''I saw Harriet pounding on you,'' she whispered, her eyes laughing. ''Was she going on again about building a parking garage? It was sweet of you to listen so attentively.''

I flushed.

''Jason, dear, I want the table with me in my apartment,'' she said, putting her soft old hand over mine. ''I want to know about it, about its *provenance*.'' Her voice put quotes around the word. ''Jacob would have thought that very important. Will you bring it and tell me all about it?''

I told her I'd come, getting the words out around the lump in my throat. Even though I'd sternly reminded myself that all this melodrama should be taken with several pinches of salt, I'd ended up awash in sentimentality.

''Tomorrow,'' she said. ''Teatime, if you can. I want to talk about Jacob.''

Her apartment was on the fourth floor of a building south of Cherry Creek, where the new mall has recently opened. Mark brought the table over from Harriet's place, then departed. Olivia's companion brought in tea and cakes and then made herself scarce, obviously by prearrangement. The two of us were to have tea alone.

When we were settled with cups and plates, Olivia did as she had promised and talked about Jacob and their youth together. She said little about either of her marriages, except to mention her second husband once:

"After Theo died, Jacob used to call me every few days. I didn't hear from him at Christmastime, so I called him. The nice young man who answered the phone said he wasn't able to talk, but he said he'd give him a message. Somehow I knew then I'd probably never talk to him again."

"You could have visited him," I said.

"We'd agreed not to do that, he and I. It was a sentimental promise. When I thought of Jacob, I thought of him the way he was before I married Tavio. He liked that. He said he liked staying always young in my mind."

Until recently, I had not thought of Jacob as an incurable romantic. "So, you left him a message at Christmastime?"

"I said, Olivia called to wish Jacob a happy New Year. He always used to wish me a merry Christmas and I'd wish him happy New Year, though I knew it wasn't the Jewish New Year at all."

"Jacob wasn't religious," I commented.

She nodded slowly. "I know. I was and he wasn't. I thought my religion meant a lot to me. I wished that Jacob's religion meant something to him, too, so he'd understand."

I said I thought he'd understood.

She shook her head at me, very slowly, making a sad clown's mouth at me. "No. He couldn't have. Because I didn't. Later on I realized what had mattered most was my parents. I thought giving up Jacob and getting married to someone they chose was a religious matter because they told me it was, but it really wasn't. It was really about other things, but I didn't know that then."

I sipped and looked enquiringly at her.

She saw I hadn't understood. "Nineteen-thirty was a different time. Oh, I know it was supposed to be the flapper age and all that, but even so, girls didn't know then all the things they know today. Not *nice* girls. We didn't have TV and movies educating us about sex. We were ignorant, and we were supposed to stay that way until we got married and pregnant. I remember whispering with a girlfriend about pregnancy and babies when we were about sixteen. She said her babies would come out of her belly button! And I believed her! That was our destiny, to believe in belly buttons and marry some nice Catholic boy and get pregnant with nice Catholic babies and never know anything until it actually happened to us. Our families and our church knew that if we were kept ignorant—though they called it 'innocent'—nature would take over and we'd be caught.''

"I can understand that," I said weakly, though I couldn't. Not at all.

"*Good* girls weren't assertive, weren't rebellious. We were taught to be passive. We got into the habit of it, and it isn't an easy habit to break. Even years later, after Tavio died, my parents were still saying I owed it to Lycia to give her a proper Catholic home, so I married Theo. Not that Theo wasn't a nice man, he was; but I didn't love him as I loved Jacob. Jacob would have married me then! I was barely forty! But, no, I married Theo because it was the right thing to do . . . .

"Of course, my making a good Catholic home really didn't matter to Lycia. After what happened to Angela, she spent most of her time in St. Louis with my mother."

I found my voice somewhere. "Angela?"

"My other daughter. Lycia's older sister. Angela."

Lycia had warned me not to mention her sister on the grounds Olivia would be disturbed. She didn't seem particularly disturbed. Weepy, yes, but not distraught. I managed an interrogative sound, somewhere between a hum and a grunt, wondering if Brother Daniel had been saying not "my angel," but "my Angela." I hadn't known her name was Angela.

Olivia stared out the window as she spoke. "When she was seventeen, Angela fell in love with Daniel Brockman, a neighbor boy a year or two older than she. She didn't need to tell me. Anyone with eyes could have seen what was going on. She glowed whenever he was around. Whenever I saw her face, it was like looking at my face in a mirror when I'd been that age.

"On her eighteenth birthday, she came to us, to Tavio and me, to tell us about him. Once she was eighteen, she didn't need our permission, not really, but she loved us both and she wanted us to approve. She was a loving girl, and she loved Tavio, even though I didn't, never had, not really. Poor child. As soon as Tavio understood what she was saying, he told her she could not marry the boy she loved because he had promised her to someone else. I couldn't believe it. The light went out of her. Like blowing out a candle. It was like my parents, all over again, like a nightmare."

I couldn't keep quiet. "Olivia, it wasn't the seventeenth century! Couldn't you have done something about it?"

She made a pushing motion with her hands, signaling impotence. "Tavio was *dying*. You don't know what it was like, Jason. I was angry at him. I hated him. But it was a *sin* to hate him. He was a wounded soldier who'd fought valiantly. He was her father. He was my husband! And I was a sinful, angry woman always trying to catch up on my penance for hating him! Of *course*, I tried to talk with him, over and over, but it was no use. I asked my parents to help me, but they refused to get involved. They'd picked Tavio for me, and it hadn't worked out as they planned. They felt . . . oh, I think they felt guilty, so guilty they wouldn't do anything to 'interfere' ever again. . . .

"The only one who could do anything with Tavio was Father Olivera. He was Spanish, like Tavio, first generation, and he talked Tavio's language. I thought maybe he could fix things, but it worked the other way. He sat us down, Angela and me, and preached at us how Tavio had sworn an oath before God, that the oath was an honorable one designed to unite two families, that the other family was a proper Catholic family, and that we owed it to Tavio to let his oath be fulfilled before he died."

This time I didn't say anything.

"Father Olivera hadn't been here long. He was wrong. I fought, Jason. Honestly, I did. But I was all alone. Poor Angela, she was like a little bird, trapped and fluttering and unable to do anything. Oh, I wish that boy had taken her away, run away with her. I wish she'd had it in her to be rebellious, but between how I'd raised her and what the school had taught her, she was just . . . lost. It had all been trained out of her, just as it had all been trained out of me . . . ."

I put my hand on hers. She was in pain, and it was too late to do anything about these ancient tragedies.

She whispered, "Even today, I try not to hate Tavio. I try to remember the unhappy life he had. He was never loved as people should be loved."

"Umm," I said, patting her hand, wondering how Jacob had reacted to these revelations.

"Angela didn't love her husband any more than I had mine. She saved all her love for the baby, for little Michael. He had a huge awful birthmark." She peered at me, waiting for something. "It was dreadful-looking. A port wine mark, I think it's called. They can cure them now, but there was nothing they could do back then."

What does one say? What I was feeling was irritation, something just short of anger, at Octavio for what he'd done, at Olivia for letting him, at Jacob for not kidnapping her and running off with her, even at poor Angela for not eloping with her boyfriend. I found all this passivity and helplessness a little unbelievable and more than a little sickening. I didn't understand how Jacob could have stood it, he who had always insisted upon honesty. How could he have loved someone like this, who had let these things happen?

"I'm sorry to hear about the birthmark," I said. It was all I could think of to say.

She glared at the floor. "It wouldn't have happened if she hadn't married that man. His father didn't even come to the wedding. He was sick, they said. Sick! He'd been sick for years, but when Michael was born, Angela's husband said the baby was cursed, someone had put a curse on the family. Oh, Angela was fierce about that! *Then* she rebelled! She said if there was a curse on the family, it was there before Michael was born. She kept Michael with her, away from his father, so the little boy wouldn't hear such talk. She told me she would save Michael, no matter what his father was like. And after all that care, all that love, it was like she was doomed . . .''

I drained the last few drops in my cup as I prepared polite reasons I had to leave.

"Huntington's disease, it's called," she said. "A genetic disease . . .''

I sat with my mouth partly open, cup in mid air.

"Tavio had sworn an oath to a man who had Huntington's disease. Three years after Angela was married, she found out what it was her father-in-law had. His family had tried to hide it, but she found out. And Angela's husband had a fifty-fifty chance of having it; and if he had it, there was a fifty-fifty chance the baby would have it too.

"Jenny came to tell me about it. She was Angela's friend, Angela's best friend. She was there the night Angela found out. She got me out of bed to tell me. She said she'd put Angela to bed, with a sleeping pill, but that Lycia and I should go over first thing in the morning to be with her . . .''

Her voice trailed away and she fell silent, grieving, unable to take the story further.

I waited for some time, then prompted her. "What happened?''

"She died," Olivia whispered. "When we got there in the morning, Angela was already at the hospital. They'd found her in her bed, unconscious. The room was full of gas. She was in a coma for a long while. Lycia and I stayed at the hospital the whole time, but she never regained consciousness. Never said good-bye. A mercy. They said if she'd lived, she'd have been a vegetable.''

She wiped her eyes. "The stupid woman who worked for her said it was suicide. It was an accident. She wouldn't have committed suicide. Lycia had nightmares about it. Everything here reminded her. Mother said if I married Theo, it would all be different and we could make a home for her, but even then she preferred to live in St. Louis. In the end, I lost both my daughters.''

"But Lycia came back.''

"Oh, yes. I shouldn't have said I lost her, because you're right. She did come back. At first she came back for visits, and the visits got longer and longer. Finally she came back to stay, but she was a grown woman then. In college."

"The woman who worked for your daughter was Simonetta Leone. Angela was married to Nimo Leone." The two halves of my puzzle had come seamlessly together.

She didn't seem surprised that I knew. Perhaps she thought Lycia had told me. "I never say his name," she said angrily, keeping her face turned away from me. "I swore I would never say the name of any of that accursed family."

This time I didn't forget to ask:

"What happened to little Michael?"

"I wanted him. Even if he had that dreadful disease, I wanted Angela's baby. Besides, he wasn't safe with that horrible nursemaid. When I asked to have him, Angela's husband said the baby was already gone. Gone away. Sent away to relatives of theirs in Italy. So *he* wouldn't be reminded. So *he* could forget."

"He?"

"Angela's husband," she said.

"You didn't protest about the baby?"

"Protest!" She turned on me. "What good was *protest*, with that family or with mine? What good had *protest* been with Octavio Desquintas y Alvarez! Every day, Jason, every day of my life since then, morning and evening, I have prayed that Michael is well and happy somewhere, that the disease passed him by."

"You've never tried to find him?"

"Theo offered to help me find him, but it was a bargain I made with God. If I didn't look for the baby, if I let him go, he'd be safe. The priest I go to now doesn't understand. He says God doesn't make bargains. Jacob understood. He knew I had to do something, make some sacrifice so that things would come right. I'd done so much to let them go wrong. God has forgiven me, so the priest says, but I'll never forgive myself for letting Angela marry that man. If God is love, how can we turn our back on love? No matter what religion says.''

Tears were dripping from her jaw, running into the corners of her mouth. I gave her my handkerchief, and she buried her face in the white linen.

When she looked at me again, she gave me an ironic glance. ''Worst of all, my parents didn't want me to marry Jacob because he was a Jew. Tavio, though . . . he was Catholic, he was a Don, an aristocrat. But when we had to leave Spain, Tavio wasn't a Don anymore. He was only an arrogant Spaniard who thought he was too good to take a job with my father. The last four years of his life, my father never even spoke to him.''

I left shortly after that, as soon as I politely could. I felt almost as grieved and battered as she obviously did. She was not the only one who had been sacrificed on the ugly altar of her parents' pride, of Tavio's pride. Jacob had been sacrificed too.

And he'd told me so, though I hadn't known what he meant at the time. There were several little lectures he used to give me when I was young: the self-reliance lecture, the work-ethic lecture, the honesty lecture, the values lecture:

''Some things that people treasure have no value at all, Jason. Ideas, customs. Scrutinized in the light, they're only husks, old worn-out things, not worth a nickel.''

I was fifteen when he'd first told me that. Olivia had long been married to Theo, but Jacob had gone on loving her. To my dismay, I did not think she had been worthy of that love.

Thursday morning the police identified the owner of the burned car as one Antonio Gabrielli (Gabe) Leone: sixtyish, pale-faced, half bald, and rather plump. He was the owner of Snowy Peaks Roofing in Trinidad, Colorado, to which city and place of business he had not yet returned. The police files identified him as the son of Canello Leone and a former associate of known felons. Both a rifle and a handgun had been found in the trunk of the car. Bullets fired from the rifle matched the one dug out of my front hall paneling. Without doubt, the brother of Olivia's son-in-law had taken a couple of shots at me. Probably he'd try it again, if he wasn't lying dead somewhere.

Grace was as intrigued and surprised by the tie between Simonetta and Olivia as I was. She became even more interested when I suggested she bring over the clinic arrest records which I'd asked her for days earlier, this time because I thought I'd made a connection with Gabe's description. Sure enough, there he was. When I'd looked at the pictures before, I'd looked right past that pale, pouchy, very ordinary face. It had been just another out of twenty or thirty, with nothing distinctive about him. This time I was looking at the long-sleeved, pale plaid shirt and the light down vest he wore. I put my hand over his baldness and imagined him with a white, curly wig.

"I think he must have arrived at the clinic wearing glasses, the white wig, and this down vest stuffed in his shirtfront to give him a bosom," I told Grace. "Later, during the confusion of the arrests, he pulled the vest out from under his shirt, put it on, took off the glasses and the wig. As I recall, he's got a lard butt and heavy thighs. That plus the bosom and the wig was enough to make me think I was seeing a woman."

"He must have killed Simonetta—he had no other reason to be there—and he must have thought you'd seen him do it."

"I remember him looking in through the glass door at me, but it didn't mean a thing at the time."

Grace showed me the picture of Gabe that had been faxed up from Trinidad, and it matched the one on the arrest report, so there was no question as to identity. She was still puzzled, however.

"Okay, we'll say he killed Simonetta, but *why* did he do it?"

I wished I knew, because the puzzle was suddenly *my* puzzle, having something to do with Olivia's family. The person who'd tried to kill me was not some nut who had seen me on TV or picked me at random from a phone book. He was a murderer named Leone who had not wanted anyone connecting him to Simonetta.

"One good thing," said Grace. "He'll know we've traced the car. It's his car. I saw him in it, and I can identify him. The rifle that fired at you was in the car, that ties him to the attempt on you. His picture from Trinidad matches the one on the arrest report, so we can place him at the scene of the murder. We don't need you to place him there. All the reasons he had for getting rid of you no longer apply. He'd be crazy to try and bother you again."

I hadn't thought of that, but she was right. Gabe Leone had no reason to come gunning for me anymore.

I phoned the clinic to tell Cynthia Adamson about Gabe, for a wonder getting to her before Grace did.

"Oh," she breathed. "Oh, God, I'm so glad it was somebody else." I knew what she meant. She meant somebody not associated with the clinic. "Why did he do it?"

I had to confess we didn't know, except that it had nothing to do with the abortion controversy. "The only reason that makes sense for him to have killed her in a crowd like that is that it gave him an opportunity to make it look like something else," I told her. "He had some reason for wanting it to look like something else, possibly because he didn't want the real reason she was killed to be known. No doubt he thought it would be blamed on some fanatic pro-abortionist, and that'd be it. And if he'd let *me* alone, that might well have happened."

She sighed. "I'd like to get the anti's off our necks. Can I tell the papers?"

"Better they get if from the police. After that, say what you will. Has it been rough?"

"You have no idea what we've been accused of, Jason. One of the nuts tried to bomb the clinic the other night. They caught him. They haven't caught the person who's been slashing our tires, though. Or the ones who call up and breathe threats. These people have so many psychological problems it's unbelievable, particularly the men. They're very, very sick.''

I knew about the men. If Tavio Desquintas y Alvarez had been alive, he'd have been right out there among the picketers. No, that would have been too undignified. He'd have hired someone to picket for him.

I phoned Dorotea Chapman and asked if she'd see me again, that we thought we knew who had killed her sister. I knew the police would probably want to see her as well, but I wanted to get to her first. She said she was coming into town to do some shopping, so she'd drop in later.

Grace had let me photocopy the two pictures of Gabe Leone, and when I gave them to Dorotea that afternoon, she stared at them in disbelief while I told her what we thought we knew.

"None of this makes sense," she said.

I was sympathetic, admitting it made little sense to us either.

"Why in heaven's name would Nello's son kill Simonetta? Now? After all these years?''

"Has anything changed recently?'' I asked.

"What do you mean?''

"I mean, has something changed recently that had anything to do with Simonetta? Anything at all?''

"Her husband died," she said blankly. "Herby. But you knew that.''

"Right. Anything else?''

"My mother went into a nursing home. That was last summer, though.''

"Up until then she'd seen Simonetta regularly?''

"Yes. Up until then.''

"Could it have been . . . perhaps something Simonetta used to discuss with your mother that she began talking of to other people? Talked of to Herby, maybe. Something she knew?''

She shook her head at me impatiently. "I told you, Simonetta didn't *know* things. Not like that. She believed things. Half the time, what she said was completely crazy.''

I shrugged helplessly. "Perhaps someone didn't know that. Perhaps someone thought she was capable of spilling a secret."

"I don't understand."

I tried an example. "We've heard that when Simonetta was about twenty-three, she came back to your parents' house one day and found no one home. She had hysterics all up and down the block. She said that Nimo's wife had committed suicide."

"I remember. I mean, I don't remember it happening—I was at school. But I remember everyone talking about it."

"Now, the newspapers said the woman died accidentally. So Simonetta had it wrong. Or, maybe, she had it right and the newspaper story was wrong."

"All I really remember is Simmy being hysterical. Her job with the Leones ended when the woman died, so for weeks after that she was in and out of the house, back and forth, throwing fits. I remember that vividly. Sometimes she cried, and sometimes she laughed like crazy. She said God had fixed it so the baby wouldn't die. The mother had died, but the baby wouldn't."

"You told us the baby died."

"Did I? You're right! Why did I say that? Come to think of it, I guess it *felt* like the child had died, the way Simmy acted. I mean, she'd been taking care of them both, the mother and the child, and then suddenly she wasn't doing it anymore. I guess the child was just taken away. I knew it was gone, because Simonetta kept having hysterics over it." Dorotea fell silent, concentrating. "I remember! Simonetta said God was the baby's father. She said, 'Just like Jesus.' Then she laughed like a crazy woman. Heavens! I haven't thought of that in years!"

It didn't really connect to anything I knew. "Could she have said something then, or at any time, that might have made people think she knew something she wasn't supposed to know?"

"What could she have known? You mean, something she overheard? From Herby? From the Leones? How on earth would I know? I haven't seen her half a dozen times in the last five years.''

I made an apologetic face, but persisted. "Would your mother know?''

She glared at me. "Mr. Lynx, I'll ask her. She has her good days and her bad ones. If I catch her on a good day, I'll ask her. If only to get you off my back!''

I chose to ignore her tone. She was no more irritable than I. "See if you can find out what was on Simonetta's mind in recent months,'' I suggested. "Ask her what Simonetta talked about. Ask your mother particularly if Simonetta talked about Herby and what he was up to.''

"You really think it had something to do with him?''

"You said yourself that one of the things that had changed was his death. I think it likely that his death and Simonetta's are connected in some way.''

"But his was accidental.''

"So I've been told.''

"You don't believe it?''

Frustrated, I threw up my hands. "I don't disbelieve it. I don't know. I know the police had no reason to question it, not then. Maybe they will now.''

At least, Grace would. Grace, who was still tracing decades-old crimes that had never been solved.

"Same M.O.,'' she chanted triumphantly, when she came over that evening.

"Cops really do say that?'' I said.

"Say what?''

"M.O. Same M.O. Why don't they just say 'method.' Same method. Why use a two-syllable shorthand for a six-syllable Latin phrase when you can use a solid two-syllable English word?''

"Jason, hush, you're spoiling my triumph! Listen to this: back in the middle fifties there were some ice pick murders over on the north side. The victims were involved with illegal gambling, which at that time implied Nello Leone, but no arrests were ever made. So now we know who probably did them, and I'm very pleased with myself because it isn't every day that a cop comes up with a probable solution for murders that happened before she was even born!''

''You think it was Gabe Leone.''

''When I say, same *method*, I mean *exactly* the same. The autopsy on Simonetta could have been written for any of the other victims. I got filthy down in those files, but the autopsy reports were still there, by God. Same weapon, same angle, same internal damage, same lack of external bleeding, the whole business. Gabe would have been in his early twenties back then. If he didn't kill those people, then it was the guy who taught him how!''

''So we know who, and we know how, but we have *no* idea why. I'd really like to know why.''

''You'll figure it out,'' she said, kissing me on one side of my chin. ''You always do.''

I was glad she had such confidence in me. All I seemed to have was loose ends.

Thursday evening I made myself go to Olivia's, ostensibly just to say hello. Actually a question had occurred to me, and I was hoping I could get the information without making a big deal of it.

She opened the subject herself. ''I should apologize for yesterday. I had no right to unburden myself that way. I haven't talked about Angela for years, except with Jacob, but yesterday was Angela's birthday. I couldn't get her out of my mind. I wanted you to know I'm grateful to you for being so understanding of an old woman.'' Tears were filling her eyes.

''You're Jacob's dear friend,'' I said helplessly, regretting my anger. ''So you're mine, too. No thanks necessary.''

''It would be so sad for Angela to go completely unremembered. After you left, Jason, I got out the old pictures. Angela's and her friends'. Daniel from next door. Jenny Bruns.'' She opened a drawer and took the photos out, laying them before me like an offering. I knew Angela immediately. She was like the young Olivia, and much, much like Lycia.

I pointed out a jolly young face. ''Jenny Bruns? She was the one you mentioned before, Angela's friend?'' That had been the question I'd wanted to ask. Who had been close to Angela?''

''Jenny Mattingly, now,'' she said. ''Mrs. Maynard Mattingly the second, or is it the third. I can never remember. She wasn't married when she knew Angela.''

''They were close friends.''

''Best friends. You know how girls are.'' She caught herself and waved her hands at me, erasing what she'd said. ''No, how would you know how girls are! Silly of me. Well, sometimes girls have real best friends. Good friends. Not the kind who are friends today and off in a snit tomorrow. Jenny and Angela were really close. Even after Angela was married, they spent a lot of time together. She was there the evening before Angela died.''

''You still see her?''

''She drops in now and then. Takes me to lunch once in a while, with her aunt and a few other old biddies. She's a great-grandmother, can you imagine!''

She showed me pictures, and I made the proper noises. As we sat there together, I toted up how many hours I'd spent in similar activities. I seem to collect old ladies. Mark has remarked upon it. I've thought it's because I have no family of my own that I collect leftover pieces of other people's families. Today I was the attentive young(er) man who sits patiently and looks at old snapshots. I did it for some little time, as penance for yesterday's annoyance.

When I left a good hour later, I promised to drop in from time to time, just to be sure she was behaving herself. She bridled like a girl, fluttering her lashes and laughing at me. For a moment I saw the Olivia Jacob must have known and loved, laughing eyes and delighted smile.

The phone book yielded no Maynard Mattingly-the-third, so I called Maynard Mattingly-the-second. No luck. The veddy haughty voice on the phone told me Mrs. Mattingly was in Mexico and was not expected to return for several weeks. Would I care to leave a message?

I left a message, mentioning that it urgently concerned Angela Desquintas y Alvarez, taking a perverse pleasure out

of the confusion the double-barreled name caused the voice.
I had to spell it twice.

Friday came and went, spent mostly inspecting the progress on the Law Firm Job: chaos incarnate. At an early stage
all jobs are chaos. Everything is torn apart; nothing is put
back together yet; nothing hints at the eventual outcome. It
would all come out right, but just now it looked impossible.

Grace would be on duty over the weekend, and I didn't
feel up to seeking other companionship. Schnitz threw up on
the kitchen floor—putting a second curse on what promised
to be a lousy weekend. I had forgotten to give him his weekly
dose of hair ball preventive, so it was my fault, not his. I
wondered, as I cleaned up the mess, what long-haired cats
did in the wild. Threw up, probably. That's probably why
they eat grass, as a purgative. The day ended in a mood of
housekeeper's irascibility.

Saturday I woke feeling no better, depressed and anxious,
as though something inimical were lurking outside the door.
This despite the fact there was no reason for Gabe Leone to
come after me now. His name and face had appeared on the
late news as a suspect sought in what the media were calling
"the abortion clinic murder." Killing me would no longer
help him a bit.

Why, then, did I vibrate with a kind of premonitory tension? I was as irritable as a bear being tracked, feeling the
need to circle and come upon my enemies from behind.

Then the phone rang.

"Cecily's back," Myra said. "She won't talk to us."

"She what?" I snapped. My irritability increased and I
felt almost clairvoyant. Somebody was up to no damned
good!

"Don't bite my head off, Jason. She won't talk to us. Her
friend Yaggie called me and said Cees was back, so I called
her in Santa Fe, but when I told her we were looking for
people who had known Simonetta, she shut up like a clam.
She wouldn't talk. And she says don't call back."

"This is the holy one, right? The one who wanted to be a
nun?"

"Right."

She gave me the address and phone number. Cecily Stephens. Two addresses in Santa Fe. One home—the one I'd tried when I was there, one office. The firm was called "Habitación." I recalled seeing it in the Santa Fe phone book when I'd looked at the contractor listings. "Casas por la gente." Houses for the people. I was reminded of Harriet's peroration on the same subject. Houses for all; information for none.

The fact that Cees wouldn't talk was actually more intriguing than Yaggie's bubbling on and on about funny old Simonetta. We'd talked to a lot of people, and none of them had had any hesitation about talking back. Dorotea had found the family history distasteful, but she'd told us what we wanted to know. Now, here, for the first time, was someone who didn't want to talk.

She had something to hide, my puzzle-solving self chortled as it sniffed along the trail and whuffed at the scent of villainy. She had something to hide, old Cees did, and I was going to find out what it was. I refused to consider that she might be simply busy, or tired, or unwilling to get involved. No, she was the person I'd been looking for, the one who knew!

How was I going to get it out of her?

I could write her a letter. Which would do no damned good.

I could drive down and try to see her. A six-hour drive from Denver. Twelve full hours, round-trip.

Or, I could fly to Albuquerque in an hour, rent a car, and drive up to Sante Fe in another hour, but the round-trip airfare was extortionate. Ever since airline deregulation, fares for lightly traveled routes have become ridiculously expensive. Persons can now fly reasonably only so long as they go where everyone else goes.

Grace and I had made the same drive the past week, and it hadn't been bad. The roads were good; the weather was supposed to be clear for almost a week. The following week, so said the weathermen, we were due for big snow. Also,

Mark would be off to New York, so if I did it at all, it would have to be now. This weekend, so I'd be there Monday.

No point in waiting around, making myself and everyone else even edgier. I left a note explaining matters to Mark and Eugenia, packed an overnight bag plus all the impedimenta that goes with traveling with pets, loaded up the animals, and headed south.

The first part of the drive was just as it had been the week before, boring. I zoomed along, thinking of nothing much, three hours vanishing along with the yellow stripe in the road, until the blue Spanish Peaks made twin indentations against the southern sky, tops lined with snow. When Grace and I had come down last, we had turned west, through Walsenburg, across La Veta Pass, and down through San Luis and Questa. The other route led through Trinidad and the Raton Pass. I decided to go through Trinidad this time. I wanted to see Gabe Leone's home ground.

Walsenburg went by on the right, endless lines of coal cars parked on a siding below the highway, small houses gathered along the bluff, every washline full of flapping laundry. Automatic dryers had not yet come to Walsenburg, might never come to Walsenburg, falling behind me among the gray hills. Abruptly, as I approached Trinidad, the vistas were no longer Great Plains but southwestern, the skyline broken in crenellated buttes and sheer-edged mesas above the town.

I stopped for dog and cat exercise, a drink of water for them, coffee for me. Acceptable coffee. The man next to me at the counter wore a sheriff's star on a chest that sloped down to a vast comfortable belly. I asked him if he knew where the Snowy Peaks Roofing Company was, and he gave me directions.

"Guy that ran it wrecked himself up in Denver last week," he said. "Now he's wanted for something or other. Musta been drunk. Never knew Gabe to drive crazy before."

"You know him?" I asked, a little surprised.

"Hell," he said. "I know ever-body. All the natives. All the refugees . . ."

"Refugees?"

He laughed. "That's the story. This here's the hidey hole for the Costa Nostra. This is where they send their guys who're in trouble. Didn't you never hear that?"

I shook my head, no, I hadn't heard that.

"Sure. This is the Mafioso Rest Camp. Also the Sex Change Capital of the U.S."

"You're kidding."

"Nah," said the counterman, shifting his gum from one side of his mouth to the other. "He's not kidding. This really is. We got a doctor here does more sex change operations than anybody else in the whole country."

They were still chuckling about that when I left. I wasn't sure whether these were local fables, used to astonish the tourists, or the truth, though later a journalist friend advised me neither story was fictional.

The Snowy Peaks Roofing Company squatted at the edge of town, a flat-roofed, cinder block building with a long shed out back and assorted tar-encrusted, wheeled machines dotted on the graveled, weed-infested lot. The shed was stacked with bundles of asphalt shingles and wood shakes and fat black rolls of roofing paper. I parked and stared. Antonio Gabrielli Leone's home base. I'd looked him up in the phone book, finding him among a number of other Leones. There were many Italian names in the book. Maybe that's where the Mafioso story had started. I tried to think up some good reason for going in and asking questions, but I couldn't come up with one. Besides, it was Saturday afternoon. They were probably closed.

South of Trinidad, piñons grew along the tumbling creek as we went up the canyon toward the pass, past beaver dams with ice frilling the banks, among winter-dark ponderosa pines, over the top and down into New Mexico, into Raton, marked on its northern edge by one of those dreadful farms that always makes me cringe: stained and rotted sheds, churned and trodden ground, with truck and automobile tires lying everywhere among derelict machinery and nothing which was or would ever be green.

I'd forgotten to get gas in Trinidad, so we stopped to fill

the tank in Raton before driving the long flat stretch south to Cimarron. Then the good part of the trip began, Cimarron Canyon, where the road slaloms upward through forests and along the tumbling stream, coming out at last at the totally unexpected lake at Eagle Nest, around it and past it and up once more, along the rock-cut road past Angel Fire, and then down, through spruce forests, past little houses lining the Taos Creek, and onto the flat where giant Rio Grande cottonwoods reach over the road with long, winter-gray arms and twiggy fingers. Suddenly there were adobes everywhere along the road, bed-and-breakfasts, art galleries, historic thises and thats.

Another hour brought me to Los Vientos once more, where the caretaker told me the guest house was mine if I wanted it. Monday morning, as soon as office hours started, I'd find out whether Cecily Stephens was present at Habitación.

Meantime, in the rounded adobe fireplace I made a tiny teepee-shaped fire, the way Mike had taught me, shared the hamburger I'd bought in Española with Bela and Schnitz, had a few bottles of Negra Modelo beer, and looked at the stars.

Mike had pets of his own, and he'd built a dog and cat run to use when he was away for brief times. After the three of us had a long morning walk down a dry river bottom, I left Bela and Schnitz sleeping in the run and spent Sunday afternoon visiting art galleries in Santa Fe and having a late lunch at my favorite restaurant, Casa Sena. They have a prime rib burrito that has to be tasted to be believed. I got back to the animals well before dark. We had another long walk before their supper, then yet another night of stars and quiet so deep I found myself holding my breath, just to listen.

Monday morning, I took the used linens up to the laundry room off the main house and got them washed and into the dryer, then called the number for Habitación. The receptionist said Cecily Stephens was in but unavailable. I did not leave a message. Instead, I put the animals into the run, got into the car, checked the location of Habitación on the map of Santa Fe I'd picked up the day before, and drove directly there.

Everything in Santa Fe is either real adobe or fake adobe, so it was no surprise to find Habitación located in a purposefully massed mud house surrounded by plantings of native, dry-land flora. Mike Wilson has lectured me on the sculptural qualities of real adobe, enough that I can appreciate the nuances. The building before me was gently curved and surfaced, made of honest mud with a weather-resistant coating. It was not the cheap imitation: square-edged cinder block covered with stucco. Beside the main building, a row of smaller structures stood shoulder to shoulder, complete with explanatory signs. These were examples of mud houses as they were built in North Africa, in Iran, in Arabia. Mud might be used anywhere, I assumed, where the rainfall was low. One of the exhibits included a ram device for making hard-rammed floor and roof tiles of sieved earth and cement.

I took it all in as I walked past, not dallying but not hurrying. I wanted some idea of what Cecily did, hoping it might give me some idea of how to approach her. The exhibits didn't give me a clue. All I could do was present myself, provoke her into saying something or other, and then be hard to discourage.

She was in a meeting. I said I'd wait. The person behind the desk announced with a fine air of self-importance that the meeting would go on all morning.

"That's all right," I said. "Twice in the past several weeks I have narrowly missed being killed by a man with a gun. I am reliably informed Cecily Stephens can help me identify who that man is. At least, waiting here, I'm relatively safe, so I'll wait if you don't mind." I gave her my card.

She stared at it nervously for a few minutes, then got up and edged out of the room, trying to do it casually but missing sangfroid by a mile. She was so nervous her eyelids were twitching.

A considerable time passed. If I had been she, or Cecily, I would have called the number on the card to find out who this maniac in the waiting room might be. I assumed they were doing that. Though maybe they were calling the police, which could cause complications.

Presumably they stopped short of the police. A short, stocky woman came striding into the area where I sat, thrust my card in my face, and said, "Why are you threatening my secretary?"

"I beg your pardon?" I asked in my most offended tone. "I have done no such thing."

"She seems to think somebody's coming in here with a gun."

I smiled ingratiatingly, which she seemed not to notice. "I do hope not. He's shot at me twice, recently, but each time I was more or less in the open. He hasn't followed me inside anywhere. Are you Cecily Stephens?"

"I am. And I'd like to know what this is all about."

"Do you want to discuss it here?" I said it politely, indicating I had no objection to discussing it on main street at high noon if she liked.

She snorted and beckoned. I followed her jean-clad form down a brick-paved hallway to a room much like the one I'd slept in last night. Exposed beams, cedar splits between them, softly textured walls decorated with Indian rugs and baskets. A slanted drawing table stood to one side with a half-finished rendering on it. The wastebasket was heaped with crumpled white-paper balls tokening inadequacy or frustration or both.

"Sit," she said, pointing.

I sat.

"All right, now what is this? And make it fast, I have people waiting."

"May I go into the history a bit first? Just so you can see the relevance."

She gestured again, impatiently. I told her about Simonetta's death at the clinic. I mentioned Herby Fixe. When I said his name, she didn't move but her skin color changed. She didn't quiver, but she turned gray. I went on talking, trying not to stare. It was like watching a chameleon. She changed color from gray to red to gray again as I talked. I told her about Herby dying. About the attempts on my life.

When I finished, she sat, unmoving. After what seemed a very long time, she said, "You misled me. You know who shot at you. This Leone person shot at you. Simonetta's dead. Herby Fixe is dead. This man who shot at you has no reason to do so again. Correct?"

I nodded, not liking the finality in her voice.

"No one is currently being suspected of a crime they did not commit, correct? The people at the clinic are in the clear?"

I nodded again.

"No one's life is in danger."

"I'm not sure of that. I don't know that Gabe Leone has given up on me."

"But as you yourself say, he no longer has reason to threaten you. It would not be logical for him to do so. Since that's the case, there's no reason for me to tell you anything. I knew some things about Simonetta, yes, but they were personal things, some of them things I would just as soon not have known. I talked about those things once before. I did so out of misplaced compassion, and evidently it only caused trouble."

I waited, but she didn't specify what trouble. Instead, she squared her shoulders and announced, "I have no intention of talking any further about Simonetta."

"Not if my life depended on it?"

"Only if you could convince me of that, and I'd be hard to convince. This Leone person was afraid you'd identify him. Well, he's been identified anyhow. Your girlfriend has seen him. Your neighbor has seen him. His car has been identified, and the weapon that was in it was the weapon he used against you. Now that everyone knows who he is, what motive would he have for killing you?"

Grace had said the same thing. I wished I felt as sure about it as they did. "Do you know why Simonetta was killed?" I asked her.

"Oh, I could make a guess," she said. "I'd guess that she got between Canello Leone and something he decided to do. That's what the note in her pocket meant. She interfered;

she's dead. That would have been Canello's way of telling the world to keep out of his way. And Gabe's way. Like father, like son.''

"Why didn't he kill her years ago? Decades ago?''

"Because he didn't know what she'd done until recently.''

"Nello died in the 60's,'' I said. "He couldn't have known recently.''

"His family,'' she said, making an inclusive gesture to show that the exact "who" was irrelevant. "I said, like father, like son. It wouldn't have mattered which of them found out. Geronimo or Canello or Gabrielli—any of them.''

"After thirty-five, forty years!'' I didn't believe her.

"After generations.'' She sighed. "Mr. Lynx, I spend a great deal of time in Latin American countries. In Brazil, for example. In that country, if a man kills his wife or his sister for some reason of family honor—because she has taken a lover, or because he thinks she has, or because someone merely has accused her of it—no court will convict him even if the woman was innocent. I vividly recall one case that received a lot of attention in the newspapers. A woman refused to marry a man and chose his rival instead. The man shot his rival. He wasn't convicted because he'd killed in the heat of passion; his honor had been bruised. The woman entered a convent. Twenty years later, she left the convent and he murdered her. He was tried and set free. He could only let her live in a state of perpetual chastity, you see. Otherwise, his honor was still offended. If he'd died in the meantime and his brother or son or nephew had killed her, no court would have convicted any of them. The law doesn't punish matters of family honor.''

"Leone was Italian, not Brazilian.''

"It's the attitude I'm talking about, Mr. Lynx, not the nationality. It's an attitude that goes with tribalism. Every tribe has a more compelling history, has suffered greater wrongs, and has a purer honor than any other tribe. They rejoice in long memories. My God, the Irish are still fighting battles hundreds of years old and the Shiites still have enemies they made over a millennium ago! You think a few decades is enough to wash out a debt of honor?

"The thing a great many untraveled Americans forget is that our country is not the paradigm of the world! We've exported a number of mercantile superficialities, enough to make us think that people who eat McDonald's hamburgers and drink Coke and watch our sitcoms must be like us. Most are not like us at all. What you tell me about Octavio's oath would be perfectly understandable and acceptable in many countries. Uniting two families by marriage would be considered much more important than the wishes of the woman involved."

"You say Octavio's point of view isn't unusual, all right. He was first-generation Spanish, maybe I can buy that. But what about Nello? Why would he agree to the marriage?"

"Who would a proud Catholic father have wanted as a bride for his son? He would have wanted a virgin Catholic girl from a good family. If she could be pretty and healthy, so much the better. The Leone family had a bad reputation. Getting a girl like that might not have been easy. And what was Angela? Someone who fit that description exactly. A girl not only from a good family but from an aristocratic one. And pretty."

"She wasn't Italian," I objected.

"Well, Nello's father was actually Sicilian, I believe, a people who are no less obsessed by the notion of honor than Latin Americans are. Nello's mother was Venezuelan. The Mediterranean-Indian mix makes fertile ground for notions of honor. Self-esteem is very vulnerable. Threats against it are serious matters." She stood up, unmistakably telling me our interview was at an end.

"You'll tell me that much, but no more?"

"Oh, I can talk to you all day about cultural differences. That's my field, after all. But I won't talk about Simonetta. She isn't my secret to share."

"You shared it once."

"With someone I thought had a right to it. With someone I thought was trying to help her."

I cast about for anything I could ask her, any scrap of information I could get. "How do you know so much about the Leone family? I can't imagine Simonetta knowing all those details of who came from where."

She shook her head at me. "I took the trouble to find out. Years ago. I needed to make sense of things Simonetta had told me. In those days, I thought if one only knew the facts, it was easy to do the right thing. As I grew older, I found the more one knows, the harder it gets."

"You found these things out before you moved to California?"

She turned gray again. "Yes. I asked questions. I looked things up. I was young and innocent-looking, people talked to me. I put together some information. A few facts I've found out only recently. Such as the significance of Nello Leone's mother having come from an area near Lake Maracaibo. The people in the surrounding villages have the highest incidence of Huntington's disease known anywhere in the world. I found that out quite by accident in a hotel room in Atlanta, watching television."

"I know nothing about the disease," I said. "Except that it strikes in adulthood and is invariably fatal."

"Some live a long time with it. Some not long. Those who die quickly are, I think, the lucky ones. Nello lived quite a long time, as did Nimo, but Nello's mother died when she was only thirty-two."

I sighed. Cecily knew what I wanted to know. She wouldn't tell me. All the principal actors seemed to be dead—except for Olivia.

"Let me take one more minute to tell you about Olivia," I said. I proceeded to do so, briefly but with some detail about her age and the tragedy of her life.

For the first time Cecily seemed to be concerned. "I . . . no, I won't. The woman's daughter is dead. Don't you understand? I will not tell you what Simonetta told me! It could cause trouble and nobody you've spoken of really needs to know! This Olivia is eighty years old, her daughter's been dead for years, she hasn't seen her grandson since he was an infant . . ."

"I didn't say anything about her grandson."

She stopped. Started to say something. Stopped. Started again. "Simonetta, of course, was very fond of the little boy, so I knew of his existence."

"How did you know Olivia hadn't seen him in years?"

"No comment. That's it, Mr. Lynx. Go back to Denver. I'm sure you've many important things to do there. If you come back here, I'll run you off." She was angry, angrier at herself than at me. She had said something she hadn't meant to.

I left. I sat in the car for a long time, adding and subtracting what she had said from what she hadn't said, coming up with only two new threads to add to the fabric of what I knew.

First: Simonetta's killing had been a matter of honor. Simonetta had interfered with something Nello Leone had wanted to do. Call it The Act. Simonetta interfered with The Act, but Nello didn't know that at the time. Which means either he thought he had accomplished The Act or he knew he had not but did not know why.

Second: years later some member of Nello's family—probably his son Gabe who was unaffected by the hereditary disease—found out The Act had not been accomplished because Simonetta had interfered. No matter that his father was dead, no matter that decades had passed, the family honor was still at stake, so Gabe killed Simonetta for interfering. Then, thinking I'd seen him, he tried to kill me.

I wondered if The Act had ever been accomplished? Had the matter of honor been taken care of?

Possibly not, else why Cecily's insistence upon silence? Though, as I had to admit to myself, it might be only that the incidents in question had been embarrassing for her personally and she didn't want to disclose them.

What had the matter of honor been? Cecily had mentioned adultery. Had Angela committed adultery? Had someone simply accused her of it? Cecily had also mentioned that rejecting a man might become a matter of honor. Angela could have married Nimo, gotten pregnant, then rejected relations with him subsequent to the child's birth. What did Simonetta have to do with things like that?

Nothing worked. Even the idea that Simonetta had somehow interfered with the cover-up of Angela's dishonorable suicide had holes in it. Everyone knew at the time that Simonetta had talked about it. She'd gone up and down the street proclaiming suicide to all and sundry!

In a mood of continued frustration and annoyance, I started the car and drove back to the Los Vientos guest house to remake the beds and put the clean dishes away. My deal with Mike was I could stay anytime, provided I left the place clean enough for the next guest. The animals and I were back in Denver by eight o'clock Monday night, March the 10th, windy but not cold. Bela wandered around the yard, reinforcing his territorial smells. Schnitz did a shred job on his climbing pole. There were a few messages on my desk. Nothing that wouldn't wait until morning except one call from Grace. When she sleepily answered the phone, I asked her if I could come cry on her shoulder, and she said I'd have to cry tomorrow; she had to be at work at six in the morning.

All in all, I did not feel terribly clever or efficient or even sensible. I was almost convinced this particular puzzle had run its course and I had unraveled all available threads.

six

OVER COFFEE THE next morning I reminded myself that some secrets remain secrets forever. Dead men tell no tales is an old saw, no less true for being old. There's no key to unlock the feelings and beliefs of people who are gone. Unless a man keeps a detailed journal, outlining his day to day, minute-by-minute emotional responses, his life-scape vanishes when he does. Even if such a journal were kept, there might be no one to read it.

Simonetta's journal, if she had one at all, had been in her housekeeping, in the obsessive performance of little rituals, the routine observances, ingrained habits, learned duties, each accomplished day by day, adding up to nothing at all. Do-rotea didn't want to think about her. Cecily didn't want to talk about her. Even Sister John Lorraine had confessed to doubt about the purpose of a life like Simonetta's. There seemed to be little reason for remembering her now.

I told myself the time had come to put her aside. Her end was like her life: beyond my understanding. All puzzles be-gin with fascination, progress through intrigue to resolu-tion—or, go on to unrequited obsession, and at that point, one is wise to stop. So I have told myself before and so I told myself now. Puzzle addiction is not unlike other addictions. One either quits chasing drink or drugs or gambling or women (or answers), or one sickens in the chase.

I told myself to forget the matter, though Grace continued resolute. By now she had ever member of the Leone family pinned to her collection board and was busy calling my at-tention to this one and that one while burbling happily that

Gabe was the last, really the last, of the Nello Leone line. There were distant cousins, but there were no dangerous Leones left, no one to take up the banner of whatever "honorable" crusade it had been. When we caught Gabe, she believed the matter would be ended. I was still curious enough to hope he would tell us then what it had been all about.

Sister John Lorraine called me and asked if everything was all right. I told her yes, the matter had resolved itself, the innocent were no longer suspected, all was well. She sounded a little miffed.

"Did you ever figure out what it was Simonetta did that got her killed?"

Here was Simonetta again! I gritted my teeth and said, "Sister, I think Simonetta upset people just being herself."

Sister said that was cool. "That's what the kids here at school say when they understand something," she explained. "That's cool." She didn't sound cool. She sounded baffled and frustrated, which was how I felt, but I let it pass. Simonetta had interfered, she was dead. Now, as at the beginning, that seemed to be all we were destined to know.

So why this hulking, suppliant shadow lurking at the edges of my mind? I heaved it aside, resolving once more to forget it.

A foul-up on delivery of carpeting for the Law Firm Job helped me think of something else almost equally irritating. The mistake involved the supplier, the shipper, and the local distributor who had placed the order. It took two days and considerable annoyance to get fixed, because everyone involved was interested in covering his ass rather than helping us fix it. Grace wasn't around to remind me of the case because she was working an odd shift which left her too sleepy to be social. "I'm filling in for three weeks," she said, yawning widely over the phone. "Then I'm back days." I marked the calendar and tried to live in anticipation.

Mark left for New York with Bryan. Without him to answer the phone, things seemed busier even though not much more actually happened. The Bonifaces came in to talk about their farm house, gave me some money on account, and asked me to work out a plan for them. I tried to get excited about their project and failed. I kept thinking of Simonetta and getting angry at myself for doing so.

Late Friday afternoon, I answered the phone with a barely civil "Jason Lynx," and heard Dorothea Chapman's studiedly cultivated tones asking whether I would be in the office for an hour or so. I said yes, I'd be there all evening in fact. She said she'd be over and hung up, leaving me wondering, reluctantly, what the hell she had come up with. Having set the matter aside with some effort, I really didn't want to get sucked back into it again.

She arrived about six, after we'd closed, and I escorted her up to my living room where I'd been having a drink before supper. She surprised me by picking Schnitz up bodily, sitting down with him in her lap and reducing him to delighted rumbles by scratching his belly fur.

"I do love cats," she said. "I always had cats as a girl. I can't have them now because Andrew is allergic. And then, too, the house is rather formal for pets." She made a moue, "So Andrew says."

I gave her the wine she'd asked for.

"I saw my mother today," she said, after a sip. "Mama had a very good day, so I asked her about Simonetta. Frankly, Mr. Lynx, I thought you were being rather stupidly obsessive about Simonetta, but it seems you were right. The poor girl had done something silly. Mother never told anyone, not until now, but you see, it can't hurt Simmy now."

"What was it?" I asked, not expecting, or perhaps just not wanting much in the way of revelations. I was tired, and I'd been trying hard not to think about it.

"Well, remember I told you about Simmy taking care of the Leone child. Did I mention about the child being born with a birthmark? I'm not sure I'd remembered that before. Evidently Nimo Leone told his associates and family there was a curse on the child because of that. It seems it was all common gossip. Mama remembered hearing about it at the time."

I told her I'd heard all about that, yes.

"What Mama told me today was that after Nimo's wife died, Nimo threatened to kill the child, or Simmy thought he did, so she took him to protect him from his father."

"Took him?"

"The child. Simonetta kidnapped him."

"Kidnapped him?" Whatever I'd expected, it hadn't been that. "How? When?"

"You'll have to forgive this being rather fuzzy, Jason. You don't mind if I call you Jason? If we're going to share all these family secrets, we might as well be on a first name basis.—You have to remember that all this happened almost forty years ago, and Simmy was never what one would call a reliable witness, even for things that happened ten minutes ago. When Mama's memory is good, it's very good, but she can only remember what Simmy told her. Simmy always called the child 'the baby,' even though she'd been taking care of him for several years. At any rate, Simmy told Mama she took the baby—that's a quote—from its nursery the day the mother died. She hid 'the baby,' and some time later, she panicked and told a friend of hers from school what she'd done. That friend took the child. Either Simmy talked her into it, or, more likely the friend offered, just to get it away from Simmy. . . ."

"Then, out of a clear blue sky, the friend left town."

"Cecily!" I cried.

Dorotea wrinkled her forehead, then tried the name on her lips, silently nodding. "It may have been. I remember a Cecily, sort of vaguely. If she was Simmy's age, she'd have been a lot older than I. Mother didn't mention that name today. Maybe Simmy never told her who it was. However, both Mama and I remember two hysterical episodes, the first one when Nimo's wife died, and another one a few weeks later."

"Cecily left town a few weeks later."

"She did? Well, at the time, no one could figure out why Simmy was so upset. If this friend left town, however, maybe she took the child with her and Simmy didn't know where it was. The friend didn't tell her, probably for good reason."

"Your mother wasn't told this at the time it happened?"

"Heavens, no. She only found out about it a few years ago. And she's never said a word about it to me until today."

"Could Cecily have given the child back to its father? Nimo said his son had been sent to Italy, to relatives."

"That's entirely possible, even probable, but Mama said nothing about that. The only reason Mama came to know about this at all is that Herby Fixe tried to blackmail Papa about it."

She watched my face, letting this information sink in before she continued. "Remember, I told you Herby used to work for Nello Leone. Well, about twelve or thirteen years ago, he came to Papa and said he knew Simonetta had stolen this child, that there was no statute of limitations on kidnapping, that he'd get her arrested for kidnapping unless Papa paid him to keep quiet." She set her wine glass down and half smiled. "It was a stupid thing for him to do, but Herby wasn't really intelligent. Clever, sly, like a rat, but not intelligent.

"I'll quote what Mama said: *'Herby should have had better sense than to mess with your papa.'* "

"I take it Papa didn't pay?"

"He not only didn't pay, he made Herby marry Simonetta at once so he couldn't ever be forced to testify against her. He also mentioned that Simonetta's brothers would break every bone in his body if he ever spoke of it again." She laughed shortly. "Papa didn't mean my lawyer brother or my professor brother, needless to say. He meant my Denver brothers, who were fully capable of doing exactly that."

"I thought your father said the marriage had to do with Herby seducing your sister?"

"That's what he told Mama and me at the time. That was like Papa. I think he didn't want Mama to know Simmy had done something illegal. Being seduced isn't illegal, it's just immoral. Mama could always handle immorality. She had the church to help her with that. She could trust in God's forgiveness, but not the law's. Not long before Papa died, though, he told Mama the truth. He told her she needed to know, so she could protect Simmy. And once Mama knew about it, she asked Simmy about it.''

''So your mother has known about this for a while?''

''Since Papa died. Evidently, Mama talked to Simmy about it every now and then. Mama didn't turn a hair when I asked about it today, just came out and told me. She said Simmy was safe with God now, so it didn't matter if I knew.''

I tried to assemble the information in a form that made sense. ''Nimo thought the child was cursed, Simonetta interpreted that as a threat . . .''

''Or she may have heard Nimo actually threaten the child. Not that it necessarily meant anything.''

''Right. She heard an actual or implied threat. So she kidnapped the child and gave it to Cecily.'' Despite what Cecily had said about other cultures, the whole thing still sounded unlikely. Children being threatened because of birthmarks! We were talking about the 1950's, after all. And why hadn't Cecily told me this? She'd told someone. Someone who had, so she said, a right to know.

''You never met Herby, did you?'' asked Dorotea, interrupting my train of thought.

I shook my head.

''He was a nasty piece of work. Ingratiating in a terribly slick way that made you feel you'd crawled through something slimy. He flattered people, sucked up to them, all the time looking for something he could use. Looking at him, you wouldn't think he could be violent, but he was bad. He ran errands for Nello from the time he was a kid.''

''Errands?''

''You know. You've seen the movies. He threatened people and beat them up. Maybe he even murdered a few, I don't know. My brothers used to bring him around, and he always made me feel dirty.''

''I take it Herby never really lived with Simonetta. I saw their house. One man's jacket in the closet, I think. Nothing else to show he ever lived there.''

"No, thank God. He didn't. Papa put Simmy on an allow-ance and bought her the house when she was married. Herby may have dropped by once in a while, to use the phone or pick up mail. When Simonetta died, the house went to Mama. As a matter of fact, after Simmy died, Mama asked me to have it cleaned out so one of my brothers can use it."

"One of your . . . ?"

"One of my Denver brothers, yes. Even jailbirds get old eventually." She sighed. "It's my brother Carlos, another one of Nello Leone's former employees. I saw him the other day at the nursing home when he came to visit Mama. I remember him as a big, burly, threatening man, but now he's just a sad old person who doesn't see very well."

"That surprised you?"

"Well, I thought he and my brother Joe were devils when I was a young woman struggling to get away from all that. Them and the uncles." She gestured helplessly.

"You were afraid they were somehow going to drag you back, drag you down?"

"Exactly. You're very perceptive."

It wasn't perception. It was what I'd gone through myself at age thirteen or fourteen with Jacob offering respectability and dignity and all that dull stuff while some of the kids I'd grown up with were offering inducements of quite another kind. Not only the kids. Some of them had by that time acquired older acquaintances, mentors, men who would have been only too glad to include me. I remembered juvenile nightmares in which I'd been caught with those men, caught doing something shameful—not necessarily something sex-ual, though there had been some of that going on, just some-thing I didn't want people to know about. My childhood friend Jerry Riggles had succumbed to that kind of life. Last I'd heard, he was back in prison for the third or fourth time. Burglary, or fencing. It had been Jerry who'd dared me to steal from Jacob in the first place.

I smiled grimly at Dorotea, and she gave me a similar smile. I realized the truth of what Jacob had said. Knowing who you had been wasn't always a help in becoming who you would be.

I told her I appreciated her telling me the story.

"It was the only thing I could do. After being so reluctant and annoyed the other day. One tries to put it all behind one, but . . ."

"I know," I said.

"They're still family," she said unwillingly. "I tell myself if I could lop certain ones off from Mama and just keep her, I'd do it, but she'd never allow that. If I take Mama, I take them all, the whole family, willy-nilly."

"I'm going to tell Grace Willis about this. Even though I don't think what you've told me is pertinent to anything she's doing, I can't guarantee she won't want to ask you some questions." If I knew Grace, she would.

"It's all right. Mother said it for all of us. Simmy's beyond hurt. Nothing we can say will injure her now."

While she was talking, I'd had an idea.

"Your brother's living at Simmy's old house?"

"Yes. The Salvation Army emptied it, all but the furniture, and I had a cleaning firm go through it. Carlos is there now. I refuse to ask Mama, but I'm pretty sure she's supporting him. Sending him a little check every week or so. You don't earn social security in jail."

She finished her wine, gave Schnitz a last pummeling, and left me. She was right about the social security. I wondered if the checks Mama sent Carlos stretched to beer.

On the theory the checks didn't stretch that far, I picked up a six-pack on the way to Zuni Street, along with a couple of double hamburgers and some fries.

The place looked the same except that a few lights were on and the porch held some empty cartons. When Carlos opened the door, I smelled something burning. It wasn't an improvement over the previous smell. Dorotea had been right about him. He was an old man with squinty eyes, a contemporary of Nimo's and Herby's, a gray sexagenarian.

He peered at me near-sightedly.

"Carlos Leone?" I asked.

"Yeah."

"I'm a friend of your sister's. She thought maybe you could help me with some information. I brought along some beer and burgers, just in case you hadn't had dinner yet."

He stepped back uncertainly, motioning me inside.

"My sister?"

"Dorotea."

"Oh, Dor'ty. I thought you meant Simmy. Yeah. I seen Dor'ty the other day."

"She said she'd seen you. Visiting your mother."

"Mama, yeah."

We stood confronting one another in the living room while he tried to see me. I lifted the beer in front of his face, so he couldn't miss it.

"Yeah," he said again. "Come on in."

He led me through to the kitchen. The pan holding whatever had burned was now in the sink. A small fan whirred, trying to clear the air. He fell into a chair at the soiled kitchen table. The house may have been cleaned before he moved in, but Carlos was busily conforming it to his life-style. I passed him a hamburger and package of fries, opened a beer and added that to the array. Hungrily, he went for the fries first.

"Ya got'ny ketchup?"

I found the packets of ketchup in the bottom of the sack. There had been a drawer full of such packets when I'd been here last. The Salvation Army had probably taken it, along with the rolled stockings and the paper bags. Carlos wasn't going to invite me to sit down, so I sat without invitation.

"Whudja wanna know?" he asked, around a mouthful.

"You remember Nimo's wife?" I asked him. "Angela Leone?"

"Sure. Ya don't forget stuff like that." He made a lewdly descriptive gesture, but there was no lust behind it. It was a meaningless, habitual response to the mention of woman.

"She had a child," I said.

"Right. Kid 'uz born 'uth this big red blotch on him.

Nimo had a fit. Kid got to look better later on, but Nimo never liked him much. Not like a son, you know.''

"Do you remember when Angela died?''

"Remember when Herby Fixe did her? Yeah.''

I guess my mouth dropped open. He laughed between ill-fitting dentures which clacked and slipped as he chewed.

"Ya didn't know that? Hell, ever'body knew that. Nimo told Herby to kill her an' the kid.''

"Why?'' I gasped.

He chewed reflectively. "I used ta think it was maybe 'cause of that blotch the kid had on him. But ya know, I think it was Nimo had that sickness. Went kind of crazy.''

"Not then, did he? I thought he didn't get the disease until later, a lot later.'' Besides, did Huntington's disease cause that kind of madness?

Carlos was still thinking about it. "I figure maybe he was already a little crazy. Didn' make sense to kill the kid over that mark on him. He was a good-lookin' kid ceptin for that. Talk your ear off, too.''

"And why kill Angela?''

"Thass what I mean. Like, it was crazy, ya know. But Nimo said kill her, so thass what Herby did. Made it look real good, lika accident. He told me about it. How he fixed the old gas pipe so gas'd go through there again. How he turned it on when she was asleep up there.''

"What happened to the child?''

"Little boy? Herb said he killed him.''

"Killed him!''

"Said he did. Nimo paid him for doin it. I always figured he did, but Simmy said he didn'. Simmy said she took the kid.''

I no longer had any appetite for food. I put the half-eaten burger down on the table and breathed deeply.

"When did Simmy tell you this?''

"I dunno. After Herby died, I guess. I usta come around, get somethin to eat. Simmy, she'd talk yur ear off. She usta talk to Mama, but when Mama went in that home, Simmy, she didn' have nobody to talk to.''

"Did you tell anyone what she said?"

"Well, probly. You know. Guys I usta know. Guys that worked for Nimo. Herby was dead, so it didn' matter. Lissen, when Nimo said do somethin, ya did it. If Herby didn' do what Nimo said, he'd've been in deep shit, I tell ya that."

I stayed a little longer, but Carlos had nothing else to tell me. When I left, I was thinking of Dorotea Chapman growing up with brothers like these. When Carlos had told me about the murder, he hadn't even stopped chewing.

All along, ever since I'd talked to Sister John and to Dorothea that first time, I'd been thinking of Simonetta as a little crazy. Now it seemed, whatever she might have been, she had not been crazy. There really had been a threat to the child, and she really had stolen the child to protect him.

Like it or not, Cecily Stephens had to tell me what she knew! She was the key to this whole mess!

I called her home in Santa Fe. Nobody there but the damned machine. I did not discuss the matter with the machine. Saturday morning, I called again, both home and business. Business was closed, said its machine, until Monday. The Stephenses were away, said their machine, until Monday. I roamed the house like a caged bear, up and down stairs. Bela whined at me. Schnitz fluffed his tail and raised his back, hissing. Both were saying the same thing. You're a stranger. Where's our two-legs? What have you done with our two-legs?

I gave up and went to a movie at an art cinema, some festival offering an Oriental film I couldn't remember ten minutes after it was over. Perhaps because I'd been too distracted to read the subtitles. Chinese histrionics don't soak in subliminally. Or had it been Thai?

At least one visual scene had penetrated my fog. A notable banquet depicted in loving detail midway through the film had started my stomach making demanding noises. I was on South Colorado Boulevard, only a dozen blocks from a good Oriental restaurant where I ordered warm saki plus dumplings with spicy peanut sauce and something monosyllabic with lobster in it. When I came out into the parking lot with my leftovers in a little plastic box, it had started to snow. By the time I got home, I skidded into the garage on the coattails of a full-fledged spring blizzard. March is the snowiest month in Denver. It looked like we'd be under a couple of feet of the stuff by Sunday morning.

I let Bela out, and he jumped around in the snowfall for a few minutes, just for the novelty of it, then came in shivering. I fed him and Schnitz before turning on the gas log in the fireplace. Wood fires are largely verboten in Denver, because of our pollution, so I lit a stick of piñon incense and tried to imagine I was back in New Mexico with Grace. I called Grace. She was out, said her machine.

The whole world was out except the machines. I decided to give up. The night was fit for nothing but sleeping anyhow. Bela and Schnitz seemed to agree. As soon as I turned off the light they both jumped up on the bed and curled against me, as though to make sure I did not sneak away in the darkness.

For a wonder, somebody had traded a day with Grace, and she had Sunday off. She called me at ten and arrived about noon. We raided both the refrigerator and the freezer, and I fixed an enormous brunch, with eggs and sausages and Canadian bacon and hollandaise. Grace ate her way through a pound of bratwurst while I told her about Dorotea and Carlos.

"It's now obvious how Gabe found out about Simonetta. Carlos told him, or told some third party who told him," I said.

"Okay, I can accept the Leones were maybe sort of superstitious, but do you really think anyone would kill a child because of a birthmark?" she asked me around a mouthful of eggs Benedict. I am very proud of my eggs Benedict, and of my eggs Florentine, and of my cooking in general. I wish Grace would occasionally pause in her ingestion of it to tell me it tastes good.

We talked about motivation. We agreed that the birthmark theory was not believable, the suicide theory had serious holes in it, and the disease theory was only marginally acceptable.

"I figure Cecily knows the real reasons for all this," I said.

"Are you going to go after her? You know, I could maybe make it a police matter, and that way you'd have some clout."

"Police matter?"

"Well, knowing about the baby maybe goes to the actual motivation for Simonetta's murder."

"With Gabe identified as the killer, does Lieutenant Linder need to know what the motivation was?"

She shrugged in her turn. "I wouldn't say he really cares, no. Even the D.A. wouldn't care why provided he could prove Gabe did it. When we catch him . . ."

"If you catch him."

"He'll turn up, sooner or later. You know, I could at least call Cecily and ask her if she minds answering some questions."

"You couldn't force her to come here, could you?"

"Not unless we arrested her for something, then she'd have to be extradited. Of course, if this case goes on developing this way, the D.A. might want to depose her, or subpoena her, but that'll be a long time from now." She chewed thoughtfully. "We could always go down there again. But you said she travels a lot. If she flies in and out of Albuquerque, she probably connects either through Dallas or Denver. She might be coming through here sometime soon anyhow. Sometimes people will cooperate just because the police ask them to, if it isn't too much trouble."

I'd met Cecily and I considered it unlikely. Still, nothing ventured, nothing gained. Grace promised she'd call Habitación on Monday.

We spent the rest of the day in a clutter of Sunday papers and sequential snacks and several bottles of wine and tangled bed clothes, trying to forget there would be a Monday. Along toward evening, Grace put her head on my shoulder, stared at the ceiling, and asked what I'd decided about keeping the shop or giving it up. It took me a minute to recollect what she was talking about. I'd gotten so involved in Olivia's life, I'd forgotten that great decisions pended in my own.

"Don't put the decision off forever," she said.

I promised her I wouldn't, wondering why she was pushing me. Maybe she wanted me gone. No. She'd have said so if that was it. Maybe she couldn't get on with her life until I got on with mine. That was more likely.

Mark was back Monday morning. A spring blizzard in New York the day of one of the auctions had kept people away in droves. Mark had bid, quite successfully, for several goodies we'd wanted, and he was full of himself over it. The things were being shipped, but by the time he was through describing, neither Eugenia nor I needed to see the actual pieces. We could have recognized them from half a mile away.

Grace called to say Cecily had been surprised by her call, infuriated at what Grace had told her about Dorotea's and Carlos's stories, and was now amenable to disclosure. "I told her we'd been told Simonetta had taken the child, and that she, Cecily, was probably involved. And I told her part of what Carlos told you, about Herby probably killing the mother, and I said maybe she'd better straighten us out as to what had really transpired, because we had some unanswered questions regarding Simonetta's death."

"And she said she'd tell us? I am astonished."

"Well, technically at least, she's probably guilty of something—aiding and abetting, maybe conspiracy to commit. I think she figures she'd better straighten it out. Anyhow, there's some kind of international conference she's attending in England, and she can connect flights here in Denver, probably on Thursday. She'll let me know when."

The following day, I dropped in to see Olivia. She looked a little tired, and said she hadn't been sleeping well, that she'd been dreaming about Angela.

"I wish I really believed in heaven," she said. "I don't, you know. I used to, as a girl. I believed we'd all meet there, those of us who'd lived good, religious lives and been scrupulous about the sacraments and worried about our sins. But the longer I've lived, the more I've thought how tiring heaven would be. Father Garson tells me I'm just worn out and going through a little spell of anomie. You know that word?''

I said I did.

"I don't think it's anomie. I think it's reality. Man has to be made for something more important than merely getting to heaven, Jason. Something more worthy than that. I mean, if we were made only for that, only to spend our lifetimes picking and prying at our consciences, it hardly seems worth it, does it?''

I saw her working away at the puzzle of that thought and wondered if this was why Jacob had loved her. She was so intent on life, so frequently disappointed and yet so intent.

"What do you think?" She looked to me for help.

The best I could do was to get her off the subject. I talked to her about getting up a dinner party at a restaurant with a couple of friends of mine (I was thinking of Nellie and her old friend, Willamae Belling). I made up an outrageous tale of love and piracy to do with the card table. I set myself out to be amusing, and when she laughed, I considered it a job well done. She might be right about the ultimate purpose of human life, but today wasn't the time to go fretting over it. It was too close to home.

All of which led me to wonder how much of what we did in our day-to-day lives was simply to distract us from certain thoughts that were uncomfortably close. Age and death, pain and betrayal, love and all the consequences thereof. Maybe football, fishing, grand opera, and all the fruits of the worlds' detective story authors are just buoys to keep us from drowning in our ancient fears.

Cecily intended to stay in Denver Thursday night. Grace and I were to meet her at the Brown Palace Hotel, in her suite, no less, at six o'clock.

We were there, on time. She'd thoughtfully laid in a tray of drinkables and a bowl of nuts.

I introduced Grace. We got through the small talk and the obligatory chat while drinks were fixed and we all sat down in comfortable chairs at a table by the window.

"I took a suite because I wanted a private place to tell you this," she said. "And I don't like talking in hotel bedrooms. Conversations in hotel bedrooms always seem illicit to me. Less than truthful."

"You have something true and licit to tell us," I said, trying to jolly her along. Cecily had the air of a woman who doesn't want to say anything, but has decided she must.

She sighed and gritted her teeth, really ground them together, making a gravelly noise. "First thing I have to tell you is that Herby Fixe got this same information out of me some years ago. I don't remember exactly what year. It was maybe '79 or '80."

"Why did you tell Herby?" I asked her.

"He came to me and told me he was Simonetta's husband. I'd never heard of him before, but he was plausible. He said Simonetta had told him she'd taken this child. He convinced me he had to know what had happened to the child, because she was having a mental breakdown and her doctors needed to know the facts in order to treat her effectively. Anyone who had ever known Simonetta would probably have believed that. She was constantly on the verge of breakdown!"

"And you knew what had really happened?"

"Hell, yes, I knew."

"So you told Herby."

"I thought he had a reason to know," she said angrily.

Grace intervened. "Well, he did. But it wasn't the reason you thought, Ms. Stephens. Suppose you tell us what you told Herby Fixe."

Cecily stirred the ice in her drink with her finger. I could see the muscle in her jaw jumping.

"I should probably have a lawyer here."

"You certainly can have a lawyer if you wish," said Grace, starting to stand up.

"Oh, no, no," Cecily waved her down. "No. If I'm guilty, I'm guilty, damn it. I've carried this around long enough!" She sighed. "Let me tell it my way, though, all right? I'd like you to understand what . . . what I was like when this happened."

I remembered Myra's report on what she'd been like—determined upon holiness. I kept my mouth shut.

"I was young," she said defensively. "I thought most of the world's problems were caused by people who refused to do good. I thought doing good was simply a matter of following the rules or following your conscience. I hadn't a clue how unreliable either one of those can be." She stopped and chewed on a fragment of ice for a while before she could go on.

"I was home from college on spring break. This was in '53. Yaggie Costermyer, she was one of the neighbors, had been in parochial school with me, and both of us knew Simmy. I won't say she was in school with us, because she wasn't but we knew who she was and what her problems were. I was very much into being . . . good at the time. Part of that included being *understanding* where Simmy was concerned."

She went silent again. I squeezed my fists and tried to be patient. Grace gave me a warning look, so I stared out the window and counted cars passing the traffic light down the street.

"All right, so on this particular afternoon, I was home. Simmy came home in a cab, then went up and down the street having hysterics because her mom was away and their house was locked. When she got to Yaggie, Yaggie suggested she come over and see me. Yaggie was being . . . well, you'd have to know her. She doesn't take anyone very seriously and she was needling me, putting me on the spot.

"So, anyhow, here came Yaggie, leading Simonetta by the hand, with Simonetta blubbering and yelling. I invited Simmy in, told her she could stay with me until her mom came home. Then, when she calmed down a bit, she told me she'd taken this baby."

"She had him with her?" I asked, confused.

"No. No. She didn't. She said she had him hidden. Only he was hurt, and she'd given him pills to make him sleep, and she couldn't wake him up. I thought she'd killed some kid, I really honest to God did."

"What did you do?"

"I told her I'd drive her to wherever the baby was, and we'd get him, and if he needed a doctor, we'd take him to the doctor. She practically screamed the house down, yelling that we couldn't take him anyplace, yelling that his father would find out, and then he'd kill the baby, yelling that he'd already tried to kill the baby."

"Did you believe that?" Grace asked.

Cecily got up, moved about restlessly, sat down again. "You've got to . . . you've got to understand this was almost forty years ago and I was only twenty. I didn't know much. However, I *did* know who she was talking about. She worked for Nello Leone's son. Nello Leone was in the papers all the time. He was a crime boss. He was into gambling and beating up on people. Everyone knew he had people killed, only nobody could prove anything. To a kid like me, brought up the way I was, he was the devil incarnate. So, yes, I sort of believed it. A kid like me . . . I could believe anything evil about him or his family. I think anybody could have."

"Why was the baby in danger?" I asked.

"I couldn't really get anything sensible out of Simmy. She said the baby was like Jesus. She said something about how he wouldn't get sick. She said his father hated the birthmark. She said she'd fixed the birthmark, but she was still afraid Nimo would kill him."

"So what happened?" asked Grace.

"So, we got in the car and went over to the Leone place, where Simmy had lived, in through the alley, to the garage. She'd been yelling about a *baby*, and I was expecting a *baby*, but she went into some kind of tool room in the garage and brought out this little kid! God . . . !"

"He was asleep?"

"Thank God, yes. She'd fixed his birthmark okay. She'd burned it off. Pushed his head down on a stove and burned it off him! The whole back of his head. God!"

I wasn't ready for this. I hadn't had a clue. The world shivered and stood still. A kind of crystalline structure formed itself around the universe, shattering light, making sound reverberate in strange ways. It was as though I had taken a drug and become suspended, outside the earth.

I said something. I must have said something, because she answered.

"She said the birthmark had been on the back of his head, but all I could see was this horrible burn. He wasn't a baby at all, he was at least two and a half, three years old. . . ."

Grace looked at me, her eyes very wide. She put her hand over mine, willing me to be still. She needn't have bothered. I couldn't have moved.

"What did you do?" she asked Cecily.

"I took the kid. Of course, I took the kid. So far as I was concerned, I was the Good Samaritan! I took him to my place. Nobody was home. My folks were down in Arizona with my gram, she was in the hospital. I bandaged the little guy's head."

"You didn't call a doctor," I said from somewhere distant.

"I couldn't call a doctor! No doctor was going to take this kid without wanting to know who his parents were, how this had happened to him! If I told them, they'd give him back to his father and he'd be killed. I *believed* Simmy when she told me that. I kept him. I got some sulfa ointment the doctor had prescribed when my dad burned his arm, and I put that on it. I used my mother's sleeping pills, quarters of ones, to keep him from screaming. I fed him. I went to the library and found a book on treating burns. I did what it said. All the time with Simmy running in and out of my house day and night, pulling at me, getting hysterical.

"Every day my folks called, wanting to know why I hadn't gone back to school, and I said I'd been sick, nothing serious, just felt too lousy to study. And then one day my mother called and said she and Dad were going to have to move to California right away because Dad had this new job, rush, rush. They said they were coming home just long enough to pack, and I'd probably want to stay at CU to finish the spring semester . . . ." her voice trailed off. She put her head in her hands and left it there.

"What?" prompted Grace.

"My mom was worried I'd take it badly, having to switch universities. Once they moved out of state, they'd be nonresidents, and they couldn't afford the nonresident fees. She was really worried about that. I remember, I almost got hysterical when she said how worried she was about that. Here she was thanking me for being understanding when all I wanted to do was escape from the mess I was in! I told her I'd already missed too much of the spring semester, and I'd go with them when they went."

She raised her head. "This . . . it all comes back. I was in such a panic the whole time. Well . . .

"There was this boy I'd known forever, we were good friends. He was living on his own for a year while his folks were in Canada, so when my folks came back, I got him to keep the little boy for me. Four or five times a day, even while my folks and I were packing and getting ready, I'd go over there to feed the little guy and take care of him. And then the night before we were supposed to leave, I picked him up and took him to the foundling home. I had it all planned. I'd looked it up. I'd even called around to be sure it was a nice place, not like in *Oliver Twist* or anything. I didn't tell Simmy where I was going. I didn't tell Simmy where I left him. I couldn't trust her . . ."

She went off into a gale of weeping, a forty-year-old tragedy being relived.

From somewhere, I heard my own voice. "Evidently Simmy believed you'd taken the child with you."

"That's what I wanted her to think. I didn't want her to know where I'd left him, but, God, I couldn't take him. My family wouldn't have stood still for that, not for a minute. . . ."

Things whirled. Grace said, "Jason, would you like to wait outside? In the car."

I said yes, but I didn't wait in the car. I went home. Later, Grace arrived, so I guess she figured out where I'd gone.

"Jason," she said. "Jason."

"I'm here," I said.

"I know it's a shock," she said. "But you've wanted to know for ages . . ."

"Yeah," I said in a blank, careless voice. "Sure. Not exactly the background one might have hoped, but who cares."

"Oh, come on, Jason. Jacob always told you that things like this didn't matter. So your dad and granddad were little mafiosi. That's not so bad. . . ."

"Not so bad," I agreed calmly from some distant part of myself, thinking I really meant it because long ago I'd come to terms with the possibility that Ma or Pa might have been a murderer or a traitor or a pimp or drug dealer or whatever. Jacob had said it didn't matter, so it didn't matter. The thing that *mattered* was the one thing he'd never thought of, and while Grace sat there staring at me, her eyes wide and a little scared, I started to laugh about that little oversight and couldn't stop.

It was a while before I could tell her why I was laughing. Nello had had Huntington's disease. So had Nimo. Which meant there was an even chance I had it too.

Friday, I left a note for Mark telling him I wasn't feeling well and shut myself into my apartment. There's a seldom-used door across the hall outside Mark's office, one Agatha got me to put in when we first moved in, to separate home from shop and give her some privacy. It had been standing open for years. I closed and locked it and the one between my living room and my office. I took my private phone off the hook. Not many people knew that number, but I didn't want to hear from any of them. I wasn't thinking. It was impossible to think. I wasn't being panicky or scared or fearing death or any of that, I was just in a void, a vacuum, where nothing connected. I lay on the bed, staring at the ceiling, thinking nothing.

I'd been very ill once in my life that I remembered—not counting injuries now and then—and this was like being ill again. My body was disconnected from my mind, occupied by some other force. My mind was on standby power only, the little red light flickered dimly and I didn't care. Bela whined, and I put him out of my bedroom and shut the door. I wanted silence to wrap around me like a cocoon, shutting me away from life and all living things.

Some time later, Grace found the doors locked, went around back and came up the elevator, came into my room and hit me in the face with a cold, wet towel. "Up," she demanded. She got me into the kitchen, put a mug of coffee in my hand, insisted I drink it, kept poking me and jabbing me and not letting me be still.

"There's a test," she said. "I called around and found some information about this thing. There's a test. You can find out if you have it."

"I don't want to know," I said.

"Don't be a goddamn coward." Her nose was inches from my own. "Anything is better than this."

Anything else meant I'd have to do something. I didn't want to do anything.

Grace wouldn't leave me alone. She fetched Mark, sat him down beside me and told him all about it, so he'd start chivying me too. "How many people do we need to get on this?" she asked me. "You want me to call Olivia? She's your grandma, Jason, you want me to call her? You want me to call Lycia? Angela's sister? She's your aunt. You've got cousins now, Jason. You want me to call them?"

As I recall, I started to cry and couldn't stop. It was Sunday before I remember being part of the world again. Sunday. She must have been working on me for two days.

I was sitting at the kitchen table with Grace, resting a stubbly chin in one hand.

"There's a test?" I asked her.

She patted me and said yes, there was a man at the medical school who knew all about it, and so on and so forth.

"You didn't tell anybody, did you?" I asked.

"Like who?"

"Olivia. Lycia Foret. You didn't . . ."

"No. No, Jason. Jacob didn't tell them, and he probably had reasons. Even though he had to have known."

"How do you figure that?" I asked dully.

"Come on!" she demanded. "Wake up!"

I tried to focus.

"Herby tried to blackmail Simmy's papa and got nowhere. He knew it had to be Simmy who'd taken the little boy after Angela was killed, but at the time he kept quiet about it because he didn't want Nimo to know he hadn't done what he said. Like that huntsman in 'Snow White.' Yeah, he said, I killed the kid. Sure I killed the kid, here's the kid's heart. Right? He didn't dare make anything of it so long as Nimo was around.

"But, after Nimo was in the hospital, Herby got Simmy to confess. He was sly, she wasn't too bright, so he got it out of her. But, he didn't know where the child was—*where you were*—any more than she did. Simmy told him Cecily took the child, so he traced Cecily. That's how he found out Simmy had burned off the birthmark and Cecily had left you at the Home, right? Now, if he knew that much, how hard would it have been to find out where you went from there? Hmm? Herby could've bribed some employee at the Home. He could've burglarized the records. Whatever he did, he found out. So then Herby puts the bite on Jacob. He says to Jacob, 'Either you pay me or I'll tell the Leones that Jason Lynx is really Michael Leone, and when I do, they'll kill him.' "

"Jacob knew I was Olivia's grandson?"

"I doubt he knew when he took you in. How would he have? Olivia didn't know, how could he know? No, that was pure coincidence. But he knew once Herby told him."

"Jacob didn't tell Olivia."

"Of course he didn't, for two reasons. One, it would have terrified Olivia; and two, he couldn't take the chance with your life."

"That was about the time Agatha and I were married," I mused, awed at everything that had gone on below the surface of the lives around me.

"Whatever," she said impatiently. "Jacob believed there was still a threat to your life, and maybe that was true."

I shook my head. "Grace, look, we've tried and tried to

find a motive here. It's no good. Neither of us really believes that Nimo Leone wanted to kill his son—me—because I had a birthmark! We're arguing backward. Because he wanted to kill me, we say there must have been a reason. But what was it?''

She nodded agreement. ''Maybe it was about the disease, Jason. Maybe he didn't want you to grow up and have to face this thing. Or, Nimo's superstitious, right? So he has this kid with the birthmark, and then *after that* he finds out his daddy has this disease. So, maybe he decides you've brought a hex on the family. I can imagine his wanting to stop it. Listen, there was a hot play back then about this kid that was born evil. *The Bad Seed*. They made it into a movie later. I've seen it on TV. I mean, it's a superstition some people have, that evil can be born in somebody. Look at that movie, *Omen*, and all those Damien thises and thats.''

I shook my head stubbornly. We were creating motives, making up stories. There was no basis for any of it.

''Never mind,'' she said, shaking me by the shoulders. ''It doesn't matter why! Just concentrate on finding out if you've got the damned disease. If you don't, then all this misery's for nothing. If you do, then you can decide what to do about it.''

''Herby should have killed me when I was three,'' I said, irrationally.

''Shut up,'' she said. ''He didn't. And you have Simmy to thank for that.''

She pushed me into the bathroom and put the electric razor in my hand. She asked me if I'd brushed my teeth. She got clothes out for me and helped me put them on. I felt like a toddler. Or an old, old man who'd been ill a long time.

Over the weekend, she talked on the phone, to Mark, mostly, and to her cop-shop. She'd taken time off, she said. Personal time. Emergency time.

It came to me that I was as bad as Ron, her brother. Doing whatever came easiest. Collapsing under the burden of life. Letting her do it all.

"I'm okay, Grace," I told her, making the effort. "Really."

"You sure?" she asked, staring at me through slitted eyes. "You sure, Jason?"

"I'm sure," I said, tugging at the edges of my life. It was like hauling in a wet sail, bringing heavy, unwieldy pieces of myself into reach. "You think it was Herby who sent those letters to me? Offering to sell me information about who I was?"

"Of course it was. He found out Jacob was sick, you were here running things, he figured maybe he could play both ends."

"He'd have had Jacob paying not to tell who I was, and me paying to know who I was." I laughed, without amusement. "Dorotea said he was slimy."

"How do you feel about finding out who your folks were?" she challenged me. "Really, Jason. You've got to tell me."

I shrugged.

"That's not good enough," she said stubbornly. "I mean, there's Nimo. A real slime ball, probably."

"Raised to be one," I said, quoting Jacob. "He might have been all right, raised by someone else. And his dad, likewise. How do we know? Look at Dorotea Chapman. She's got the same parents Carlos does. So, one brother's a jailbird and one's a lawyer."

Grace made a joke about there being less difference than one might suppose, and I actually managed to smile. Nimo being a criminal didn't bother me that much. Anybody could be taught to break the law. Rectitude, so Jacob had always said, was inculcated, not inherited. All babies are born lawless.

Despite my assurances, Grace didn't leave until Monday morning, when Mark arrived. By that time I was seated at my desk with the phone number of the man at the medical school in front of me. I dialed it at eight-thirty. His secretary told me the doctor usually arrived at nine. At nine-oh-two I called again. An appointment had just canceled, he could see me that morning. Maybe that was true. Maybe he heard the panic in my voice and made room for me.

I found the department of genetic diseases. I found the doctor's office at the end of a long corridor, an institutional space littered with computer terminals and piles of books and stacks of paper with holes down the edges. The doctor himself was insignificant-looking except for his eyes. They knew things. I told him I was adopted, that I'd recently found out my biological father had Huntington's disease.

"Ah," he said, frowning. "Do you know any members of your father's family? Do you have siblings? Does he? How about grandparents?"

I shook my head. "My father is dead. His father is dead, of this disease. If my father had any uncles or aunts, they are now dead. My father had a brother, but he is dead."

He frowned again. "Mr. Lynx, let me explain something to you. You obviously know this is a genetic disease or you wouldn't be here."

Since this was the department of genetic disease, it was a fair guess.

"We've made a lot of progress in recent years, not in curing the disease, we can't do that, but in finding out if people are carrying the gene."

"That's what I want to know," I said patiently.

"Let me explain, please. We don't know exactly what the gene looks like. When we test for it, we don't even look for the gene itself."

He saw my incomprehension.

"The gene for Huntington's disease is located down at the tip of chromosome number four. We know it's there, but we're not sure what it looks like. What we do know is that elsewhere on the chromosome, family members with the disease have a different DNA sequence from family members who do not have the disease. We call this other sequence a marker."

I still wasn't with him.

He said, "Let me try an analogy. There's a buried prehistoric village along a certain stretch of coast. You don't know where it is, but you do know that ninety-nine times out of a hundred, prehistoric villages of this kind were accompanied by shell middens on the shore, places where the village people threw away their clam and oyster shells. You with me so far?''

I said I was, impatiently, wondering what the hell he was getting at.

''Villages are buried, but shell midden aren't. So you look for the midden.''

''And that's a marker.''

''That's a marker. If we have access to your relatives we make DNA sequence maps of a long section at the end of chromosome four. We do maps of your kinfolk who have the disease, and maps of your kinfolk who don't. We run these maps through computers that are programmed to look for identical sequences in the people who have the disease and, we hope, a different sequence in people who do not. We find the sequence that's the marker in your family, and then we see if you're carrying that marker. If you don't carry the marker, you're probably not carrying the disease.'' He looked pleased with this explanation.

I said, ''But you can do this only if there are enough relatives to test.''

His face fell. ''Yes. Only if there are enough relatives with and without the disease for us to find the marker that works in your family.''

We stared at one another for a long time.

''It's only a matter of time until we'll be able to identify the gene itself,'' he said, rather weakly. ''A couple of years, maybe.''

''A long time to live in doubt,'' I said.

''Some people prefer not to know,'' he remarked, holding the idea toward me, like a toy for a kid, a distraction.

''Some people do not live well with uncertainty.'' What I was actually thinking about was my son, Jerry. He had never lived to grow up. Perhaps there had been good reason for that. I was ashamed of the banality of the thought. I remembered Jacob telling me that any God who could create this universe wouldn't stoop to being purposefully sadistic with man. "Omniscience," he'd said, "is incompatible with horseshit of that kind."

No, I told myself sternly. Jerry had not died young to prevent his dying later. This disease was not why he had died. This was not *why* anything. It was not *because* of anything. It simply *was*, and it was up to me to handle it. One way or another. But thank God I had no family to worry over.

"You've shown no signs of the disease, right?"

"Not that I know of," I said.

"You'd know. You're, what? Thirty-six, thirty-seven?"

"Forty," I said. "Almost forty-one." Then I laughed. I didn't know that! I assumed that. "I'm not sure, doctor. I've only recently found out about my biological parents. Now that I know, I can get a copy of my birth certificate. Then I'll know exactly how old I am."

He asked a few questions about my childhood, which I answered absently.

"You might be older than forty, but surely you can't be younger. The people at the Home thought you were three when you were abandoned, right? It's fairly easy to tell the difference between a two-year-old and a three-year-old. You might have regressed a little, because of the trauma, but the reverse wouldn't have been true. You might have acted younger, but not older. If you've shown no symptoms by now, I'd consider that an extremely good sign. Onset of the disease varies, but it often happens in the twenties and thirties."

"Or waits until the forties and fifties," I said. "I think it did with my father and grandfather."

As a hopeful sign, being healthy now wasn't hopeful enough.

I promised to stay in touch, to keep *au courant* with all the wonderful progress they were making. He gave me some Xeroxes of articles about the disease. I didn't go home. There were people at home who knew all about this and I didn't want to be with them.

Instead I went to the library where I could sit at a table and read and no one would bother me. The articles I'd been given were mostly about current research, technical and dry and full of what I thought of as cumbersome evasions about the possible side effects of counseling or treatment. Sometimes I think the human body is only a battlefield to doctors. They fight disease across it, paying no attention to the person inside. I left the articles lying on the table when I went to ask the librarian if there was a list of associations or societies set up to deal with various diseases. She had a whole book full of associations and groups, charities and educational institutions. I found a National Huntington's Disease Society of America in New York City. I called them from a pay phone down the block, and they said they'd send me materials written for the layman. The man I spoke with also came up with the phone number of a "support group" in Denver for patients and families of patients. He said absolutely nothing about people who had no idea whether they would ever be patients or not.

I thought of going out to the department of vital statistics to get a birth certificate, but it was too late in the day. Mark and Eugenia would have gone home by now, and Bela and Schnitz would be hungry, wondering where I was.

Bela and Schnitz didn't know anything about genetic diseases. Whatever I did, they would not look at me with pity in their eyes. I went home to them.

seven

DURING THE NIGHT, I came to a decision. I would sell Jason Lynx Interiors to Mark. He had plenty of money to buy it. He was as qualified as I to run it, more qualified, really, since decor is what he really wanted to do. I would set up the sale the way Jacob had, payments every month, enough to support me, to let me travel a little, see the world—at least those parts of it one could see without meeting a bullet or bomb in the process. Maybe I'd go to some places formerly behind the iron curtain, places people couldn't visit easily until the last few years. I could go to museums, add to my art education. Then, if I was permitted the time to live normally, I'd be more qualified for the kind of job I'd once hoped for.

There was no longer any question of marriage, not to anyone. The sooner I went away and let Grace find someone else, the better. If I didn't develop the disease, I'd hate myself for having left her, but if I did, I'd never forgive myself for having stayed. The next few years were the years in which she should have children, if she was going to, and I wouldn't father a child who might inherit this tragedy.

I told myself it was my decision to make. I could imagine Grace doing something fine and sacrificial, and that couldn't be allowed to happen. Olivia had sacrificed herself for her parents' sake. Jacob for Olivia's sake. Angela had done it for her father. Daniel for Angela. Even Cecily had made sacrifices for poor Simonetta, and carried the guilt for years. I wouldn't let Grace repeat the pattern.

Though, I reminded myself with a certain wry honesty,

she said she wasn't in love with me and might not be inclined to do any such thing. Continuing the attempt at honesty, I admitted I didn't want to know if that was true. The doctor had said some people preferred not to know. About Grace's feelings in this matter, I agreed. I preferred not to know. I was going to say goodbye to her, but not just yet. I had to work my way into it. Little by little.

When I saw her next—it was Wednesday evening—I told her there was no test they could do for me. She looked shaken.

"Nothing they can do?" she whispered.

"Nothing," I said in the calm tone I'd been practicing all day. "I'm not sure I'd have had the test done even if they could have done it."

"Why not?"

"The doctor was very frank. Some people get along better not knowing for sure. If they know in advance, they kind of give up on life."

She dropped her eyes, and I knew she'd been thinking about something else. Children, maybe. She needed to know for her own sake if I had the damn thing, and there was no way I could tell her.

"Grace, hey," I said. "What I'd really like is for us both just to relax for a few weeks. Let time go by. Let me get used to the idea. Then we'll talk."

She hugged me and left me alone to consider a small dilemma I'd come up with. Did I tell my grandmother anything? Olivia, my grandmother: did I, for example, make up a story abut Angela's son being alive and well in Sorrento or someplace? I could explain that he didn't know who he was, and therefore she could not write to him, or see him, but the knowledge he was safe and well would be a relief to her. I had no moral compunctions about telling her a new lie to replace the old one. My lie would at least be more comforting than Nimo's lie had been.

I did not consider telling her the truth.

I did decide to get a birth certificate. If I was going to travel, I'd need a passport, so why not get one with my own birth certificate? The legalities didn't even occur to me: the problem that would arise with a change of name from the one I'd been using, the different dates of birth. I just trotted over to the Department of Health, Bureau of Vital Statistics, paid my money, gave the name of my parents and the year of birth—"Nineteen fifty, I think. There's been some confusion in the family, and it could have been the year before or after. . . ."

It was nineteen fifty. December 1. I went back home and sat down at my desk to look at this document. Mother's name, Angela Leone, née Desquintas y Alvarez. Father's name, Geronimo R. Leone. Mother's birthdate, March 5, 1932. Place of birth. Attending physician. Date of marriage, March 25, 1950. She had been just eighteen years old.

I found myself counting weeks. Angela had gotten pregnant on her honeymoon, and I felt a wave of pity. She'd certainly been given no time to adjust to anything. Not to her husband, not to being a mother, not to anything. My poor mother. I tried the word on, *mother*, to see how it sounded, but it didn't work for me. Angela was, and forever would be, only a girl, less than half the age I was now. If I remembered her—and perhaps I did remember her, for she looked a lot like Lycia, and I'd always thought Lycia looked familiar—it was as a girl. Forever young. Never to be white-haired. Never to be the baker of cookies, the helper with homework. Only the girl in love who died tragically soon.

I put off making any decisions about Olivia. I was desperately resolved on keeping everything very loose and very calm. I went on automatic pilot. Bela and I went back to our pleasant routine of running twice every day. Schnitz got his fur rumpled regularly. I paid scrupulous attention to what Mark and Eugenia were doing in order not to think about what I was doing. Of course, I woke up a lot in the middle of the night with my heart pounding, terrified. It usually took an hour or two to get back to sleep. I drank more than usual. I tried not to think, not to feel. I kept going. March went out, the days warmed, crocuses stuck their heads up beside the portico out front. Blue crocuses and some little yellow cup-shaped flower with a green fringe around it.

It was a Wednesday I first saw the old guy. A derelict, really, a typical skid row type in layers of clothes. He was considerably the worse for the contents of the paper bag he kept tipping to his mouth. He was at the corner when Bela loped by with me staggering in pursuit. A stagger was the best I could manage because I hadn't totally recovered from the fall I'd taken the day Grace had saved my life. I'd twisted an already injured leg, and it was still stiff and painful. So, as I staggered by I saw the old guy and he saw me, stared at me in fact.

The same man was there when we returned.

He was there again Thursday afternoon. And Friday evening, about suppertime, when Bela and I returned from our run. This time he stepped out on the sidewalk, blocking my way.

"You're Jason Lynx," he said.

I stepped back from the miasma he was exhaling and admitted I was.

"I have some letters which refer to you by name," he said with owl-eyed, professorial dignity.

All I could think of was that he'd been pilfering mail, reaching through mail slots, maybe.

He must have read my mind. "I found them," he said. "In the course of my du . . . duties. With the Salva . . . Salva . . . shun Army." His careful diction was starting to slip.

It still didn't connect.

"Inna pocket of this coat," he cried desperately. "We took all the stuff outa this house on Zuni Street, an they was inna pocket!"

The quarter dropped. Simonetta's house. Dorotea had had the house cleaned out for her brother. "Letters with my name in them?" I asked. "Did you want to give them to me?"

"Mushisit worth to ya?" he asked, giving up all pretense at enunciation.

I shrugged. "I don't know. What do they say?"

He shook his head drunkenly. "Not 'less you pay me."

"Okay. Who're they to? Who're they from?"

"One's to you," he said. "Thas who."

I fished out a ten. He reached, then craftily said it wasn't enough. We settled for twenty. He shambled away with his money, and I walked along the sidewalk examining the first of the two wrinkled documents he'd handed me. It was completely familiar in appearance. I'd seen several almost exactly like it; cut-out letters, glued on a sheet of typing paper.

"Jason Lynx. You need to know who you are because somebody wants to kill you. Ten thousand buys it. Put an ad in the personals, say J.L. wants to know."

Found in Herby's jacket, where I'd have found it myself if I'd looked. Where Herby had left it last winter, intending to mail it, but not getting around to it before he died.

Bela whuffed at me. I looked up from the paper I was holding, totally at a loss.

Before he died?

Why would anyone have wanted to kill me *before* Herby died? Gabe had wanted to kill me only since Simonetta was killed, only because I was a witness, but he hadn't wanted to kill me last November. Had he?

The idea was fairly chilling. Since Gabe's car had crashed, I hadn't worried about taking precautions. Everyone said he had no reason to come after me now; *I* thought he had no reason to come after me now. If he did, Bela and I had been inviting assassination each day during our slow circuits of the park. Preoccupied with this thought, I stuffed the papers in my pocket and went around to the back of the house in a considerably chastened mood. I approached the back door. Bela hung back. He whuffed at me, sniffing along the fence, then growled at the back door. I reached for my key with one hand and the knob with the other. The knob gave. Unlocked.

Bela went on growling.

The light over the back door was sufficient only to throw a dim glow on the steps. It was not designed to illuminate the lock, a fact which had annoyed me in the past. I leaned down and peered at it from four inches away. Maybe there were scratches. Of course, I could have made them myself, fumbling with my key in the inadequate light. On the other hand . . . I hadn't left the door open.

If someone was in there, where would he be?

I slipped through the door, into the laundry room which opens at the left into the old kitchen, used for showing country-style furniture, mostly Shaker stuff. To my right was the small storeroom, the back staircase, and the slow, cumbersome elevator Jacob had installed. Bela slid in behind me and faced the kitchen, rumbling very softly. Both stairs and elevator go from the basement all the way to the attic. I went down the basement stairs in the dark, Bela beside me, nose down. He was silent. He didn't smell anyone on the stairs.

The square piano was in the storeroom next to the furnace with the holster still taped to the inside of the leg where I'd left my Smith and Wesson thirty-eight automatic, model 52, a target gun, one no longer made. I'd left it with one round in the chamber and six in the clip. When I released the safety and cocked the pistol, the soft double click seemed as loud as a gunshot. I held my breath, waiting. Bela remained quiet.

Though there'd been a time when I'd known the thirty-eight very well indeed, I had not fired it in years. Relying on reflexes from ten years before was probably not a good idea. I told myself not to take any stupid chances. I did not tell myself the sensible thing: to call the police. Later I wondered why. At the time it seemed self-evident. Somebody was after me. It was up to me to stop him.

A flashlight from the furnace room enabled me to find my way to the front stairs without tripping over anything, including Bela. A lighted Exit glowed over each door, as required by the fire code, but they give very little light. The front stair leads to a service corridor at the rear of the ground floor hallway. From that service corridor, doors open in every direction: west into the old pantry by the kitchen, north into what was the dining room, south into the main showroom at the front of the house.

I stood on the top step, my forehead against the door, silently counting the possible hiding places on the ground floor, including the north front parlor and the south back parlor and the two toilets I'd put in, one for staff, one for customers, plus a number of nooks and crannies and several capacious closets. Normally we keep the closets locked, but an intruder who could pick locks might be almost anywhere.

With the flash off, I opened the stairway door very slowly. The exit sign threw a dim greenish glow on a shadow crouched before the pantry door. The shadow turned two glowing circles on me. Schnitz, his eyes reflecting the dim light like two moons. He turned back to the door, crouched once more.

Beside me Bela trembled. I laid my hand on his shoulder and felt the silent growl.

My intruder was somewhere behind that door, in the pantry, or the dining room to the right of the pantry, or back in the kitchen. Maybe he'd been waiting for me to come past him from the back of the house. Probably.

There were a number of ways I could get into the pantry and dining room. I could come at him from almost any side, if I knew exactly where he was. Which I didn't. Besides, he could be somewhere else by the time I got there and would be if he'd heard me come in.

I said "heel" to Bela in my fiercest whisper, stepped forward, scooped Schnitz off the floor, and went to my left, into the main showroom, continuing the circle around into the front hall and up the curving front stairs, quickly and quietly. Bela came beside, still rumbling softly. I was counting on his letting me know if there was anyone ahead of us, but he didn't bark.

We went through the door between my office and my living room. I locked it and bolted it. Out in the hall, I closed the seldom-used door across the hall and bolted that as well. The intruder might pick a lock, but he could not pick the bolts. I put Schnitz in the bathroom, shut the door on him and went to the top of the back stairs. Until then, I'd been as quiet as possible. Now I talked loudly to Bela. "You'll be a good dog and go out if you need to go, won't you, Bela boy. Yes, he's a good dog. He'll go downstairs if he needs to go, won't he. Sure he will."

At the top of the stairs, quite loudly, I told Bela to lie down and stay. I wanted the intruder to hear me moving around, but I didn't want him sneaking up on me. Bela would make sure of that. We'd been gone almost an hour on our run to the park. Whoever was in the house, assuming he had watched us leave, had had plenty of time to get the layout of the place. Whoever was in the house had no doubt watched us for several days before he came in. He would know all the ways there were to get at me.

Schnitz yowled in complaint, and I took him a bowl of food. He could drink from the toilet bowl and usually did. I left him shut in. After a while he shut up.

Meantime, I moved around, rattling pans, shifting this and that, making a pot of coffee—the person hiding downstairs would smell that—taking up time. It had been almost seven when we'd come home. It was now almost eight. A little early for bedtime. Still, I'd been under stress lately. Early bedtime might be believable. Believable or not, I couldn't continue the charade for much longer. My stomach was doing back flips.

When as much time had elapsed as I had patience for, I took Bela down the hall to the front bedroom, the one Agatha and I used to share, and put him inside. "Lie down," I whispered sternly, then, "Stay!"

He looked at me reproachfully, but he lay down and did not move when I closed the door on him. That would keep him safe, as well as Schnitz. One final thing. I took both phones, business and private, off the hook. Nothing like an unexpected phone call to distract people's attention from the work at hand!

The door to the back stairs is across the hall from my bedroom. I pushed it almost closed. Another of the ubiquitous exit signs glowed greenly above the door, and I unscrewed the bulb, leaving only the dim light coming from the tall, narrow window at the end of the hall. I went into my bedroom and pulled all the curtains tightly shut.

My bed is on the same wall as the door, which means it can't be seen very well from the hall. My favorite leather wing chair and its hassock are near the north window, across from the door. Once my eyes adapted to the dim light, I could barely make out the stairway door in the streetlight filtering through the hall window. If someone pushed open the door and came into the upstairs hall, I could see him, but he could not see me. So I believed.

I've never liked ceiling fixtures in bedrooms. Lamplight is warm and intimate. Ceiling fixtures are cold and remote. So, my bedside lamp and the floor lamp beside the chair are on a three-way circuit, one wall switch beside the door, one switch on the bedside table, one beside my chair. I unplugged the floor lamp before I sat down in the chair and took off my shoes, dropping them one by one. Then I waited. Every ten minutes, the furnace cleared its throat. People went by on the street and in the alley. The luminous dial of my watch said nine-thirty. I stayed where I was.

The first sound came a quarter of an hour later, from the door across the hall, the second one I'd bolted. Not much of a sound, really. A creaking. As though someone had leaned on it, hard. Then the same thing from the door between the living room and my office. That took care of his coming at me from the front of the house.

Would the fact the doors were bolted scare him off? Probably not. So far as he knew, I bolted them every night. But he'd heard me telling Bela to go downstairs if he needed to go, which implied a way left open back here. I'd have been more frightened of the dog, myself. Though he could have made plans to deal with the dog. A silenced gun, perhaps. The idea infuriated me.

I put my left hand on the light switch beside the chair, shifting slightly and breathing slowly, deeply. Anyone coming up the back stairs would expect to hear someone breathing slowly, deeply. As though asleep.

On the back stairs, the fourth step from the top creaks. I heard it sooner than I'd thought I would. The barest whisper.

The door opened. I saw the shadow emerge. It paused there. I went on breathing. The shadow came to the door. From my position in the chair, I waited until it was inside, beside the bed, before I pressed the switch and said, "Drop it."

He didn't drop it. He swung it toward me, wide-eyed, panicky in the sudden light. I saw the gun come around toward me, saw his black torso silhouetted against the bedside light, and my hand took over. I didn't even think about it. He was a target, that was all. The old reflexes I hadn't wanted to count on did it for me. I shot him. He fired at me then, a whisper, but the bullet came nowhere near me.

"Why?" I cried at him, as I crouched over him, trying to stop the bleeding. "Why!"

He only looked at me stupidly. I thought he tried to speak, so I leaned forward, but he was trying to spit, instead. His mouth was full of blood. "You bastard," he said. By the time I got back from the phone, he was dead.

One does not need a license to own a gun. One needs to be licensed to carry a handgun, but I had not been carrying one. I had merely kept one in my house. I had heard an intruder. The intruder had entered my house and come into my bedroom with the intent of doing grave bodily harm. No one, least of all me, doubted that, especially since he was quickly identified as Gabe Leone. A rather battered, bruised, and bandaged Gabe Leone, probably injured when he jumped from his car before it crashed, and only recently recovered enough to come hunting me. So the police theorized while I was being questioned briefly. They took my good old S&W for evidence, then both the body and the police were gone.

There was blood on the bedroom floor, less of it than one might expect, most of it on the braided rug beside the bed. I took the rug down to the laundry room and put it to soak in the tub. I got most of the rest of it up with wet paper towels. I let Schnitz out of the bathroom, then opened the door to the front bedroom and joined Bela on the bed.

I didn't start shaking until later, until I was stretched out in the bed, warm under the blankets, with the tension slowly draining away. Then I thought how simple it would have been if I'd just let him kill me. All my troubles would have been

over. All these terrified nighttime panics I'd been having. All
these attacks of horror at the thought of what might happen
in the future. All over. And I hadn't even considered it. In-
stinct had taken over. Preserve thyself, said all the little cells.
Well, I had.

I prodded my conscience, seeing if I felt guilty over killing
my uncle Gabe. Not much. I'd warned him; I'd given him a
chance to drop the gun; I'd intended to turn him over to the
police. He'd been the one who'd tried to kill me, and though
I would have given anything to know why, I didn't figure it
was my responsibility to grieve over him. The Leones had
not behaved in what I'd call a familial manner toward me.

Morning found me hollow-eyed, not precisely sleepless
but not rested, either. I got up early, made coffee, cleaned
up the bathroom where Schnitz had demonstrated his irritation the night before by tearing a whole roll of paper into
confetti, fed him and Bela, gradually worked myself up to
going through the motions in a kind of weary haze, where
nothing quite connected.

Still, I was shaved and dressed when I went down for the
morning paper. It was about a quarter to eight. I arrived at
the front door coincident with a shiny older car driving up in
front. It slowed, backed up, and parked at the curb as I
searched the portico for the paper boy's newest hiding place.
A chauffeur got out and called to me, "Mr. Lynx?"

I stopped where I was. "Yes?"

He came around the car and opened the near door. First
out were two canes, the kind with braces that go around the
arms. Next out was a little woman who took the canes and
began a slow progress toward my front door. Her driver
walked beside her, up the short flight of stairs to the portico.
She moved slowly, carefully, obviously in pain. When she
was beside me, she fixed me with a birdlike stare. "Jason
Lynx?"

"Yes, ma'am," I said. "What may I do for you?"

"I rather thought you wanted me to do something for you,
young man. You left a message at my home. I'm Jenny Mattingly. Angela's friend."

My mouth dropped open. I didn't plan what came out, it just emerged. "Jenny," I said. "I'm Angela's son."

She made a little cry and sagged on the canes. The driver caught her and supported her weight while I unlocked the front door. I didn't try to take her upstairs, not even in the slow old elevator at the back. We went into the showroom, where the chauffeur seated her on the nearest sofa, hovered around until she waved him away, then went back to the hall. I could feel him out there, within earshot.

"Ma'am, may I offer you some coffee? It's fresh."

She thought that would be nice. I took the stairs three at a time, my leg screaming protest, though I came down more sedately, bearing a tray. I'd brought a cup for the driver, too, and he nodded his conditional thanks at me.

I put the tray on the table before her and poured us each a cup. "I'd forgotten I'd called you," I said. "Olivia showed me your picture. I should have recognized you."

"I've been away. I go to this clinic in Mexico sometimes, for my arthritis. I'm so sorry I was away when you called. I got back yesterday, late yesterday. I got your message, but it was so late, and I was tired. Then I heard your name on the news this morning. That man, trying to kill you. I said to Bentley, I have to go see Jason Lynx. I know about the Leone family. I have to go see him right now. Bentley thought I was being hysterical, I'm afraid. And then, when you told me! I thought you were dead. I thought Angela's son was dead."

I shook my head at her. "Not yet, no. I think there was some confusion about that. I get the distinct impression I was supposed to be dead."

"You were," she said. "Oh, yes, you were. I heard it all. I knew all about it."

"Why don't you tell *me* about it?" I asked her.

She reached out to take my hand, as though she couldn't believe I was there. "Angela was my dearest friend," she said.

"I know. Angela's mother told me."

"I mean, really my friend. I've never had another like her,

not in all the years since. Did you know about her marriage?''

''Her mother told me.''

''It was so foolish and tragic. I told her not to do it. I told her she and Daniel should run away, anything would be better than marrying that man. But that priest talked to her and talked to her—about her duty, about her religion. Any other priest in Denver would have told her not to do it, but that man! He was like that Russian, that Rasputin! He hypnotized her. We all knew what he was like! Machismo, isn't that it? Proud as the devil. . . .

''Poor Angela. She was as white as her dress the day she was married. I stood up with her because she said she couldn't go through with it otherwise. There were only a dozen people there. Her parents. His mother. Angela didn't even *know* him. It didn't get any better after she got to know him. I used to go over there every chance I got. She'd phone me and beg me to come. He didn't like for her to go out. If she went out, one of his goons went with her. That's what she called them, goons. I don't know what you'd call them now.''

She meant Herby, or Carlos, or men like them. ''I'd still call them goons,'' I said.

''Angela got pregnant right away. Really, that was good, because she told him he had to leave her alone then. And he didn't care if I was there with her. He had this retarded maid who watched her all the time, a great, huge woman.''

''Simonetta,'' I said.

''I guess. Simmy. That's right. Well, Angela had the baby, and he was beautiful, except for that blotch, but when his hair grew in, it hardly showed. The way Nimo took on, you'd have thought he was deformed. He kept howling about the evil eye, and how bad luck was settling on the family. . . . Listen to me. I keep saying *he* and *him*. Not *you*. It was *you*, when you were a baby. . . .''

She sat back, shaking her head and saying it over and over. ''You. You as a baby.''

I patted her hand and refilled her coffee cup, and after a while she calmed down.

"I was afraid she'd get pregnant again, right away, but she didn't. I think she was using something." Jenny Mattingly blushed. "She wouldn't have told me if she was doing that. Either that or she wouldn't let him . . ."

I nodded, to show I understood. Jenny blushed again.

"The baby . . . you, you grew up, such a handsome child. You would have been, oh, about three when the terrible quarrel happened."

"The quarrel?"

"I was there. I'd had supper with Angela. Nimo had been out somewhere, but he came home about eight. Then his mother came from the hospital to talk to him. They were right in the next room when she began to cry and tell Nimo about the disease his father had. His father had been in a hospital for a long time, but no one had ever said what exactly was the matter with him.

"Angela and I heard every word she said. And we heard him, too, when his mother told him he might have the same disease. He was screaming like a crazy man. They were right there, in the next room, where we could hear everything!

"When his mother said it wasn't only him, but his children too, I reached for Angela, thinking she'd be horrified, but she was shaking her head at me and smiling this tiny little smile . . .

"I couldn't belive it. She was smiling. And she said, 'Don't be afraid, Jenny. Michael's all right. Nimo isn't Michael's father.' Just like that. 'Nimo isn't Michael's father.' "

I had no sense that the woman sitting beside me was talking about me. She was talking about a stranger, not me. Michael, not Jason.

"And?" I choked out.

"That maid heard her say it. And she came at Angela, gabbling, waving her hands, demanding to know who the baby's father was, whether Angela had committed a sin. And Angela smiled at her—oh, so sweetly, and she said, 'Simmy, God is Michael's father, just like God is Jesus' father.'

"The maid began to laugh, this loud, hooting laughter she

had, and Angela gave me a look. And that's when I knew she'd been pregnant before the wedding.''

I couldn't believe it. I'm sure I stared at her stupidly. It had never occurred to me. Even though I'd noticed the dates on the birth certificate, it had never occurred to me!

Jenny took my hand again. "But that crazy woman went straight to Nimo, I heard her. The nursemaid. She walked out of the room where we were and went to him, laughing like a crazy woman, and told him not to be so upset. The baby wouldn't get sick because he, Nimo, wasn't the baby's father! I couldn't believe she'd do such a stupid thing. What she was saying was all garbled up, but he heard part of it. He came raging into the room where we were. He said he'd always had his suspicions, she'd always been cold toward him, now he knew he wasn't the father, she'd taken his honor from him, she'd have to die, her and her bastard baby both! Oh, he used language . . . language people never used in front of women.

"Angela was frightened, really frightened. She tried to reason with him. She said she'd told Simmy that God was the baby's father so Simmy wouldn't be upset about the disease, but he didn't listen. He just went on screaming, and then he left. Angela was shaking all over. I got her to bed. I gave her a sleeping pill. I wanted her to take the baby—you—and leave with me, go over to her mother's house, but she wouldn't. She said her husband would calm down the next day and she'd talk to him then. But the next day she was dead. They said an accident. I always thought she did it herself, just to escape.''

I remembered the last letter I'd had from Herby. I remembered what Carlos had said. I remembered the look on Gabe Leone's face as he died. "She didn't do it herself," I said. "It could have been an accident, but more likely it was murder. Nimo meant what he said. He killed her. He tried to kill . . . me. If it hadn't been for Simmy, he would have. She saved me. Maybe only because I was Angela's son.''

"But not Nimo's," she said. "Angela knew you weren't.

That's what she was telling me. I'm sure you're not. You even look like him. Or like he did.''

I'm sure I looked at her stupidly once again. "Like him?"

"Daniel," she said. "Daniel had hair the same color as yours. Nimo was dark, but Daniel had that same auburn hair. He was the only one who could have been your father. The only one."

And, of course, she was right. He was the only one who could have been.

We sat there for a time, each lost in our own thoughts. "You never told Olivia about Nimo threatening Angela and . . . me?" I asked at last.

"No, no," Jenny said. "Poor Olivia. I told her about the disease, I had to tell her about that, so she'd know the reason. I didn't tell her the rest. She felt badly enough as it was. Why add to her pain? I thought you were dead, but Nimo told her you were in Italy. I let her believe that."

After a time, she asked me to call her driver, then got herself levered up onto her canes and left. I know my face was wet, maybe with relief, maybe with sorrow. I remember going upstairs and falling into bed again. All those nights of waking up in terror had taken their toll. My body and mind had some catching up to do. When I got up later that day, Mark was there. He'd heard the news about the shooting and had come over in case I needed him. He greeted me with a good deal of concern, but when I told him about Jenny Mattingly, he yelled so loudly it brought Grace running in. The two of them had been keeping watch over me. She said we had to have a celebration. It occurred to me while all this was going on that it was the only time I had ever heard of a celebration in honor of someone's finding out he's a bastard. I hoped I was a bastard. Gabe had thought so. He'd accused me of it with his last breath. Even so, a tiny, lingering doubt remained.

Monday morning, on the strength of what I remembered reading about all the children who had disappeared in the Argentine and how blood tests were used to determine what parents or grandparents were related to what children, I went

back to the physician at the genetic diseases department and
told him my problem. Nimo had died in a hospital within the
last twenty years, I said. There should be records. Angela
had died years before, but there had probably been a post-
mortem, and there might be records. If they had not been
kept all these years, Olivia might not mind giving a blood
sample for this particular purpose.

"Can you get a sample from the man you think is your
father?" he asked me, eagerly setting down the names and
dates and facts I had.

I shook my head. "Who my father is is unimportant," I
said, really, honestly meaning it. "All I'm interested in
knowing is who he's not."

He said he could understand that, under the circumstances. He took a sample of my blood and promised to do
what he could. He could find out where Nimo had died by
getting his death certificate. He would call me if he needed
a sample of Olivia's blood.

Grace was free that evening, and though we'd already cel-
ebrated for two days, we went to Charkeys for dinner, a new
place that specialized in mesquite-broiled everything. I
showed her the last letter from Herby and told her about
Jenny once more. She cried, and wiped her nose on the nap-
kin and then cried again.

"So she didn't just go along," she said at last with great
satisfaction. "Good for her!"

"Who?"

"Your mother. They may have talked her into making that
stupid, stupid marriage, but she didn't just go along. She
loved Daniel, she wanted his child, and she made sure she
had it. I like that!"

"I'm still not entirely sure . . ." I said.

"I'm sure," she said stoutly. "It just feels right. I never
could believe you were related to the Leones. Not even to
the nicer ones, like Dorotea. You just don't look anything
like that family!" She turned her attention back to her second
helping of cheese-crusted onion soup, warming up her stom-

ach for the very large steak which was coming next. "How did Gabe find out you weren't dead, after all those years?"

"I believe that once Simonetta's mama was in a nursing home, poor Simonetta had to talk to someone else about her sins. So, she told her brother about the child she'd stolen when she worked for Nimo, and Carlos talked about it to someone. The word somehow got to Gabe. That's why he killed Simonetta."

"But how did Gabe know who you were? Simonetta didn't know."

I got out my wallet and took from it the much-creased letter the old man had given me the night I'd found Gabe in my house. Not the one with the cut-out words; the other one. I'd forgotten it was in the pocket until after Gabe was dead. I handed it to her.

"It looks like a draft," she said. "You can hardly read his handwriting. Or his spelling."

"Right. It's dated a few years back. I figure he wrote a clear copy to leave with Walt Huggenmier, and he stuck this one in his pocket, and forgot about it."

"Dear Gabe," it said.
"I'm leaving this with somebody to mail in case something happens to me. That kid of Nimo's, he isn't dead. He grew up. His name is Jason Lynx now. He has a place here in town on Hyde Street. I never did him like I told Nimo. Since you made that promise to Nimo, I figured you should know.
"Herb Fixe"

She laid it down on the table and stared at it. "Herby left this for Gabe?"

"Don't you remember Walt Huggenmier saying Herby left a letter for him to mail?"

She looked stricken. "I'd forgotten. And this was it?"

"I think this was it, Herby's protection. The proverbial letter-left-to-be-mailed if the bad guy gets killed. Good old Gabe found out about Simonetta from Carlos, but he found out about me from Herby. He'd made his brother a promise, and he tried to keep it.''

"Sick," she said, with an expression of distaste.

"Sick," I agreed.

"I simply can't imagine anyone doing such a stupid thing, after all those years. It's ridiculous. Angela hadn't done a damned thing to make the Leone family behave that way.''

"She'd broken their code of honor. She'd been represented to them as a virgin whom Nimo had to marry to keep a promise made by his father. You know, the one thing we've never considered in all this is that Nimo may not have wanted to marry Angela any more than she wanted to marry him. Their fathers had sworn an oath, however, and that was it. So, he married this girl who was certainly not loving and undoubtedly sexually frigid toward him. She was pregnant immediately and asked him to leave her alone, which he may have been only too willing to do. Then the child was born with what Nimo saw as a deformity. That would have been a blow to masculine pride, so it had to be her fault. Then, later on he found out this thing about Huntington's disease, which was definitely his family, not hers, but it would be human nature to try and deflect the blame onto her or the baby. And then, hard on the heels of that discovery, here came Simonetta saying the baby wasn't his anyhow.''

"So he blew.''

"He obviously did more than merely blow. He swore to avenge his honor, and Gabe was his surrogate. Angela was dead, her child was supposed to be dead, but Gabe was prepared to act if the real father of the child ever showed up . . .''

"I guess Brother Daniel wasn't available as a victim," said Grace.

"Myra located Brother Daniel purely by chance. I doubt Gabe ever had a hint as to who he was.''

She ate in silence for a time, then asked, "Have you thought any more about what you're going to do?''

I almost told her what I had decided before Jenny's revelations. I caught myself in time. "God, Grace," I said soberly. "Up until today, I thought I was doomed. This changes everything. I need to take a while just to be relieved!"

My relief was confirmed when the doctor phoned to say Nimo Leone's records were complete as to blood type. He had been type O, and I was type AB. No matter what Angela's blood type had been, a type O father cannot produce a type AB child. It was one of those results which didn't require equivocation. There were no maybes. Nimo Leone had not been my daddy.

Which meant everything was solved except a few final and minor puzzles.

What should I do about Olivia? What should I do about Brother Daniel? What about Grace? And what about me?

A week or so went by.

Grace and I were playing kneesies at my kitchen table when she asked me when I was going to tell Olivia about me.

"I'm not," I said, without even thinking about it.

She gave me a long look.

"No reason to," I said defensively. "She's accustomed to the idea that Angela's son is in Italy. No point in rearranging her world."

"I thought you always wanted a family," she said.

"Well. Yes. But I can be familial toward her without telling her anything. Being Jacob's son allows me to do that. I'm taking her to lunch with Nellie and Willamae next week, as a matter of fact."

"So she's just another of your old ladies," she said. "What about Lycia?"

"Lycia's fine. She has plenty to keep her occupied, she's not grieving over her long-lost nephew."

"And you? What about you?"

I shrugged. I hadn't figured that out yet.

Grace was very silent the rest of the meal. I'd planned on her staying over, but she excused herself, saying she had some things to take care of at home. The whole episode left me irritated, first at her, but then at myself. By morning, I'd decided it was time I quit fooling around and did something about Grace. Put up or shut up, as they say. Did I want to marry her or not?

I did. However I looked at it, yes, I did. If that meant staying here in Jacob's house, in Jacob's business, well, so be it. If that meant buying a house in the suburbs and raising two point one children, so be that, as well. I loved Grace, and it was time I made that clear to her. Enough fiddling about!

I'd bought tickets, months ago, for the road show of a recent runaway Broadway hit. The tickets were for the following Friday night, a long-agreed-upon date. We enjoyed the show, which was mindless fun, and went on to supper at a little place off Third Avenue which would have picked up a lot of after-theater business by merely remaining open after ten, but also happens to have an interesting menu. The food's always tasty, the wines are exemplary, and the place stays crowded into the wee hours.

So, we scrunched together at a tiny corner table, enjoying our meal, and when I figured Grace had had enough food to be able to concentrate on something else, I asked her to marry me. I said, "Grace, will you marry me?"

She put down her fork. Her face turned pale. She got that pinched look she gets sometimes, when she's upset.

"Hey," I said, suddenly very worried.

"I don't think so, Jason," she said. "I don't think you'd be happy with me."

I'd been prepared for a yes. I'd been prepared for a "No, there's someone else." I'd been prepared for "I don't love you, Jason." I was not prepared for her thinking I'd not be happy with her.

"Why would you think such a thing?" I demanded a little angrily.

"Because I'm not perfect," she said, staring at my chin, avoiding my eyes. "You only want a family that's perfect. I knew that when you said you weren't going to tell Olivia you're her grandson. She's not perfect. You told me that. You said she wasn't worthy of Jacob. You had Jacob and you believe he was absolutely perfect. You had Agatha, and she was perfect. . . ."

"That's not true," I cried in an outraged whisper. "You know that's not . . ."

"Oh, I know she wasn't, but you *think* of her as perfect. You don't think about the dumb things she did. She's dead, and all her failings are sort of washed away. You didn't live together long enough to grind on each other."

I held on to my temper. "That's true, Grace. We didn't live together very long. But Agatha and I knew we weren't perfect, for God's sake. . . ."

Grace interrupted, "And I'll tell you something else. Jacob wasn't perfect either. Jacob decided he'd rather play the part of the faithful lover than be a real live person. All his life he was faithful to Olivia, but he never once *did* anything about her! You told me Olivia wasn't worthy of him because she didn't save your mother, but you might just as well blame Jacob for not doing anything about Olivia!"

"There was nothing he could do!" I cried, stung.

"Shit," she said. "He could have tried. If not when she married Octavio, then before she married what's-his-name Meyer. He could have offered his home as a sanctuary for Angela. He could have talked to her, tried to undo what that priest had done. Fact was, he never did anything. And he didn't get on with his life, either. His whole life he spent mooning over her. No wife, no children, just mooning. Kind of a sentimental warm bath. You may call that perfect, but I don't."

"He was wonderful to me!"

"To you, yes. Well, he was over fifty when he took you in. He was doing well financially. It wasn't much strain for him, was it? No diapers. No up all night with the colic. You were easy, weren't you? You didn't give him a hard time. That's one thing about you, Jason, you're basically really a *nice* person. But he never adopted you. That way, you didn't have any real claim on him. So, it worked out, and he felt good about it. Especially after he found out you were Olivia's grandson. That must've made it really romantic. Paying out all that money, year after year, never once doing anything sensible like trying to put the extortioner in jail and put an end to the threat.''

"He thought it would endanger me!"

"Yeah, well. Maybe. As it turned out, it endangered you a hell of a lot more not to tell you about it!"

"Grace, I don't know where you've come up with all this, all of a sudden. . . ."

"It isn't all of a sudden. It's been months. I've watched you, and I've talked to you, and I've made love to you, and I've thought about you all the time. And I've wondered if maybe we could make it together, but we can't. We can't, because you've got this dream of some perfect family to match up to Jacob and Agatha, and I'm not perfect. I'm just not, but I'd try to be for your sake, and I'd end up destroying us both by trying.''

She got up, spilling her wine in her haste, and went out. I thought she'd gone to the restroom to cry and then fix her face, so I waited, angrily marshaling my arguments. Only when she'd been gone about twenty minutes did I realize she wasn't coming back.

What she'd said was unfair. It was unfair to Jacob, unfair to Agatha. I was sure of that. As the night wore on, however, with me sleeplessly replaying what she'd said, I wasn't at all sure it had been unfair to me.

She didn't call. After ten days, it became obvious she wasn't going to call. When I called her, I got a machine.

I talked to Mark. We had quite a long, involved conference during which I yelled some and sulked some and listened to someone else's opinion about my character. Always enlightening, that. Salutary, I suppose. After which, he went to see Grace on my behalf. His message was simple. If she and I were going to split, we owed it to one another to split as friends, to leave things peaceful between us. Would she please have dinner with me.

He had to go back twice, but he got her to agree. Yes, Saturday. Yes, I could pick her up.

I did, dressed in my conservative best.

"Where are we doing?" she asked in a subdued voice.

"A place we haven't been before," I said. "I hope the food will be good."

When we drove up in front, she said, "I didn't know there was a restaurant in this building." It was the first thing she'd said since we left her house.

When we got out of the elevator and walked down the hall, she gave me a curious look, maybe a little hostile. "I have to pick up something," I said lamely . . . and truthfully.

She didn't know the woman who opened the door. She did know the people assembled in the living room.

"Grace," I said, "I'd like you to meet my grandmother, Olivia Meyer. This is my Aunt Lycia and her friend Ross. Grandmother, Aunt, this is Grace Willis. I'm trying to talk Grace into marrying me."

She was too dumbfounded to say anything at that point, and by the time she thought of something (I could see it in her eyes) it was too late. Dinner was served.

Not that I got an answer. I didn't. She seemed to enjoy herself, however, as did everyone else, even though I'd forgotten to warn Aunty and Granny about Grace's appetite and we had to stop at a fast-food place on the way home.

From the time we left Olivia's to the time I dropped her at her house, Grace didn't mention my proposal. I didn't really expect her to, not this soon. I didn't bring it up either. Maybe she won't marry me, but she'll damned well have to refuse me for some other reason than the one she gave me. She's got to know I'm ready to accept a family, perfect or not. She's got to know I want her to be part of it.

A few loose ends.

Cecily: I wrote her a letter, thanking her for her intervention on my behalf. I told her who I was and that she had saved my life. I thanked her for that. I told her not to blame herself for telling Herby where she'd left me as a child. In the end, it had all worked out all right.

Brother Daniel: My father. I called the monastery and

spoke with the same voice I'd spoken with some weeks before. Brother Daniel, said the voice, had died several weeks before. He'd had cancer for some time. It had been only a matter of weeks even at the time I'd seen him.

I counted up the days and realized he'd died before I'd known he was my father. There had been nothing I could have told him at that time. Perhaps there had been nothing I should have told him, even if he had lived. "Remember me in your prayers," he'd said. I was not much for prayers. But I would remember him.

Simonetta: The day after our family dinner, I went to see Sister John Lorraine to remind her of what she'd said about Simonetta being proof of God's inscrutability. I told her the whole story, starting with Olivia and Jacob and including Brother Daniel. If I wasn't one for prayers, I supposed Sister John was.

"If you're looking for purpose in Simonetta's life," I concluded, "consider this, Sister John: She saved my life. All her craziness saved my life. I'll be remembering Simonetta."

"Kindly," she said in a hushed, wondering voice, tears in her eyes. "Remembering her kindly."

I agreed. Despite the burns and the craziness and the long years spent in the Home, I'd be remembering Simonetta— and Cecily and Brother Daniel—kindly. And Jacob. Who, despite Grace's calumny, had been a fine and wonderful man. Though not perfect.

None of us is perfect. Thank God. What would we do for puzzles if we were?

Look for these novels
of mystery and suspense
in your local bookstore.